The Problem With Fae

Emma Bradley

WATCH. LISTEN. LEARN.

DEDICATION

For the unfailing supporters of *The Trouble With Fairies*, you kept me going and made this possible – thank you!

CHAPTER ONE
A SPECIAL GUEST

"Freak!"

The verbal punch landed exactly where my sister, Jenny, meant it to. Right smack-bang on the anger button. She'd been taunting me all morning about 'knocking the fairy out of me', and finally had me cornered by the airing cupboard at our mum's house.

"What would you know?" I shouted back.

If I yell, Mum will come to break us up, I'm sure of that. Well, pretty sure.

Jenny's eyes glittered with hatred as she grabbed my upper arm with super-strong fingers that were forged by smacking other people with a hockey stick for years. I struggled and pushed against her shoulders, but I had no hope of breaking free. She jostled me backwards until I was squished in between a suitcase and a pile of towels.

I took a deep breath despite the pounding in my chest and tingling in my veins. I could feel my skin flushing hot, a sure warning sign I'd learned to recognise.

"You really don't want to do this," I pleaded.

Her expression hardened. "Oh, I *really* do. You don't belong here, *Demerara*, but while you are, I'll give you a lesson in knowing your place."

She always used my full name whenever she could, pronouncing it like acid on her tongue.

The back of my head pressed against the towel shelf. My fingers buzzed on her shoulders, bare without the gloves I'd taken to wearing over the past few days. If I took my hands away, Jenny would try to hurt me properly. If I kept pressing, who knows what I'd do.

"Fairy scum. I wish you were dead," she hissed.

I couldn't find my breath as my temper shot out, along with Faerie knows how many volts of what I assumed was some kind of magic energy.

I stared at the pale skin of my fingers now glowing white-blue. The fabric of Jenny's t-shirt started to smoke. Acrid burning filled the air. She released me with a scream, stumbling back. I pushed myself forward away from the shelf and shoved her out of the way, dizziness whirling upwards. If I didn't get air soon, I was going to be sick.

Will I puke energy now? The question was ridiculous and valid at the same time.

Ever since I'd gained the random ability to give people electric shocks three days ago, this reaction had been splurging out whenever I was stressed or frustrated, which in this house was all the time.

I grabbed the banister with one hand and groaned when the wood beneath my fingers started to smoke. As I broke into a run down the stairs, I could hear Jenny bashing about behind me. Knowing my luck, she'd lumber straight over the banister, break her neck and I'd be done for killing my sister.

I whipped around the turn in the staircase and caught a glance of her dashing after me. I stumbled downwards, reaching out for the front door at the bottom. My gloves were in my pocket, but Jenny had jumped me coming out of the bathroom and I'd had no time to put them back on.

Stupid, stupid, stupid. My mind chanted along with my pounding feet as I reached the front hallway.

A hand closed on my shoulder and caught a painful chunk of

hair with it. Kicking back, I landed a heel on Jenny's shin. She grunted, but she was used to worse than that on the hockey field. She switched her hold. With my hair free, I twisted and pushed my hands toward her.

She veered back, eyes wide with alarm, but didn't let go.

"What the hell is wrong with you?" She whispered, and the sound grated on me. "Some kind of weird mutant? I'm not scared of you."

We both knew that was a lie.

"You are," I goaded. "You're scared of me because I have stuff you'll never get. Skills. Abilities."

I ducked just in time to avoid the fist that came flying at my face.

"JENNIFER DARCY!"

Mum's voice filled the hall. Jenny stared at me, brown eyes wild, chest heaving. I glared back, petrified but too angry to back down now.

"Out." Mum pointed to the kitchen, meaning the back door. "Out now. Don't come back until you've cooled off." Jenny lifted her fist, her eyes still on me. "*OUT,* or don't come back!"

Mum had never threatened that before, but it broke through Jenny's rage. She glared at me, span ninety degrees and threw her fist into the wall instead. The punch wasn't enough to break right through, but a couple of paintings jumped off their hooks and crashed to the floor.

Jenny pushed past Mum and stormed along the hall toward the kitchen and the back door, but Mum followed her. Their voices echoed through the house and no doubt halfway down the street.

"She's still your sister."

"She's a freak, and we'll *never* accept her. I wish she would go away and never come back. I wish she was dead!"

I ignored the familiar stab of hurt that twisted in my chest.

The never coming back would suit me just fine, but she'd never actually wished me dead before, at least not when I was in earshot.

I sighed as the backdoor slamming echoed through the house. All I wanted was to get back to Arcanium, headquarters of the Fairy Deity People who took on assignments in the various realms of Faerie. I was in my first year of training there to be a Fairy Deity Person, or FDP as we were known, but I'd been all but forced to come back "home" for a visit over the mentee break. Mum had been happy to see me, but my sisters not so much. I used to tell myself it was because they were twins and two years older than me. They had each other so they ganged up on me. The fact I was a fairy and the rest of the family wasn't only added to their determination to torment me.

I glanced at the front door. Through the frosted glass, I could see misshapen blobs of colour, their stillness indicating whoever was standing on our porch had been there longer than a few seconds. Possibly we'd missed the sound of the doorbell, or more likely they'd heard the commotion and didn't dare interrupt.

Mum rushed past me, her cheeks flushed. I hastily pulled my gloves on and brushed my hands over my unruly curls, black except for the sheen of oil-slick colours. I noticed now that Mum had gone to a lot of effort to pin her hair back in an elaborate bun, very unlike her. She and my sisters had nut brown hair all straight and flat, not curly or sheeny like mine. They all had brown eyes too, very unlike my bright icy blue ones, so even with genetics I was singled out as *different* in almost every way.

Mum threw open the front door to reveal the two people we'd been expecting. The two people I really didn't want to hear my awful sister spouting off about me.

My best friend, Taz, stood on the doorstep with his mother at his side. Embarrassing enough, but his mother also happened to be the Queen of Faerie.

Taz gave me a quirked eyebrow, intimating without words that they'd heard something of my fight with Jenny. Beside him the Queen looked radiant with hair the colour of honey, curling and glossy like Taz's, but long over her shoulders where his stopped around his ears. I'd been expecting her to be in some kind of dress, perhaps hair set in an elaborate creation, but she wore tailored dark blue jeans, black suede boots and a smart navy jacket. She looked as though she was off to a casual meeting or a day out lunching with friends.

"Hi," Taz muttered. "This is my mother, Tavania Elverhill. Mother, this is Demi."

I froze. All my carefully prepared greetings sailed straight out of my head. The Queen smiled with a shine in her green eyes, as if she guessed how nervous I was.

"Hello, Demi. Oakthorn has told me next to nothing about you, but it's good to meet you."

I'd all but forgotten that Oakthorn was Taz's actual full name in the eyes of Faerie and the royal court, and almost questioned it without thinking. Taz had already given me a quick course on what he called 'the parent-gauntlet', so I didn't want to let him down now.

The first time he'd gotten in touch, two days into the mentee break, he'd orbed me. I'd been watching a scary film on my cruddy old phone at the time, headphones in so my sisters wouldn't see it as an opportunity to try and make me jump. The sound went silent just before a really scary bit, then Taz's face popped out of my orb, looming in the air in front of me with ghostly, pearlescent clarity. I screamed. Loudly.

I'd forgotten Taz had no mobile phone, but had already had

several long text conversations with our friend Ace, whose family lived in London. Where Ace was full of flirty wink emojis and x's at the end of his messages, Taz was short and to the point.

The parent-gauntlet advice was that I shouldn't bow or do anything embarrassing or 'courtly', as the Queen was visiting us as a mother and not a regent. I wasn't to mention her status to anyone other than my mum. Above all, he told me, I should probably try not to speak much at all.

"Hi, Mrs Elverhill," I croaked, my throat dry. "It's nice to meet you too."

There, that will do fine.

"Demi, don't leave guests standing on the doorstep." Mum nudged me. "Hi Mrs. Elverhill. I'm Jane, we spoke on the phone."

The Queen shook Mum's hand. What with all the squabbling between me and Jenny, I'd not noticed Mum wearing what she called her 'going-out jeans' and a floral blouse. She was also wearing her best make-up face that she usually only bothered with for important occasions.

"Come in, please." Mum shuffled me sideways to leave a space. "Come into the parlour."

I bit my lips together, not sure if to be alarmed or amused. Mum never used words like 'parlour'. As we turned to go into the living room, I noticed that both my sisters were now suspiciously absent. Jenny wouldn't come back until she was sure I'd left, but Mary had been upstairs still.

"Well, welcome." Mum went into full hostess mode. "It's not much but it's home."

The Queen smiled and looked around at the hastily tidied room with a motley bunch of sweet-peas in a pint glass on the chipped pine coffee table.

"You have a lovely home." She sounded completely sincere. I wondered how, as fairies and Fae couldn't lie, but then maybe being Queen came with perks. "I admit it would be nice to have all my children closer, but I don't think the furnishings would survive for long."

Taz snorted and I risked a quick smirk in his direction. The Queen didn't acknowledge his outburst, moving swiftly on.

"I'm afraid we do need to be on our way," she continued. "I believe the first day back is always one of the most exciting. Demi, do you have your things ready?"

I recognised the direct command hidden beneath the pleasantries and stood up, hurrying over to the dusty old bookcase. Mum insisted on keeping some educational books there in case we had special visitors who liked to inspect people's bookshelves. I guessed it was also because she didn't want anyone seeing her entire history of Mills and Boon which was stashed upstairs, but I knew nobody used the bottom cupboard. It was the perfect hiding place. I pulled out my satchel and my suitcase that had all my clothes in.

If anyone thought the hiding place was weird, at least they didn't show it. I slung the satchel strap over my head and smiled as Leo, my pet chameleon, popped his head out. He noticed Taz and made a crooning noise, but I tapped the top of his head with a hesitant finger and he disappeared back inside the satchel.

At least I didn't shock him as well.

I sagged with relief. The gloves had proved a good barrier so far, but I didn't exactly get close enough to anyone on a normal day to test it, let alone when I knew I had some kind of electric shock gift.

"Ready," I announced.

Everyone stood and shuffled back to the front door.

"We'll wait in the car, let you say your farewells," the Queen insisted. "Come along, Oakthorn."

They walked back to the car and I turned to Mum. She smiled at me.

"No need to tell you to be good." She pushed a lock of hair back from my face, the shimmer of its oil-slick colours catching the light. "Make sure you let me know how you're doing. Oh, but just remember we're off to see Aunt Cara next weekend, so nobody will be at home. Then I'm taking Mary and Jenny to see their university the weekend after, so best keep it to messages or evenings."

I pretended to listen to the family schedule. Part of me felt the usual residual hurt that it didn't include me, that I was barely a part of my family. But now most of me yearned to leave it all behind and escape back to Arcanium. At least people smiled at me there and said hi when they passed in the halls.

Mum gave me a hug and I flinched, but she didn't react like I'd shocked her. I stood there letting her hold me as I silently said a proper goodbye. After this visit, I doubted I'd be coming back for a long while, not if I could find excuses to stay at Arcanium over any more mentee breaks. I took a deep breath.

Time to go home.

"Okay, bye Mum."

I struggled free, grabbed the handle of my suitcase and fled toward the waiting Land Rover. I'd expected some kind of limo or fancy antique car, but apparently the Queen was determined to blend in. The driver took my suitcase, but I clung onto my satchel. It had all my important things in it, my FDP manual, my Jelly Babies stash and most importantly Leo.

With the Queen sitting in the passenger seat up front, I put my fingers on the handle of the rear door but froze as something caught my eye.

Panic flared inside my chest at the sight of the man walking along the street toward me.

It's okay, he doesn't know about my new 'gift'. But then, what is he doing here?

My old mentor from fairy classes smiled at me as he approached.

"Xavio? What are you doing here?" I asked.

He had his long grey beard in a French plait like a pony's tail, which somehow drew more attention to his bald head. I eyed the khaki shorts that exposed his bony knees, and the vacant smile that sat beneath fiendishly bright blue eyes. He stopped beside the bonnet, giving me a superior look.

"I am still part of the Arcanium flock, am I not?" he asked. "I can still check-in and visit, can I not?"

I often forgot how tetchy he could get when asked a question he thought was stupid. I didn't look behind me to see what Taz and the Queen made of this, but I could see Mum still at the front door with a frown. She'd met Xavio before in passing, always reticent to do more than kick me out of the car when she dropped me off at his fairy classes.

"Yeah." I couldn't bring myself to say any more.

Xavio smirked at me. "I have been extended an invitation, don't worry."

"To Arcanium?"

He shook his head and gave me another despairing look.

"I hardly need an invitation there now, do I? No, the Queen offered me a lift."

He rounded the car and just like that, where there had been a Land Rover with two rows of seats, now it had three like a mutant 4X4 space cruiser.

So much for blending in.

Xavio got into the middle row, so I slid into the back beside Taz. My heart pounded as he gave me a quick, questioning look, but I could only shrug in reply and turn my face to the window instead. I'd have to find a way to explain everything later.

I went through the routine of waving goodbye to Mum as the car set off and let out a tumbling sigh of relief as my street sailed past. At least we were on our way home now.

I was quite happy to sit in silence if the others were, but the Queen didn't seem to get the memo.

"Oakthorn, don't be rude," she chastised. "Why don't you tell Demi about your time back at court?"

Taz glared at the back of her head before turning to me with a theatrical eye roll. It gave me time to notice that he now had two black rings pierced through his left eyebrow instead of one, but his stormy turquoise eyes were as bright as ever.

He gets a piercing, while I get a gift I can't control. Sounds about right.

"It was okay," he said. "I did stuff. Yours?"

I could match that. "It was okay. I did stuff."

His lips lifted at the corners, highlighting the sprinkle of freckles across his nose and cheeks. I considered that the conversation closed, but the Queen clearly wasn't done.

"Oh, congratulations by the way on your gift, Demi. That's a great achievement for one so young."

Taz stared at me, his mouth dropping open, but it was Xavio's stiff shoulders and sudden stillness that took my attention.

Is he annoyed I didn't tell him, or annoyed that someone gave me one at all? He should have been paying more attention to what happened when I was helping out at fairy classes then.

I shook the residual irritation away. The Queen was right about one thing - being given a gift when I didn't have any Fae family to give it to me was a huge deal. I hunched lower, as Taz prodded my elbow.

I froze, but he didn't recoil.

No shock, phew.

I saw him gawping and sighed.

"It's turned out more of a curse than a gift," I admitted, keeping my voice low. "I can basically zap people with electrical currents. Oh no, wait, it's not a case of 'can', I do. So, don't come anywhere near me or you'll be zinging for hours."

Taz's gaze swept over my gloved hands. I tipped my head back against the seat.

"Go on," I grumbled. "I can tell you're dying to dissect me."

"So, if I touch you it'll hurt?"

I nodded. "Like a static shock, yes. As my sister found out when you arrived, hence the shouting. I tried so hard to keep it hidden as well, but she cornered me. It's cliché, but this time it really was in self-defence."

Taz went straight into detective mode. "Can you control it, like dial it down or is it only one type of shock?"

"I'm not a dimmer switch." I glared at him. "Besides, I've only had it like three days, so I haven't exactly tested it on people yet, not by choice anyway, unless you're offering."

Taz shook his head. "Er, no thanks. Do you feel anything when you zap someone?"

"Not really, it doesn't hurt me. Tingles a bit, like the connection to my fairy side does. But basically it means I can never pass someone a pencil, or have another hug, or shake someone's hand without potentially hurting them."

I turned my face to the window. The enormity of it dawned again, the realisation swelling as it had done for the past few days in crashing waves. I couldn't find a single thing to say for several excruciating moments.

"Ace is going to get a shock then," Taz quipped. "No pun intended. He's always trying to be buddy-buddy touchy-

touchy."

It was perhaps a bit unfair, but Ace had a habit of slinging his arm around people in a matey-type way. I thought about the many enthusiastic texts Ace had sent me during half term and felt my lips twitch.

"So, does this mean you're going to threaten to zap me every time I do something dim?" Taz pressed.

I shrugged. "Maybe. When my sister was trying to lock me in a cupboard, I accidentally zapped her." I caught sight of his darkening expression. "She wasn't hurt or anything, just had, well, a shock. I shot out of the cupboard and took about half her arm with me, so there are a few minimal upsides."

Taz chuckled at that, and I realised the dark expression had been on my behalf rather than my sister's. I half expected the Queen to reprimand him, or Xavio to reprimand me, but they were both silent.

"I won't ask if you had a good time for the rest of it either," he said.

"I'm unscathed. I helped out at fairy classes and spent the rest of my time skulking around the local bookshop. My sisters are off to university, which would be a blessing except they'll be going local and staying at Mum's still. After the week I've had, I'm just so glad to be going home."

Taz crossed one leg over the other and shifted to face me.

"Do your sisters bewitch your clothes to disappear when you're wearing them in front of visitors from neighbouring courts?" he asked, challenging me to up the stakes.

I forced the accompanying image straight out of my head, my cheeks burning with embarrassment.

"No, but they've tied me between the goalposts in the garden before and done target practice. The footballs you actually get used to as long as they don't hit you in the face. The hockey pucks not so much."

Taz's nostrils flared and his eyes flashed electric blue just for a second. They were usually a northern lights-style turquoise, but the electric flash of lightning I hadn't seen before. After a few seconds, I blinked and turned my head away so I wasn't caught staring.

"So, who gave you the gift then?" he asked.

I froze. "Doesn't matter."

Knowing him, he probably would have pushed me, but the Queen cleared her throat.

"As much as I don't wish to disturb your delightful competition, we're here."

I twisted to stare out of my window in alarm. Arcanium was on the south coast and at least a two-hour drive away from Mum's house in Salisbury. But there it was, the flashing lights of the dingy amusement arcade that hid the entrance to the Arcanium headquarters.

"Is that- we can't have-" I tried again. "How could we have gotten here so quickly?"

Taz gave me one of his withering looks. "Simple court Fae trickery."

He got out of the car and the Queen followed a moment later. I checked on Leo nestled in my satchel out of habit and slid out into the blustery autumn wind. The driver handed me my suitcase and I inched a few paces away to give Taz a chance to say goodbye to his mother.

"I'll make sure your account is up to date." The Queen glanced up and down the street. "Try to be positive."

I bit my lip. I couldn't hear any affection in her tone, or any sign that she was even paying much attention to him.

Taz shrugged. "Okay. Bye."

He turned his face away from her and I saw the lightning

quick crumple of emotion. I gripped the handle of my suitcase tight in one hand, knowing better than to try comforting him right now. The Queen stepped forward, her face relaxing into a gentle smile as she regarded me with determination.

"Thank you for bringing me," I said.

"Go on inside, Demi," she said without taking her eyes from mine. "I need to have a word with Oakthorn."

Taz looked up, startled. Xavio strolled past us, whistling to himself as he held the door to the arcade open for me. I couldn't exactly refuse, so I had to give Taz a rueful grimace and go inside.

Xavio shut the door behind me but remained outside on the pavement. Despite knowing I should give them privacy, I dodged behind the nearest flashing arcade machine and peeked out. I couldn't hear what they were saying, but through the window I watched as Taz stared at his feet, his brow furrowed and his mouth sulky. The Queen said a few things, I had no hope of knowing what, but Taz's expression didn't improve. Then the Queen leaned forward and kissed him on the forehead.

I winced, a flash of three days ago flickering in my mind's eye.

The good-looking face leaning toward me, and me closing my eyes like an idiot. A kiss landing on my forehead, instead of my lips like I'd been expecting, and a tingling fizzle spreading warmth throughout my entire body. Then the contact disappeared and I opened my eyes to the sound of the previously charming voice turned full of malice.

"Consider that gift as payback from an old friend, Sparky."

I shivered and pressed my hand against the nearest arcade machine, the cool plastic grounding me. The Queen could have been kissing Taz goodbye, but I knew now how gifts were given, and they didn't seem like the huggy-kissy type of family.

She had given him some kind of gift.

I turned quickly as Taz and Xavio came toward the arcade door. I peeked into my satchel the moment I heard the door open, pretending to be checking on Leo. He barely fit in the main compartment now but last term I'd been given proper permission to keep him. He'd taken to riding around on my shoulder, but after Jenny had tried to snatch him when I arrived at Mum's and he'd almost taken her finger off, he'd stayed in the satchel to be safe. He'd become my constant, and I couldn't bear the thought of being made to give him up.

But now we were finally home.

Taz's cheeks were flushed but the rest of his face was pale. When I caught his eye, he looked away. Xavio hummed to himself as he strode past us and headed straight for the door at the back of the arcade. He seemed chipper enough, but then his moods were legendarily unpredictable.

Through the door and down the short corridor was the lift that would take us into Arcanium. We squeezed into the lift, surrounded by the metal walls as the door clanked shut. I cast another quick glance at Taz but he seemed determined not to catch my eye or show he had any knowledge I was here. I bit my lip and did the same.

If the Queen's given him a gift, most would be pleased, but then he's not like other Fae. Maybe it's a curse rather than a gift, like mine.

The lift jolted, throwing us sideways, but I was ready for it, unlike the first time I'd arrived. Taz might normally have thrown me a knowing grin, but he didn't so much as blink. Even Xavio was completely silent. The moment the lift came to a stop and the doors slid open, I sagged with relief.

I pushed out of the lift first and forgot all about Taz and Xavio, Jenny, Mum, the Queen, my new gift, all of it. I stood in the middle of a chaotic crowd of people and took a deep breath of delight. Usually the mayhem of Arcanium's atrium was a bit much for me, too overwhelming to stand still in for long, but now I barely noticed the loud buzz or the flickering sway of people rushing about.

The atrium looked the same as it had a week ago. Broad, dark red beams reached upward, covered in ivy with butterflies flitting in and out, and a glass ceiling hanging much higher above that, not even visible beyond a bright light beaming down. The circular reception desk dominated the middle of the marble floor, flanked by a couple of cherry blossom trees in huge terracotta pots on either side.

I turned to grin at Taz and remembered his sudden detached mood. He still looked pale, but when I stared directly at him, he took the couple of steps to reach my side and bumped my shoulder with his. I tensed, but it seemed that through the fabric of clothing he'd avoided getting any shocks off of me.

"Home," we chorused.

Xavio apparently felt much the same and powered past us toward the reception desk.

"Henry!" he cried with his arms out wide. "How's the stationery?"

We watched in horror as Xavio gave Call-me-Henry, Arcanium's longest serving Head Receptionist and Stationery Organisation Director, a not entirely welcome bear-hug. Given that Call-Me-Henry was rumoured to have shoved stationery somewhere unmentionable on someone who had dared call him by his first name once, I wondered if Xavio had some kind of importance in Arcanium circles after all, or if Call-Me-Henry just knew how bonkers my old mentor could be.

Taz leaned closer to me. "Is he all there, you know, in the head?"

"Er, I think so." I hesitated. "He's very bright."

Taz scoffed. I wanted to drop a few choice experiences I'd had with Xavio into the mix, but wasn't sure Taz would believe such crazy tales were real.

"He's from one of the old Fae families, I think," Taz added. "He isn't involved in the court politics much though."

I raised an eyebrow. "And you know a lot about Fae court politics?"

"More than enough to know I want nothing to do with it. So, this gift of yours. How did you go about getting it? You don't seem pleased."

I folded my arms and tapped my thumb over my fingertips, my normal habit when I was anxious. I could feel a headache needling behind my eyes, and suddenly the atrium was too bright.

"It doesn't matter how, but I know it was Diana's payback for last term."

"How do you know though?"

I clenched my gut and tapped my fingers faster. "I just do, okay? I can't control the frigging thing and I'm stuck with it, so why does it matter how I got it?"

Taz stood quiet for a moment. "I'll help you figure out how to control it, don't worry. It would be easier if I knew exactly what the wording that they used to gift you was though."

My shame increased. "There wasn't any."

I heard his sharp breath despite the chaos around us.

I knew that had to be a bad thing.

His eyes narrowed, but he didn't say anything more. Xavio turned back to face us, but I'd seen someone else on their way to say hello, and joy mixed with anxiety at the thought.

"Hi, guys!" Ace steamed toward us. "Welcome back."

His black hair was cut shorter, and he looked even taller and broader than I remembered, which was ridiculous after only a week. Despite being a year older than both me and Taz, and in his second year of mentee training, Ace had started hanging around with us most of the time.

He held his arms out as he drew closer and I knew he was about to get us into a hug. I had no idea if my powers were just in my hands or not yet and took a step back. In the three days since I'd been cursed with my 'gift', I'd only touched Jenny and Mum, both earlier today. I hadn't shocked Mum when she hugged me, but then I hadn't hugged back, so I couldn't be sure. I definitely didn't want anyone here finding out until I'd had time to speak to some of the tutors and maybe look through the library for a way to control or contain it.

Taz appeared half in front of me, his arm and shoulder blocking me from Ace before I could figure out what I was going to do.

"Hi, mate," he said. "Demi's not feeling too good, so don't squish her or she'll go projectile."

Oh great, thanks.

I grimaced a weak smile at Ace, burning with embarrassment. My mind flitted back to some of the over-enthusiastic text messages Ace had been sending me over the last week, and I wondered if perhaps the mention of me going projectile might at least put him off a bit. As much as I loved him as one of my closest friends, the mere thought of him maybe feeling anything more than platonic made me irrepressibly anxious.

Xavio appeared beside us with the kind of smile that suggested he was a few biscuits short of a crumb, all wide-eyed and bunch-cheeked. Ace blinked at him for several moments before looking at me.

"Sorry Dem, hope it's nothing too bad." He gave me a soft

smile. "I'm guessing you'll want to get to your room and veg, but you'll have a chance to do that after, hopefully."

I blinked. "After what, and why hopefully? I don't like the sound of that."

"Emil just collared me on my way in." he grimaced. "Queenie wants to see you."

CHAPTER TWO
HERE WE GO AGAIN

I managed not to groan out loud, especially when Taz, Ace and Xavio all gave me doubtful looks at the news. Queenie, Arcanium's Director, hadn't exactly warmed to me last term. Then again, she didn't seem to warm to anyone, but her wanting to see me couldn't be a good thing.

"I've only been here two minutes or so," I grumbled. "I've not even had time to muck anything up yet."

Xavio frowned. "Well, best get it over with. Down and to the left, is it?"

"Up and to the right actually," Taz said.

Ace grinned. "I'll take your suitcase to your room, Demi, if you want? And Leo? Then we can catch up properly. I finally got my hands on that book you recommended."

I let go of my suitcase handle, but transferred my gloved hands to the strap of my satchel instead.

"I'll keep Leo on me, but yeah the suitcase would be great, thanks Ace." I gave him my room key and the biggest smile I could dredge up.

Ace hurried off to one of the waiting internal lifts with my suitcase in tow and Taz led the way to another.

As I followed Taz into the nearest lift, I realised Ace hadn't offered to take his bags as well, but then Taz only had a rucksack on his back, no suitcase or anything. Whether he'd left stuff at his mother's or not bothered taking much in the first place, I couldn't be sure. I'd just packed everything I could possibly fit, hoping that I'd not need to go back to Mum's any time soon.

I shook the thought off as we got into one of the internal lifts. While the one coming in from the arcade was a dingy metal box, the internal lifts were ornate golden cages built so that you could see the brick shafts behind as the lift moved. I'd gotten used to that and the rush of wind that came with travelling in one now, but it was always a good idea to be mindful of where your elbows were and not to pick arguments until you got out, just in case.

I bit my lip as we sailed upwards. I had no desire to see Queenie again. It wasn't so much her enthusiasm for skin-tight velvet or the thick purple lipstick, but the sharp nails and the piercing eyes, like a hawk searching for a potential morsel.

"Maleficent might only want to give us a warning after last term," Taz suggested, a tinge of hope in his voice.

I thought Xavio, who was always keen on politeness when it suited him, would chastise him. He didn't. Instead, he hummed a few tuneless bars of *Rise of the Valkyries*. Worried that he would start playing percussion on his bald head, I cleared my throat and willed the lift to go faster. Xavio's drumming was not something that anyone wanted to see.

The lift stopped. Taz opened the gate and hurried out first. I let Xavio go ahead of me, despite being determined to get Queenie's summons over and done with. Once she was done, I could say a quick goodbye to Xavio and head straight to my room.

The doors to Queenie's office loomed at the end of the hall, the Arcanium insignia carved on them as an orb surrounded by ivy.

"Best wait outside, kids." Xavio tipped me a wink.

I stood beside Taz to watch as Xavio strode forward in his rain-mac and shorts, entered Queenie's office without knocking and closed the door behind him.

"He's bold, I'll give him that." Taz sounded impressed.

"Say that after you've been made to recite the entire Faerie code in the original language while standing on one leg."

I respected my old mentor but it didn't mean I had to appreciate every single learning tactic that had been thrown at me over the past three years.

Taz grinned and slouched against the nearest wall.

"I'd love to see that," he said.

I shook my head. "Not in a million years. That wasn't as bad as-"

"Abso*LUTE*ly not!"

Xavio's voice fired like a gunshot through the wood of the door and off down the hall. I froze. Taz folded his arms and widened his stance as if preparing for a showdown.

The buzz of voices continued inside the office like a swarm of furious bees. Taz straightened up, no doubt on his way to eavesdrop at the door. Before he could do anything, it swung open.

"Demi, Queenie would like to speak to you." Xavio didn't look pleased.

My mouth went dry and my tongue seemed to grow three sizes. When I swallowed, my throat got stuck. Taz shoving a hand against my back to hustle me forward didn't help. I waited for a yelp, or a sign I'd shocked him, but none came.

"Why?" I asked Xavio without thinking.

Queenie could probably hear me through the open door. I stood up straight. She might still scare the pants off me, but I'd taken an assignment on my first day last year and succeeded, mostly. I'd faced a lunatic Fae woman and two fearsome, illegal lizard hybrids.

I was now, without a doubt, feeling like throwing up everywhere instead.

I took a deep breath and walked into Queenie's office with my shoulders breaking a sweat. She sat behind her imposing grey wooden desk with its spiky carvings, surrounded by purple wall fabrics and grey-framed mirrors. Her dark hair was scraped back from her face and tied tight, making her vampiric purple lips and heavy eye make-up even more prominent.

"Ah, Demi, come in and shut the door."

I did as I was told while trying to keep my shoulders square and my chin level with the floor. Despite my aversion to maintaining eye contact with people I didn't know well, because it made me feel like their gaze was crawling over my skin with thousands of tiny legs, I managed to meet Queenie's eyes.

"We're a little thin on the ground in the FDP department at the moment." She started to drum her purple nails on the desk with a loud clacking. "There's a task I need done."

I shivered, my gut clenching at the noise. I wanted to stride over and slap her hand still, but I probably wouldn't get out of here alive if I did.

"You're giving me an assignment?" I asked.

"It's more of a quick jaunt." *Clack. Clack. Clack-clack.* "Emil will fill you in."

Before she could dismiss me, a loud knock made me jump. The door opened and a familiar young woman strode in with Xavio close behind her, and another man I recognised, Emil, Head Mentor of the FDPs. He had another one of his boilersuits on, this one a dark blue, with a flat cap over his hairless head. I managed a weak smile for Petra, who I'd met in passing, and forced myself not to smirk at the sight of Taz inching in behind them, trying to look as if he belonged here.

"I was summoned." Petra stood with her arms folded. "Oh hi, Demi. Welcome back."

She wore her dark hair in a long ponytail, but I knew from

last term that the leggings, black dress and floral t-shirt masked a very no-nonsense fairy indeed.

I smiled at her, nerves stopping me from speaking as I turned back to face Queenie, my fingers curling around the strap of my satchel.

"Right, yes." Queenie stopped the infernal clacking and eyed us all. "As I said, we need you to complete an errand. It's nothing much, find some information and report back. Petra has been appointed your mentor, so you are both on the normal probationary watch. I'm sure after last year we can count on you to be back in a flash. Emil?"

I eyed Emil, noting his unimpressed frown.

"Right." He dug a sheet of paper from his pocket. "This is the brief. It's not a realm I'd have chosen for you, but I've done what I can to send you in prepared this time."

I reached forward and took the paper. Taz stood with his fingers twitching, no doubt desperate to shove me aside and take the page himself. For his benefit, I read the words out loud.

"Realm 191 – mixed hostility, medium magic. Pose as assistants and ascertain the location and any other information, such as participants, of the elite 'Forgotten 24 club'."

I read it over once again to myself, just to be sure, and looked up at Emil.

"Um, where exactly do we have to be assistants?"

"What's a '24 club'?" Taz asked.

"Are we aware of what exactly the 'mixed hostility' is?" Xavio stroked his beard thoughtfully.

Emil hesitated. "To answer you all in that order: I can show you, don't know and you don't want to know."

I wondered if I had a fair shot at dashing for the lift, my insides flipping with fear.

You can do this. You've done an assignment before, and

succeeded, just about. If you say no now, they'll never consider you for the FDP trials next year.

I held my head up high despite my shoulders shaking underneath it.

"Okay." It was all I could say.

"Is this wise?" Taz asked, frowning as he folded his arms.

Emil gave him a withering look. "No it's not, mainly because I'm sending you with her. Realm 191 is Fae-strong and Gallows Oak is a prestigious club, but less standing around chatting."

Taz gasped. "You're sending us to Gallows Oak? But-"

"No buts," Emil warned. "It can't be avoided, and I'm sure you'll be able to handle yourselves."

Xavio's expression was only marginally more sympathetic.

"It'll be fine." He didn't sound so sure. "The quicker you go, the quicker you can find this club, expose it and get back here."

Petra sighed. "I suppose it could have been a worse assignment, somehow."

I nodded and took a step back, noticing Queenie had already lost interest in us and was reading a glossy copy of *Faeshionista* magazine.

"Then let's get this done," I mumbled.

Taz gave me a sympathetic look before leading the way out of the office. Emil strode off along the intersecting corridor without a word, leaving Taz, Xavio, Petra and I to head toward the lift.

"Maybe Queenie got Demi confused with someone else," Taz suggested as we squeezed into the lift.

"Ouch," I grumbled. "Say what you really think, don't hold back."

He pulled a face. "Well, first years aren't meant to take assignments, even if you did last time. Even second years don't. Maybe she's just not in her right mind or something."

"We're being tested," Petra said. "Demi and I are on probationary watch."

Xavio nodded sagely. "That's standard, or at least it used to be, in my day."

Silence fell and I let my fingertips ghost over the flap of my satchel. Leo had been suspiciously silent inside it for a while, almost as if he knew I'd send him to my room if I noticed him. No time now, and having him with me felt safe, right. I knew Ace would look after him if I asked, but I didn't have time to ask and Leo belonged with me.

Petra opened the gate the moment the lift stopped and hurried out first. I let Xavio go ahead of me, then Taz. As I stepped onto the walkway that led to the circular despatch platform, I felt a stab of nostalgia. An FDP's life was never settled, always in and out of different assignments and realms, and we never got to hang around after other people's happy endings.

I accidentally looked down at the Atrium far below as we strode along the walkway, and gulped down a wave of disorientation that turned my knees to jelly. There was no railing, nothing to stop us plummeting hundreds of feet to our doom at the slightest mistimed nudge.

I focused instead on the enormous wall of white quartz ahead and the rickshaws that surrounded it. Waiting for me on the circular platform was someone I knew would be glad to see me.

Trevor jumped down from the seat of his rickshaw. I was used to the trolls now, short with warty green skin and bat-like ears, and hearts of gold from what I'd experienced so far.

Trevor beamed at me.

"Hi, Demi! Glad to see you off adventuring again."

I raised a shaking hand. "Hi Trevor, thanks."

"So, you will check in regularly," Petra insisted. "Time passes similar to our own here, give or take an hour, so keep it sensible unless you're in serious trouble."

Taz folded his arms, his bottom lip peeking out. "What am I there for then, decoration?"

"If you like." Petra rolled her eyes. "You know Fae-folk better than Demi does. Help her. Got your orb, Deni?"

I nodded. It was always in my pocket. All that remained, I realised when I saw them all staring at me, was to get in the rickshaw. It was a small one and a tight squeeze, but I had enough space beside Taz, who seemed to be all elbows and knees, to lean forward and catch Xavio's eye.

"You'll be fine, just keep your head." He gave me a thumbs-up sign.

"Okay," I took a shaky breath. "Trevor, please take us to Realm 191. Somewhere discreet and can we go steady on the landing please?"

I'd learned the long way that you had to be very specific with instructions for realm-skipping. Trevor grabbed the wooden handles at the front of the rickshaw and grinned over his shoulder.

"Hang on then!"

I clung onto the front rail as he wheeled around to face the huge wall of Quartz. It picked up the weak sunlight filtering through the dome ceiling, dazzling if stared at too long.

Trevor launched into a run. Taz clenched his eyes tight shut. I copied him moments later.

Unlike my first ever landing on my previous assignment, I didn't land in a stinky bog. But that didn't give us much of an advantage. I opened my eyes again and stared at the dense forest surrounding us in all directions.

Taz clambered out and I followed, taking the hand he held out to help me without thinking. I flinched, expecting him to get a mighty shock, but he didn't even blink.

Phew. Perhaps I exhausted the zap-power on Jenny earlier.

As Trevor whirled in a circle and disappeared with a cheery farewell, I tried to squelch down the tremor of anxiety fluttering in my gut.

Before I could say a word to Taz, a throat cleared nearby, making us both jump.

"Hi, I'm Milo. What are you doing out here?"

CHAPTER THREE
INTO THE THICK OF IT

"Umm, hi." Alarmingly, I recovered my wits before Taz did. "Can you give us a minute?"

Milo appeared to be relatively normal in that he was a teenage boy, a somewhat bulky one with shaggy ash blonde hair and even broader shoulders than Ace under his blue duffel coat. I ignored my brain pestering me with Paddington Bear references as he nodded.

"Okay, sure."

Milo waited patiently with his hands clasped in front of him. I turned to find Taz right beside me and we sidled a few paces away behind a nearby tree.

"What do we do?" he murmured.

"Well, he's as good a guide as any," I whispered. "I'll ask him if he's heard of the 24 club."

Taz's turquoise eyes flashed. "It's an elitist Fae place, so the club is bound to be a secret! Orbs alive, use your head."

Ruffled by his tone, I prepared to ask Milo some very awkward questions about where we were. But before I could drum any up, Taz jostled past me.

"Hi, mate." He approached Milo, all easy smiles. "We're a bit lost. Where are we?"

"You're in the forest outside the Gallows Oak social club," Milo explained. "I don't think people are expected to be here. Are you meant to be visiting someone?"

Before I could answer, a vibration shook my pocket. I pulled out my orb, the pearly ball dangling on the end of its silver keychain. Taz flashed a scowl at me, but it was too late to hide it now. I had no idea whether people in this realm like Milo would recognise it or think it was witchcraft, so different were the variations of understanding in the many realms of Faerie.

A ghostly, pearlescent image of a familiar face loomed right in front of me with such horrific clarity that I squeaked in alarm. Queenie's sharp features, made no less severe by the shades of grey, seemed to bore right into my nervous system. My hand started to shake and Taz gave me a withering look as Queenie's voice boomed through the trees.

"All inter-realm travel has been suspended, following a breach in security. I have been advised to tell you to make yourselves safe as much as you are able, and your mentor will communicate when you are allowed to return. That is all."

As Queenie disappeared again, my insides twisted with panic. A breach in security could have been another attack by the Forgotten.

If travel's been suspended, then Trevor can't come back for us. We're stuck here. I can't risk doing anything wrong either if I'm on probation.

Milo stood staring at the orb in my hand, his jaw slack with shock.

"Um, sorry," I grimaced at him. "Could you just give us one more minute?"

Milo nodded and shuffled a few steps back, clasping his hands in front of him again as if obedience was his default reaction.

At least he's not running screaming to the nearest pit of Fae civilisation.

Taz's head appeared right beside mine, but I couldn't dwell on the anxiousness of having someone right over my shoulder.

"Do you know anything about this place, or the club we're

after?" I asked.

Taz shrugged, glancing back and forth at the empty space between the trees. I knew he was keeping watch for anyone else that might come across us, but I had to think of a plan and quick.

"Gallows Oak is where all the elite Fae hang out," he said. "But I've only heard whispers, rumours, and none from my mother's court would be caught here. I don't know anyone who would be influential."

"Do you think the breach has anything to do with last summer, or the Forgotten?"

He shrugged. "I wouldn't be surprised. The Forgotten have always wanted to overthrow my- the Queen, but for them to actually attack a stronghold like Arcanium, then there must be a branch of the Fae dynasty family ready to step in now, powerful and influential. This is exactly the place they would turn up at."

"Not exactly encouraging," I sighed.

"Well, we're stuck here." Taz huffed. "First, we need to get ourselves in. Emil said we're meant to be assistants, so we go up and find someone to give us something to assist with. We can learn more about the situation once we're settled."

I resisted the urge to comment on how he seemed to be taking charge, mainly because his idea made the most sense. Taz stared at me expectantly.

"Well?" He raised his eyes upwards in disbelief. "Aren't you going to go and get started? You are the "FDP" after all."

Okay, the air quotes hurt.

I blinked back at him and experienced the strangest urge. I couldn't quite put my finger on it, but it felt rather like I wanted to throttle him. I knew it would be pointless to pick a fight when he was in a mood though, so I hurried back across the grass toward Milo instead.

"Hi, sorry." I had no idea what I was apologising for, but did it out of habit anyway. "So, yeah, um, we're meant to be starting at Gallows Oak as assistants today."

Milo frowned. "Assistants? You look as young as me, no offense. What kind of assistants?"

"Agency staff." I said, at the same time as Taz piped up, "Apprentices."

I glared at him. He frowned at me.

"Apprentice agency staff," I offered.

Milo blinked. "Oh, okay. You've come to the right place then I guess."

"Great." Taz straightened up and looked around at the forest. "We should go get inducted then."

Milo eyed us with quick, furtive glances as if he was scared that we were going to shout at him for staring too long.

"Are- Are you sure?" His voice rang clear but hesitant. "You still have time to get away, if you're quick. The ground patrols may not even catch you."

I wrapped my fingers around the strap of my satchel, unnerved.

"Is it really that bad?" I asked. "A place that needs ground patrols doesn't sound very welcoming."

Milo shrugged and stared at his feet. My doubts were screaming at me to flee, but we couldn't exactly go back home now, even if we wanted to.

Ignoring the cold grip of fear squeezing icy around my chest, I tried to think like someone generally brave and cool. Ace would have been perfect for this.

"It's- you'll see if you're intent on going there," Milo said. "I mean, you might be alright if you keep your head down and do as you're told." He eyed Taz. "But they might take more of an interest in you."

"You know who I am?" Taz asked.

Milo nodded. "Yes, um, sorry, should I be bowing? I've never met Fae royalty before. Is there an honorific I should be using? I figured if you were back here, you might be trying to be incognito."

I wanted to laugh, but the sheer depressed resignation wiping across Taz's face stole any hint of amusement away. Although people at Arcanium were used to him, he still had to deal with everyone else treating him differently because he was the prince of Faerie. I'd never actually considered it in any depth, but with him not being fully pure-blood Fae his sisters were, I didn't know if that meant he was first in line by virtue of being a boy like the human world, or not in line at all due to his lack of pure Fae blood.

If Milo knows who Taz is, then this is likely one of the realms that are aware of the courts and the overall set-up of Faerie itself.

That at least made things slightly easier to navigate in terms of talking to people, but also painted more of a target on my back considering I was half-fairy instead of Fae. The pure-blood elitists, like the Forgotten, looked down on half-Fae, who were termed as fairies, but a half-fairy half-human like me was lower than dirt to them.

Despite my own lowly status, my gut twisted with pity as Taz continued sulking.

"If you're being proper about it, just call him 'idiot' and move on." I suggested.

Taz looked at me with horror written across his face, which made me laugh. He started to smile, and I had to remind myself we were in a potentially dangerous situation still.

"I'm more than capable of looking after myself," Taz retorted, sticking his tongue out at me. "But I guess I should go for some kind of anonymity here. Don't make a big deal though, okay? I hate having to do this.”

I couldn’t help gawping. I’d seen him glamour once before, but it still amazed me. Where Taz had been standing a mere split second ago, there was now a completely different boy. Taller, slender and yet with hints of muscle under the dark green t-shirt he wore. The no-longer-Taz had wavy chocolate brown hair and bright blue eyes big enough for a Frozen character. I started scanning his face for signs, as if I could find magic seams that stitched the effect together.

“Oh to be a proper fairy,” I sighed.

Most fairies and Fae at Arcanium learned to glamour in their second year of mentee training, but by virtual of being royal, Taz had learned as a child. He faced me, his lips pressed in a disagreeable expression that was still so unmistakably him somehow.

“Don’t be an idiot,” he said with a huff. “We’re all Fae to some degree. I’m just a bit more tainted than the rest of you. I’m direct half-blooded, so it’s only my family that’s full. Milo, is this place as bad as the rumours make it sound? Like, traditionally, typically Fae?”

Milo nodded. “Pretty much, sorry.”

“Great.” Taz wrapped his arms over his broader-than-usual chest. “I’ve heard of Gallows Oak. We’re basically walking into a country club full of egomaniacal, manipulative people, all of whom probably have been given token fairy gifts from relatives without actually earning them, therefore have no respect for what they’re capable of, that about right?”

Milo nodded again, a look of abject misery passing across his face. Feeling sorry for him, I copied Taz’s stance.

“You don’t like Fae, we get it.”

I gave him a look which seemed to surprise him into momentary silence. Either way, fairy or Fae, weren’t going to get anywhere standing around in the forest.

"Milo, can you take us to someone who can get us started?" I asked.

Milo shrugged. "If I have to, although I still think you're mad, sorry."

He set off into the trees and I started after him, Taz stomping along behind.

"So, why are you here if you're not full Fae?" Milo asked. "Couldn't you ask- I mean, I'm guessing the agency thing isn't real, if you're... um?"

Despite the hesitation, I knew what he was getting at.

I should have thought of this, should have made Taz glamour before we even got in the rickshaw. I should have insisted on twenty minutes to do some research before we left, anything would have done.

Then again if we'd left it twenty minutes, Taz and I wouldn't have made it into the realm at all.

I sought for the best way to explain things to Milo without doing something dim, and guessed vague honesty would probably be best.

"It's a long story but, um, I'm a Fairy Deity Person, or FDP."

Milo's eyes widened. "Wow, really?"

"Well, sort of. I'm just a mentee, but they sent me here- well, us. I shouldn't be telling you, but I feel like we can maybe trust you not to say anything. Can we?"

I bit my lip, relieved Milo couldn't see my face from up front. Everyone knew Fae and fairies couldn't lie, but I didn't like having to word-tangle him into answering me honestly. If he said nothing, then that was a no.

"People don't pay much attention to me," Milo said. "They never have. I won't say anything about who you really are, assuming I don't get tricked into it. I'm not that great at most things, to be honest, so they probably won't bother asking me."

That was as close to a yes as I was going to get.

I didn't mention needing to find any clubs or deviant nests of evil Fae, hoping to gain Milo's trust first. Above all, we needed to keep an ally in what was beginning to sound like enemy territory.

"How long have you been here then, Milo?" Taz called up.

I focused on not stumbling over embedded roots as we trampled through the undergrowth, running my hand over my satchel to feel the reassuring lump of Leo inside. I would need to be so careful with him here as well, and the foolishness of not handing him over to Ace after all made my face burn.

"I've been here since I was nine," Milo said. "I'm a nobody so my uncle dumped me here. It's never mentioned, but I think the Director owed him a great debt and offloading me onto the club as staff was it. They keep telling me I don't really belong here, even though my mother promised me I was Fae before she died."

I wasn't sure how to respond to that but tried anyway as we came to the edge of the trees.

"Oh."

Milo shrugged his burly shoulders. "I shouldn't complain. I get a room of my own, mainly because nobody else would have me in theirs and people are housed according to familial importance, but they feed me the same as the other staff. That's the club there."

A grassy hill led up to a towering red-brick building in front of us. Long corridors reached out on either side of the main structure built at angles to accommodate the slopes underneath them, like a tall spider with two arched legs splayed out. I bit my lip, trying not to associate the sharp metal decorations on the edges of the roofs as barbed wire hemming in a prison. In comparison, the entrance had been decorated in astonishing glamour against the brick, with pale marble columns flanking towering statues and a set of semi-circular, white stone steps leading up to vast doors of what looked like shining black glass.

"Yep, that's Fae alright," Taz remarked. "Total ostentatious shark tank. We should have formulated a plan first."

I shot him a look to imply he wasn't helping and focused on the facts.

"Before anything else, we need to figure out how to explain our presence to people inside. It's either that, or consider running back into the forest to live in the wild until the realm-skipping ban is lifted."

My sisters had forced me to put up a tent once, and I reckoned that building a shelter out of branches and foliage couldn't be anywhere near as traumatic.

"And here comes Director Cornelius," Milo added glumly. "For the record, I did give you the chance to get away."

I eyed the tall, imposing man striding down the grassy incline toward us.

"They let you call them by their first names?" I asked.

Taz snorted. "Of course not. Cornelius is his last name."

Milo glanced at him, alarmed. "You know him?"

"Unfortunately, yes, in passing. Let's just say we should be glad I can pull on a glamour after all."

I had no suitable outlet for the hundred questions boiling in my mind, like how it was that he knew the Director at all if he and his mother's court didn't associate with these social circles.

The Director moved with innate grace toward us, a cloak of the finest black satin billowing atmospherically behind him. When he stopped in front of us, I noticed the initials *A.R.C.* on the left breast of the cloak, but Milo's entire body shaking beside me took all my attention.

"You'll be the new assistants I've been told to expect?" Director Cornelius asked. "You are Demerara and Roger?"

I froze, the urge to laugh tickling my insides like a gigantic feather as I saw Taz's scandalised expression. Someone, Petra most likely, had smoothed our way into the realm after all.

At least she had the foresight to give Taz an alias, even if I didn't.

"That's us." I jumped in. "I'm Demerara, but everyone calls me Demi, and he's Roger."

"We were lucky Milo found us," Taz said, his tone icy. "I'm surprised we weren't met at the gates."

The Director regarded Taz for several, tense seconds of silence. I wanted to shake him, but couldn't. I guessed fairy assistants, even half-Fae ones like him, weren't supposed to be hoity-toity to the employers. Milo's shaking escalated to a full-on tremble which gave me the jitters too. If Taz had any nerves he was a master at hiding them, and he held the Director's gaze without a shred of anxiety. Cornelius eventually relented and held an arm out to invite us up the hill.

"All new recruits are welcome." He gave Taz one last, appraising look. "We have only the highest standards here and not everyone can thrive in such an elite environment, but we shall see."

When we didn't move immediately, Cornelius set off back up the incline first. Taz powered after him, leaving Milo and I to trail behind. I cast a furtive glance at Milo but the poor boy was still a bag of nerves, staring at the ground in front of him. I knew what Fae could be like, tricksy, manipulative and often downright cruel. Milo's reaction to the authority figure didn't fill my half-fairy soul with any confidence.

As we neared the building, I couldn't help ogling the guests arriving in all sorts of frippery and finery. Several motorbikes in shining black, red and chrome were parked to one side, some of them still beneath their riders.

Taz appeared beside me and I held in a squeak as one rider turned their head, showing off what looked like a long snout amid a huge mane of hair.

"Werewolves," Taz muttered in my ear. "Don't let them catch you staring."

I transferred my gaze to a group of impeccably dressed women, their silvery blue gowns trailing trains and their faces a matching hue of pale blue.

"Water nymphs," Taz added. "Don't drink anything they offer you."

He nudged my elbow with his and I had to tear my gaze away to catch up. Cornelius dodged toward a side door in one of the long corridors either side of the main building and flung it open.

"Milo will show you to your accommodation." His eyes flickered with a spark of cruelty as he looked Milo up and down. "I believe he has plenty of spare room on his floor for other assistants. See that they're inducted sufficiently, Milo."

Milo nodded. "Yes, Director Cornelius."

Without another word, the Director disappeared inside with an elaborate swirl of his cape. When Milo let out a tumbling breath of relief, I felt several links of tension unravel in my gut.

"So, escape rates aren't high around here then," I asked, knowing the answer.

Milo managed a meek smile. "Not really. I guess it could be worse. The meals are second to none and it does give you good life skills. Well, if you manage to survive the clients that is."

He started toward the door. Taz gave me a dark look as I hurried after Milo in horror.

"Wait, what do you mean, survive the clients?"

CHAPTER FOUR
AN UNEXPECTED ALLY

Milo waved us through the door that Director Cornelius had left open behind him.

"I'll explain everything," he insisted. "There are some parts of Gallows Oak that aren't as respectable as others, and you don't get to choose which tasks you get given, but don't worry."

That didn't sound like something not to worry about, especially as I looked around at the lamp-lit, windowless halls of plain grey stone, adorned with various swords, bows, pikes and other weapons.

"You're here at a busy time as well," Milo continued. "The Grand Puzzle Tower is in two days' time, but I'll give you all the advice you need for surviving, as best I can at least."

Taz gave him a reassuring smile. I still couldn't get used to looking over and seeing Taz in his Roger glamour rather than the boy I knew, but there were similarities in the voice still that reassured me, the intonation and the depth of it.

"Sounds like we're lucky it was you who found us," he said.

Milo smiled shyly. "I think I'm the lucky one to have met you two. Not many people here acknowledge me but now I have roommates! Also, I do a few odd side jobs for some of the nicer people here, like Mrs Paget who looks after us assistants. You've missed our dinner, but she lets me have the keys so I can sneak down to the kitchens and get you something if you're hungry."

He pulled out a jangling bunch of tarnished metal keys and headed toward a wooden door at the far corner of the hall.

Him having keys could be useful at some point.

I didn't like the idea of potentially having to pick them if we had to go looking for the Forever 24 club, but here it was clearly going to be a case of doing whatever it took to survive.

I checked Leo was still asleep inside my satchel and we followed Milo through the deserted halls. Despite the lamps lighting our way, Milo picked up his pace as if he didn't want to linger.

Three flights of stairs later, I stared down a narrow, dingy corridor with the wallpaper peeling at the corners. There were floorboards instead of flagstones and runners like previous floors. Then Milo picked up a lantern which he lit with a match from a box in his pocket.

"This floor used to be staff quarters but now it's for storage," he explained. "They moved the paid employees into better rooms long ago, but it's more than good enough for me."

I didn't want to mention how cold it was. I guessed if Milo had no lighting, he'd also have no access to heating either. If the mention of cold showers was brought up, I decided I would wait until I was alone to moan in despair. Fairies and Fae couldn't lie, but I couldn't imagine saying what I really thought out loud either.

"We don't need much compared to some." Taz's tone didn't quite keep up with the smile. "Do you get heating up here, like for water and things? I know how to start a contained fire, if needed."

Of course you do.

I resisted the urge to ask him why he knew such things. Milo shook his head and opened two doors at the far end of the hall, one on each side.

"Bathroom is on the right." He pointed. "It has hot water and we have heating. There's lighting too, just not in the hallway. I keep meaning to put a new bulb in but never get round to it with all the other chores I have to do."

Relieved, I followed the others into the bedroom. Milo flicked a switch on the wall by the door and several lamps began to glow. He swivelled to face us.

"It's not much," he apologised.

I blinked, diverted from negative thoughts. The bedding looked clean and there were two pillows on each of the three beds. Milo even had a couple of books on the desk. Apart from that, and a wardrobe in the far corner, the room looked all but unlived-in.

"This is great." Taz sighed, his shoulders sagging with relief. "It's the kind of place you could hide secrets and nobody would know."

A cheap shot and a lazy attempt at digging for information, but when I gave him a look he winked at me.

Milo chuckled. "No secrets, just me I'm afraid."

"I imagine this is the type of place where you'd have clandestine meetings of all sorts," I added. "I used to love those stories as a kid, where you'd find panels in the cellar that opened hidden tunnels. Or there was one where there was a society in an old summer camp and they had passwords and everything."

Milo's eyes widened and he glanced at the shut door behind him.

"There's initiation, where newcomers are tested by their peers. Some of the staff set each other silly dares sometimes as well, like stealing things as trophies. But I doubt you'd get invited as initiates though, no offense."

His eyes widened, his mouth twitching with anxiety. I wondered if he was regretting being so forward, if he expected us to punish him for it. My heart squished for him, a kindred spirit. But where I'd had to put up with my sisters tormenting me, he'd had to put up with a whole club full of Fae by the sounds of it.

"I doubt we'd want to join," I said with what I hoped was a reassuring smile. "Not our scene."

His expression brightened. "I tell you what, I'll go down and sneak some cocoa up from the kitchens. The cooks make the best cocoa."

"You can use the bathroom first then, Dem, while we wait," Taz offered.

I nodded and clutched the strap of my satchel. It would be tricky keeping Leo hidden, let alone properly fed, but at least he was behaving himself so far.

Sensing me hesitating, Taz shot me a determined smile and sat on the middle bed.

"So, Milo, before you rush off for cocoa, tell me all about you."

I took that as a veiled dismissal and went to check out the bathroom. Milo clearly kept it very clean. Spare towels waited on a wooden rack and I investigated the bottles of shampoo and body wash with intrigue. I had no idea what 'flower of Oia' was, but it smelled nice, like berries and cream.

I set my bag on top of the toilet lid and pulled out the contents. I had Leo of course in the main pouch, and the latest *Carrie's Castle* book in the flap pocket.

I turned my attention to my orb next. While Milo had seen Queenie's broadcast, and this was definitely going to be the kind of realm where orb-communication was commonplace, I had to be cautious. I couldn't risk people overhearing that we were searching for the Forever 24 club, or anyone else knowing I was from Arcanium. I held the orb up in front of my face.

"Petra? Are you there?"

Seconds passed. The vision of Petra's head appeared in

ghostly grey just as I was lowering my arm, so her chin bounced momentarily through the toilet.

"There you are." She frowned. "Are you okay?"

I sat on the edge of the bath as Leo slid into it and started to drink from the dripping tap.

"We're fine. We met a boy called Milo who's helping us find our way around. I haven't found anything about secret clubs though yet, and apparently the Fae hospitality isn't great to staff like us. What of this breach though? Is it *them* again?"

Petra's eyebrows disappeared beneath her hairline.

"Nothing to worry about, it's Queenie overreacting." Her tone was firm, and I knew not to push her for any more information. "At least you're established in the realm now. But you're okay other than that, aren't you?"

Endeared by her concern, I managed a smile.

"I'm fine, although we don't have changes of clothing or anything." I lowered my voice, conscious of the silence around me. "I guess it could be worse. I don't know where to even start looking though. The instructions were less than vague and I can't exactly go up to anyone and ask if there's a super-secret Forgotten club around."

Petra rubbed her nose. I saw glimpses that her usually neat hair was messy.

"I wouldn't hold your breath for an easy solution, no," she admitted. "I don't have much to report from here. I managed to get you on the rota as staff members, but my meagre influence won't reach much further beyond that I'm afraid."

"I know, they were expecting us. Also, Roger?"

Petra grinned. "Was he mad?"

"Indignant." I had to laugh. "The physical side we took care of as well, like looks and everything."

"I know, I'm watching the Ogle screen every spare second I

can. I'm also keeping on at everyone to reopen the wall so you can realm-skip back, but it's come from top level and you know Queenie. I'm working on other avenues and finding out what I can about where you are, if we have anyone we can do a deal with to get you some level of reassurance or help, but you need to stay safe for now. You'll be careful, won't you?"

I nodded. "Yeah, I will, thanks Petra. I'm going to get a shower and an early night, but seriously thank you."

"Keep me updated as often as you can. Stay safe, Demi."

"I will, thanks."

Petra's face disappeared and I stuffed the orb back in my pocket. I'd already hogged the bathroom for a while talking to her so I washed as fast as I could bear.

When I re-entered the bedroom with Leo back in my satchel, I found Taz and Milo completely at ease with each other. Or at least Taz looked at ease, lounging back on the middle bed like he belonged there, hands clasped behind his head. As Milo hurried off to get the cocoa, I sat on the bed furthest from the door with my satchel in front of me.

"So, deep in the thick of it now," Taz said. "Does it bother you, sharing a room with boys by the way? We can try and find you somewhere else, although I don't think the girl staff will be much friendlier than the clients in a place like this."

Touched he was being thoughtful, I eyed the four feet between his bed and mine.

Not ideal, but I'd rather share with Taz and Milo than the kind of Fae I assume are going to frequent this place.

Even so, I couldn't fight the blush creeping across my cheeks.

"I think I'll cope." I peeked into my satchel and ran a finger over Leo's sleeping head. "If all else fails, I've got Leo."

Desperate to distract us from any awkward silences, I got up and started pacing beside the bed. How was I going to explain any of this to Milo without giving the game away? I'd already told him I was an FDP.

"Want me to make something up?" Taz's unusually soft voice disturbed my thoughts.

"Huh?"

"Want me to make up a story about why we're here? I'm experienced at word-tangling, been doing it for years. I'm used to these people."

I shrugged. "We still don't know why Milo was conveniently out there in the forest when we turned up, or if it's coincidence that he has two extra beds ready and waiting for us. Petra can't have had much time to let them know we were coming for them to sort extra beds. But if you're offering to pitch in, I won't say no. That's probably why Emil sent you with me anyway, I'm the FDP mentee but you're the one who actually knows about Fae stuff."

Taz frowned and opened his mouth to say something, but the door swung wide and he didn't get a chance. Milo inched into the room with a feast teetering on a wooden tray and my stomach forced my brain into freefall.

"I got there and I wasn't sure what you ate," he explained, setting the tray down on the end of Taz's bed. "Some people don't eat animals, others have allergies, so I thought best get something for everyone."

I eyed the tray, marking out a bowl of salad which would do for Leo, but I wasn't sure I could risk Milo knowing about him yet.

"We agreed it would be best I explain," Taz announced. "Have you heard ever that there are other realms besides this one?"

Milo nodded. "I know some of the Fae don't live anywhere

near here, but I never wanted to pry. Alcartan, where my uncle lives, is definitely somewhere else completely. I've read some books as well about it, but a lot of the ones around here are written in ancient Faeish so I can't understand them anyway. But the man in the club's bookshop lets me work the counter a bit to pay off any books I want, so I'm a huge *Carrie's Castle* fan."

I grinned at the sound of that. A *Carrie's Castle* fan couldn't be a complete monster.

"Have you read the latest one?" I asked. "Where the castle turns into-"

"-the Mount of a Hundred Horrors?" Milo's eyes lit up. "Oh that was amazing-"

We jumped as Taz cleared his throat. He sat with his arms folded, his foot now tapping on the floorboards.

Apparently, he is a complete monster.

"As fun as this is, we should keep things on point." He gave me an irritable look.

"Sorry." I nodded and hurried over to grab a plate and a pile of food. "I don't get to talk about it much with anyone as you and Ace aren't fans, but go ahead."

Milo hung his head a little as Taz ploughed on.

"So, these other realms are like a flower. Arcanium, where we're from, is one of the petals, and this place is a different petal. So are all the realms of Faerie. Then to get from realm to realm, you need a skip-way. Either that or you need to be gifted with translocation, but that's unbelievably rare as the person giving it has to be super powerful."

Milo stared at Taz with his mouth hanging open. I wondered if he would start laughing or worse, start backing slowly out of the room. He seemed to be thinking something through, his brow furrowing up and down and his lips twitching through words.

"So, why are you here?" he asked after a long pause.

Taz eyed me and I bit my lip.

"As I said earlier, I'm an FDP and we get given assignments," I explained. "I was told my assignment was to come here, but not much else. If I had my way, I'd be getting some more instruction from them right about now."

It wasn't a lie, just a half-attempt at word-tangling, but Taz's smile suggested I hadn't completely mucked it up.

"We do have the slight complication of being stuck here though," I continued. "Arcanium have closed all realm travel for some reason. We just need to keep safe until it's available again. I mean, we're at a sort of social club, right? How bad can it really be?"

Milo gave me a worried look. "You have no idea."

I had no answer to that, and my anxiety climbed until I couldn't stop myself pulling my hand inside my sleeve to tap my fingers back and forth.

Taz sighed. "We have to play along for a while it looks like, until we can move things forward."

Milo looked so sad for us that I had to change the subject. I decided the situation probably couldn't get much worse if I risked asking Taz a personal question instead.

"So, how do you know the Director then?"

He glowered at me, the effect marred by the glamour he still wore, making him look mildly disgruntled instead of the moody teen effect he usually had going on.

"Through Fae circles. He's definitely no friend of my family."

"Do any of your family hang out here?" I asked.

"No, they wouldn't be allowed. Not our sort of establishment, and the restrictions on royalty are always harsh for protection. Anyway, this isn't to do with me."

I wanted to ask how he could possibly have been allowed to come on this assignment anyway, but decided not to push my luck.

Him not being half-Fae probably diminishes his value in the eyes of Faerie so he'd be the last one to get kidnapped. His ability to glamour also helps.

Milo passed around mugs of cocoa and my mouth started to water. I grabbed the one he held out to me, complete with whipped cream, marshmallows and chocolate flakes. I downed half in a few greedy gulps, stopping only to wipe cream off my nose. Even Taz gave me a look and started laughing, but he'd already finished his and had a foam moustache. He wiped it off with the back of his hand and stretched with a groan.

"Guaranteed to give you the best night's sleep ever," Milo said, clearly not as enamoured with the cocoa as he'd barely touched his.

I hid a yawn behind my hand and slumped on my pillows with one hand on my satchel. Now that I had a comfortable bed to settle on and no immediate danger pressing in, it surprised me how sleepy I was.

I'll need all the rest I can get by the looks of it in this place.

CHAPTER FIVE
THE KING IS COMING, LOOK BUSY

I opened my eyes to a vast sea of brown. Blinking, I realised this was a) the flat surface of a bedside table and b) not my bedside table at Arcanium, or the wall next to my bed at Mum's house. I sat up with a start to see a boy in the bed next to me rubbing his eyes. It took me a couple of moments of sheer unfamiliar panic before I remembered the day before and Taz's glamour. His disguise as 'Roger', all brown flicky hair, straight nose and big eyes, disorientated me. Then I eyed his healthy-looking tanned skin with a sigh.

Of course he'd wake up looking flawless. Stupid half-Fae boy. I frowned and lifted a hand to my hair. *Yep, and mine is doing the whole ball of wool after the cat thing.*

Milo's bed was empty, but the sound of water running suggested he was in the bathroom.

"Morning." Taz nodded.

I nodded back. "Morning."

Okay, that's not awkward at all. I ignored the flush creeping over my cheeks. *Focus on the reason we're here. We need to find out about the 24 club, then we can work out how to get back to normality.*

"Did you sleep well?" he asked after a long pause.

I nodded, frowning. "Yeah, surprisingly well actually."

Taz opened his mouth to say something, but the door swung open and Milo came bustling through, already dressed in a red t-shirt and black jeans with a pile of pyjamas in his arms.

"Morning! You've got about twenty minutes each left to

shower, then we need to be downstairs for breakfast and to report in."

Taz glanced at me and held out his hand to the door. I shrugged and grabbed my satchel. It didn't exactly have anything useful in it other than Leo, like fresh clothes, but I wasn't letting it out of my sight.

I washed quickly and wrangled my hair into a half-neat ponytail, then went back to the room to give Taz his turn. The moment I stepped through the bedroom doorway, I had to stop and stare.

Both Milo and Taz wore the same uniform of black jeans with the deep, blood-red t-shirt over the top. I noticed a suspiciously similar bundle on the end of my bed and pointed to it.

"Mandatory?" I asked.

Milo nodded. "Yeah, we all have to wear it, but it could be so much worse."

Granted, a fresh pair of jeans and a t-shirt was the least of my worries. But what if they didn't-

"I got Mrs Paget to choose the size for you," he added. "They should fit. She has expandable waist ones apparently for safety's sake."

I grabbed the t-shirt and the jeans and stalked back to the bathroom to change. Of course, the clothing fit perfectly. Not perfect for me, given that the t-shirt was all but skin-tight and the jeans were not nicely baggy in the slightest, but ideal in that they fit someone my size.

I emerged from the bathroom for a second time to find Taz and Milo waiting in the hall.

"I'm forgoing my privileges so we've got fifteen minutes to explore instead." Taz grinned. "Just need the loo."

I ignored the suggestion of bathroom habits and faced Milo

instead.

"What kind of things can we expect to be doing?" I asked.

Milo rubbed the back of his neck. "Oh, kitchen duty probably, or laundry. You need to achieve higher level training before they allow you to interact with the club members, which neither of you have. But Director Cornelius has told me to guide you, so that means I don't have to interact with them for a while either."

I couldn't help smiling at that. "You don't like the guests?"

Milo looked up and down as if the light fittings might be eavesdropping, although in this place literally anything was possible.

"Some of them are okay, but I just want to avoid it for the next few days."

I leaned back against the wall. "Why's that?"

Milo blinked. "Because the King is coming, of course."

Of course, silly me, I should have somehow magically intuited that.

I took a deep breath and almost choked on it as the bathroom door flew open.

"The Old King?" Taz flew out, almost crashing into me as he turned toward us. "The Old King is going to be here?"

Milo cowered as if he expected to be hauled up by his collar, although he was half a head taller and much broader than Taz.

"Um, yes. He's arriving this morning. It's all everyone is talking about, a big deal. He does sometimes frequent the club of course, but only privately on a need to know basis, and nobody ever knows exactly when until after he's left again. But this is public, a big to-do."

I watched the internal implosion on Taz's glamoured face, visible only through the narrowing of his eyes and the twitch of his teeth rolling over his bottom lip. Time to do what I did best:

embarrass myself.

"Um, sorry to be dim, but aren't we meant to have a Queen instead?"

Milo stared at me, but Taz didn't even blink as he replied.

"The Queen overthrew the Old King, long ago. The initial rumour was that she killed him, but those close to her always knew he'd been exiled. Lately, he's been gaining favour in dark corners of Faerie that m- the Queen can't reach. The more favour he gains, the more of Faerie the Queen loses."

I remembered the calm, smiling woman who'd picked me up from Mum's. She didn't strike me as the kind of person who was losing parts of her kingdom, but then I guess I didn't look like the kind of person to be charging into FDP assignments either.

I glanced at Taz's furious face, wondering if it was just family loyalty that had riled him, or something deeper that I had no idea of.

"Right well, nothing we can do about that right now," I said, despite my brain itching with questions and worries. "Let's do our quick tour, get some breakfast and find out all the club's dirty secrets."

Taz nodded, but I could see his mind was still stuck on the Old King's imminent arrival. Milo hurried down the hall but I kept pace with Taz, giving him space to think.

"The Old King is the worst of the Fae," he muttered. "I can't even mention some of the things he did, but if I see him, I should be honour-bound to kill him on the spot."

I blinked and tried to keep my face neutral.

"Since when do you care about family honour?" I asked. Finally, he glanced at me. "Come on, you're no killer. Pain in the arse maybe. Besides, who else would keep getting me into trouble if you were imprisoned for murder? Or murdered?"

Even as the words danced out of my mouth, the mere thought made me anxious. I couldn't read his expression for a long moment, and my mind wandered off wondering where Fae convicted of crimes ended up. It wasn't something we'd ever learned about in fairy classes, but perhaps now wasn't the best time to ask Taz.

Milo stopped at the bottom of the stairs to wait for us, but Taz kept our pace slow. Then his shoulders sagged.

"Thanks, I think. We need to focus on finding things out first, you're right."

"First time for everything," I joked.

Taz rolled his eyes. "Oh, the modesty. Just don't expect me to be polite to him, or not to curse him if I get the chance."

We reached Milo, who smiled hopefully like a bear with a toothache.

"I'll take you through the central chamber," he said. "That's worth seeing. There won't be much time for more than a quick look at what's where, but maybe in a couple of days we can do a proper tour."

We followed him toward a door at the far end of the corridor. Milo hesitated with his hand on the handle and threw the door open with a flourish.

Lights and colours flashed like a media storm on the television, but it was just the hustle and bustle of a huge hall. I inched through the doorway, overwhelmed by the loud hum of noise and the nauseating pong of combined expensive perfumes and colognes.

"This is the central chamber." Milo's head appeared between mine and Taz's. "You can see the entrance there on the right, then straight ahead you have the wellness and training centre. There's stabling for one hundred animals, the spa, the fighting pits, the race course- oh, and the climbing arena."

I stared at the entrance to a large hallway on the other side of the chamber, covered by a vast golden archway. For all I knew, that was real gold.

Idiot, this is a Fae stronghold. It's probably something even more valuable than gold.

"Over to the left, you have the shopping district," Milo continued. "It's thirteen floors and extends back for longer than I've ever wanted to wander. Come on, we can have a quick look in the window."

We trailed after him through the crowds. He held himself tall and walked fast, but I was too busy gawping to be mindful of my place.

One woman wafted past with a dress made of jewels. The whole dress, train trailing behind her, was glimmering. She had a pinched look around her eyes and walked like a snail dragging a hefty shell.

"The length these idiots will go to fit in." Taz snickered. "I bet you she's exhausted."

I nodded. "Yeah, that and one of those shoulder straps could probably buy a normal person a conscience."

We joined Milo at one of the huge windows, lit up bright so the items inside stood out to passers' by.

I eyed a shiny black pen with a curling plume at the end, along with the price tag.

"Two hundred percats," I murmured and glanced at Taz. "That's Fae currency, right?"

"Yeah. I'm not sure exactly what the currency rate to human money would be though."

"A percat is approximately one thousand human pounds," Milo chipped in. "I sometimes get sent to work in the exchange here. We often have customers asking to transfer human money, but humans must call their exchange process something else."

"Why do you say that?" I asked, still reeling from the idea that a *pen* could cost two hundred thousand pounds.

Milo frowned, glancing around the chamber.

"They come in, put human money on the counter and say it needs washing."

I blinked. "You mean laundering?"

"Yes! I assume they're used to the human world and its ways, but we wouldn't dare ask questions of our customers."

I shook my head. *Fae getting human money through trickery no doubt, and coming to turn it clean. Nobody would ever be able to trace it then.*

Before I could fathom the inner workings of the inter-world financial systems, Milo gasped.

"Oh, we're going to be late! Sorry, here's me going on. We won't even have time for breakfast now. Come on."

Taz descended into discontented grumbling, always one who wore his emotions on his stomach, but Milo was heading back toward the door we'd entered through. We hurried after him into the long corridor and straight through to a dingy canteen. The buffet bar at the far end was nothing like the gleaming chrome counter in the Arcanium canteen, and the seats looked as though they might leave a stain if you sat on them too long. It was as different to the glitz we'd just been walking past as anything could get.

Nothing like polar opposites to remind everyone of their place.

"Ah, Milo, there you are." A woman bustled up, her expression sharp despite the grandmotherly face. Even she was dressed in the uniform, but held a clipboard with several bits of paper shoved on at random angles. "And you must be Demi and Roger. I'm Mrs. Paget, your team leader. Right, it'll be kitchen duty this morning for you, ease you in with Milo. You'll soon learn our ways. But first, we need to be up at the entrance."

Milo froze. "Out front? Why?"

"Why do you think, boy? We're being trotted out for the King's arrival."

Taz stiffened beside me. I shuffled a step closer, as if me hiding his clenched fist could wipe the scowl off his face as well.

"Well, off you go!" Mrs Paget waved her clipboard at us.

Milo inclined his head to the door and we trouped back into the hall.

"We won't have to do anything," Milo said. "Just stand there and clap or whatever we're told. Bow low if addressed, don't make eye contact. Once he's inside we'll come back down and start washing duty. It's fairly easy but takes a while."

I kept one eye on Taz as Milo chattered on, but he didn't give me any reassurance that he wasn't suddenly going to go kamikaze and try to assassinate the Old King or anything dim. I took a deep breath, reminded myself that I couldn't be responsible for his actions, then started planning ways to either distract or disarm him.

We emerged into dazzling sunlight, like the very depth of summer. I blinked against it and held up a hand so I could squint across the grounds. I could see the hill we'd walked up yesterday to my right, and to the left of that the long, wide drive. Banners of dark blue and red were fluttering in a breeze, and the scent of something floral filled the air.

"Our guest arrives," Director Cornelius' voice echoed, magnified across the grounds. "To attention everyone."

We stood at the back of a sea of red and black. Everyone in a uniform stood on the right of the main entrance, and everyone else to the left. I gawked at the collection of impeccably dressed Fae in the opposite crowd, all decked in outlandish dresses and suits that dripped with jewels, and hats that seemed to get bigger and madder the closer the wearer was to the front. The separation between the two sides couldn't have been clearer.

A clattering noise drew everyone's attention. Heads craned and handheld fans began to flutter as a large horse-drawn carriage came into view.

"That's obscene," I whispered to Taz out of the corner of my mouth.

He grunted but didn't reply as the coach loomed closer, pulled by a team of eight golden horses and driven by a man dressed in a gold top-hat and tails. Behind the carriage were the entourage, a long train of people on horses, and motorbikes, and in cars, all carefully coordinated in gold.

Milo stood to attention with the rest, but it took a sharp jab in Taz's ribs and a stern look from me to get him to stop slouching with his arms folded across his chest.

The coach came to a halt in front of the entrance, and there seemed to be a communal breath being held as the driver hurried to open the door. I don't know what I expected from a Fae King, but I lifted my chin like everyone else to get a glimpse.

A black boot emerged, shining but more like a riding boot than a fancy one with buckles. The boot was accompanied by a leg in a fitted pair of black trousers. A man emerged, decked in a suit of golden velvet that fitted effortlessly to his muscular frame. I managed to get a few glimpses of his face through the crowd, surprised to find him much younger than I'd expected. Golden hair waved effortlessly around his temples and wide jaw, and he was more rugged-looking than I'd imagined a Fae King would be. When he smiled, all perfect white teeth and full pink lips, several of the people assembled had a variation of flutters.

I squinted harder. He was sinfully good-looking, in a too-perfect-to-be-real sort of way, but if I focused, I could see the sharp edges that all pure-blooded Fae had. The eyes a shade too glassy and the skin too much aglow. I tried to remember the Queen, for surely she had been much older than this King she'd supposedly overthrown. When I dredged up an image of her in my head, I realised she hadn't looked old at all, or maternal. She'd been suitably and deceptively ageless, just like the King now in front of me.

"Going to have a swoon?" Taz muttered.

"No." I scowled at him. "Why, are you?"

The King waved to the now cheering crowd and strode up the steps to the entrance with impulsive energy. Taz stood with his jaw tense and his fists pulsing at his sides. His gaze tracked the King's movements, a falcon waiting to pounce, but two huge men flanked the King and moved a few paces behind him. With bodyguards like those, I didn't fancy Taz's chances of even getting close.

The moment the King disappeared inside, silence fell, almost as if everyone was counting to ten.

Three... Two... One...

A hum of excitement broke out, feverish like swarms of bees meeting other swarms and deciding to party.

Milo pointed toward the side door and I nodded. We followed him inside and I blinked with relief at the cool dimness of the hallway. Taz was walking with his arms folded, but something else was bothering him now. I'd known him long enough to get familiar with his various expressions, even with the Roger glamour. The one-sided crumple of his mouth meant he was puzzling over something rather than silently fuming. Milo led us into a kitchen, all dingy surfaces, yellow lighting and brown cupboards.

"Right, stuff comes through this hatch here," Milo said as he passed around aprons. "We load it onto that wire rack. Once the rack is full, press this white button here and the conveyor belt will take it into the washer. Grab another rack from that pile there, and keep going."

I tied my apron on and took my place beside Milo at the rack. Taz stood on my other side and eyed the hatch doubtfully.

"So, things come down and I just put them in the rack?" he asked.

Milo looked at me, his eyes wide. He didn't want to tell Taz that the instructions had been simple, but I could handle this easily. My chore at home had been the washing up.

"When the stuff comes down, take it out and hand it to me. Milo, grab two racks and we can double up, move things faster."

Milo grinned at me. "Yes, boss!"

I rolled my eyes as a loud rattling noise filled the air. A moment later, the metal door of the hatch sprang up, revealing a pile of dirty plates and cutlery.

Taz wrinkled his nose. "I have to take those out? They're all grimy."

With a huff, I leaned over him. By the time I'd grabbed the tray underneath it all, the hatch was buzzing again. Milo appeared beside me with a pair of bright pink washing up gloves which he handed to Taz.

"I never bother with them," he said. "But you can wear them if you like."

Taz stared back at us like he suspected a huge joke at his expense. I finished putting the dirty bits in the nearest rack and found another tray waiting in the hatch.

"Just put them on, we're backing up already." I reached past him to grab the next lot.

With Taz gloved up, we started working. He wrinkled his nose every time he picked up a tray, but he'd hold the tray steady while I pulled bits off of it. In mere minutes we'd sent four racks into the washer and were picking up speed.

I tried not to smirk at Taz's dainty behaviour, knowing he couldn't help his royal upbringing, but every time he pulled a face I had to smile.

"Okay, there must be some kind of speed gift or initiative that can get this done without the need for us," he insisted. "Why can't they just gift someone with super speed, or a whole bunch of people?"

Milo smiled. "Because this is the way it is. I'm sure you could create something automatic or magical, and have one person to monitor it, but then there'd be little need for us assistants."

"Not everyone can just magic up a solution either," I reminded him. "Some need these roles to live on."

I bit my tongue before saying that not everyone had a wealthy family who could provide the essentials at the click of their fingers either.

The kitchen door slammed, making us all jump. We whirled around to see a tall, slender girl leaning against the doorframe as if she owned the place. Her auburn hair was set in perfect curls around her face, her figure draped in an elegant monochrome wrap dress. Something about her, the pert nose lifted high in the air or the stark blue eyes, set my anti-mean-girl alarm on high alert.

"Well, new recruits." Even her voice was a confident symphony. "I'm Penelope."

Given her dismissive tone, I wondered if she expected us to bow. A boy appeared beside her, his straight black hair swept back from his forehead as if he'd been born to look naturally tousled, his angular face framing bright green eyes. He looked every inch a beautifully sculptured Fae, just as flawless as she was.

"This is Demi and Roger," Milo mumbled when nobody answered her. "They're new assistants I'm training."

Taz bristled beside me, but I knew Milo was trying to draw attention away from us.

"Oh." Penelope sighed. "Well, I daresay a bunch of runts like yourselves can find a suitable place in the pecking order."

Her mean words didn't fit her friendly tone, but I hadn't expected someone like her to be genuine. She kept her eyes widened to make her expression look welcoming, but her smile was thin and cruel, hidden with a lift of her chin.

"I think you'll find we have plenty to recommend us." Taz said.

Penelope eyed him up and down and chuckled. Behind the sound of gently tolling bells of her laughter, I heard the sharp, harsh notes of reality.

"I doubt it," she scoffed. "One half-fairy girl and a boy with tainted Fae blood. I didn't think even you could stoop so low in your acquaintances, Milo."

Taz's arms bunched with the clench of his fists. I tried to find something that I could say to calm the situation, but my mind was typically blank, so I went for the first thing that came to my lips.

"I doubt you'd know anything beyond surface appearances anyway given the look of you. You sit here in your cosy country club, playing at 'earning your dues' I'll bet, with less knowledge of surviving the real world than a common garden ant."

A bit harsh. Ants are actually fascinating creatures.

Everyone turned to stare at me. I caught the acidic curl on Penelope's lip, and the amazement on Taz's face. Even now, for some reason it still shocked him when I stood up for myself.

The slightest twitch beneath Penelope's facade suggested my words had found a chink to bat against.

"Well, I'm too busy for the likes of you," she sneered. "See you around, runts. Oh, I'd watch your back as well if I were you, Demi."

I watched her swish away, the unnamed boy following.

"Well, that was eventful," Milo murmured.

Taz only scowled deeper. I didn't risk reminding him that he didn't look like a prince of Faerie anymore, so now people were going to treat him like every other person.

"Penelope and Friese are both determined to win the Annual Puzzle Tower event," Milo said. "One of them will obliterate everyone else but then they're ruthless like that. Right, I think that's break time, but we're probably best off hanging out here if we want an actual break. You're not allowed to say no to anyone once you're away from staff areas, or even if you're in staff areas. If a client told you to clean fifty rooms for the hell of it, you'd have to."

He tapped a big red button on the wall, and the hatch door clanged shut. I assumed that was a signal that no more dirty things were to be sent down for a while, but couldn't get the image of the shoot filling up and overflowing into some posh dining room out of my head.

Tempting…

"What's this one do?" Taz asked, striding across the room to tap his hand against the shutter of another hatch.

Milo grimaced. "That's the hatch for Director Cornelius' private quarters. He's very particular about meals."

"Maybe he's afraid someone might try to poison him," Taz suggested.

He slouched against one of the counters with a disagreeable frown and I rubbed a hand over my face. I needed a few minutes of quiet thinking time and with him showing no signs of coming out of his sulk, I wouldn't get it here.

"Where's the bathroom?" I asked.

"There's one in the hall a couple of doors down from here," Milo pointed to the door. "Just out into the hall, turn left and count two doors. I can show you?"

"No, I'll find it. Thanks, Milo."

I strode toward the door. The corridor was teeming with staff rushing about, but I ducked my chin down to my chest to slip by unnoticed. I kept one eye on the doors I passed, looking for a toilet sign.

Someone backed out of a passing hallway, looming in front of me like a giant. I stumbled to a halt too late, bouncing off a sturdy, cloaked bicep that must have been the size of my thigh.

"Sorry!" I squeaked, looking up. "Oh."

A large face loomed down at me, the chin and mouth obscured by a wiry tangle of russet hair. I recognised him immediately. One of the Old King's bodyguards.

CHAPTER SIX
A VERY DEMI THING TO DO

"Look," the man's voice rumbled. "A tiny bird caught mid-flight. On you go tiny bird, be careful now."

I blinked at him, frozen. He was smiling, I was sure of that, but it was a wide, toothy grin rather than a dangerous expression. The smile faded, the beard drooping.

"You're scaring the staff." Another voice boomed down the hall. "Hurry up, the King is waiting."

The red-bearded man glanced at his companion, a man much the same size as him but with an even wilder black beard and bushy head of hair. Now I looked closer, both were adorned with tattoos, although one of the markings on the red-head's huge forearm was of knitting needles and a ball of wool. He frowned at me and sidled backwards, giving me ample space to go past. I mumbled a flustered thank you and found the nerve channels to my legs.

When I reached what I had to hope was the toilet, I glanced back. Both men were standing close, muttering to each other. When the dark-haired man pointed in my direction and lifted his head as if to look my way, I pushed open the door and fled into a less busy hallway.

"I told Father it was absolutely unfathomab- Hey!"

I yelped as someone ploughed straight into me on their way past. I staggered back to right my balance for the second time in as many minutes and looked up into a very narrow pair of jewel green eyes.

"Um, h-hello." I grimaced at my own hopelessness. "I'm

sorry! I was trying to find the toilet, um, the bathroom."

The boy who had come into the kitchen with Penelope only a few minutes ago took a step back and shot me a dazzling smile. He had a clipboard in one hand, a pen in the other and the air around him brightened as he tinkled a laugh at me.

"Oh, not to worry." He waved my apologies away. "Don't mind Penelope either. She likes to think she's in charge and to establish her pecking order early."

I nodded, dazed. "That's really okay, I mean, I understand."

His laugh sent tingles rippling over my arms. "That's very big of you. It does get a little tiresome, the hierarchy act, especially when you know she has no need to prove herself here, what with her familial connections. I'm Friese by the way."

I tried to think of something unidiotic to say.

"Uh, huh?"

Friese didn't seem to mind that I sounded like a complete idiot. He leaned a little closer, the subtle scent of roses mingling with something sharper. I gulped as he settled his fingertips gently on my sleeve.

"Alas, those not blessed with such lineage must do their bit," he sighed. "I'm just hunting for entrants to the annual Puzzle Tower event, in vain I fear."

I was still in my worst pair of trainers and hadn't brushed my hair properly. I hadn't brushed my teeth either. I fidgeted on the spot.

Yet, here's a very pretty Fae boy talking to me. Touching my arm.

"What is it?" I asked. "The Tuzzle Power, um, thing I mean?"

"Chuh! It's only the most stunning event of the Fae calendar. Competitors enter the old tower on the edge of the club grounds and solve puzzles. Staff are allowed to play too of course. Ooh, would you like to enter?"

He blinked at me with the beguiling wide eyes and I found my mouth preparing words without intervention from my brain. I swallowed the yes back down before it could get me into trouble and shook my head.

"Um, no, thanks," I hesitated. "I doubt I'd be any good at that I'm afraid."

Milo appeared beside me before I could find anything to say that would continue the conversation and not make me look pathetic at the same time. Taz almost knocked my shoulder clean off as he swooped in to stand on my other side.

"Of course she's not going to enter." He folded his arms across his chest. "Don't be stupid."

I winced at the vehemence in his tone.

"What, because you think I'm so hopeless I can't even manage a competition?" I asked.

Taz stared at me then averted his gaze to scowl at his boots without another word.

"I'm sure you'd do great." Friese pounced. "So I'll put you down then?"

He brandished the clipboard and pen at me. I saw Taz's hand twitch, as if to snatch the clipboard before I could do anything rash with it. I ignored the temptation to grab it and hit him with it instead, shaking my head.

"Okay well, would you at least sign a petition?" Friese gave me another winning smile. "If it were to campaign for a bigger tank for the waterpoises."

He waved the clipboard under my nose and I took it automatically. It was the least I could do after refusing to take part in the competition.

"Um, the waterpoises are fine," Milo interrupted as I scrawled on the page. "They live better than we do, I don't think they need a new tank?"

I inspected my signature, wondering if it looked like a little kid's handwriting. I handed the clipboard back.

"Thanks-" I began.

Friese rushed off before I could finish thanking him.

"Um, Demi?" Milo shuffled in front of me. "I think he just tricked you into signing the entry form for the competition. There is no campaign for the poises, or Mrs. Paget would have told me. I'm the one that usually cleans the tanks, you see."

I could just see Friese at the other end of the hall, then he was gone in a swish of perfect hair and sunshine. I shook my head, a sense of disorientation swimming around me. Given Taz's open-mouthed gawping and Milo's weary resignation, I realised I'd been had.

"Um…" Milo actually raised his hand. "Do you think now might be a good time to return to work?"

I followed him down the hall, my insides thundering as my entire body burned with shame. I'd been fooled so easily. I'd not even made it to the bathroom either. I decided not to try and listen to whatever damnations Taz was muttering under his breath.

I kept silent all the way through our next shift, the hurried lunch and the afternoon of steaming hot kitchen work. I didn't dare try and cover my uselessness with chatter either. The only small blessing was that Taz seemed so furious with me his productivity doubled and he only broke three plates and a glass in the process.

"Right, dinner!" Milo called, hitting the big red button. "Someone else will come in to do the evening shift soon."

We followed him, but nobody said a word as we walked to the staff canteen. I managed to lift myself out of my shame spiral enough to notice that while the dingy interior was still the same as it had been during the morning, now the dirty benches had been replaced with finer furniture.

I eyed the round tables that had clean cotton tablecloths, places set with three different types of fork and actual wine glasses. When Milo found us a table, we also had labelled jugs full of water, various soft drinks like cherry bubble juice, and also *Beast*, the fae equivalent of an energy drink which seemed to be popular.

I made a big effort not to look directly at Taz as we ate. Milo had been right about the food being good but my nerves wouldn't let me eat much of it. I'd skipped breakfast and barely eaten a bite at lunch, but even though my stomach rumbled, every time I lifted a fork of stew or potato to my mouth, I got the feeling I was being watched. I'd look across the main hall to find Penelope laughing at me and Friese sending me a little wave.

All of the opulence served to make me feel completely out of place. Only when we retreated back to our room did I sink onto my bed and risk speaking.

"So, on a scale of one to me, how doomed am I?" I asked.

Taz flicked a glare at me. "Oh, definitely you, times a thousand. You can't pull out either, not now you've signed up for it. It's a binding Fae contract."

Knew I shouldn't have asked.

He threw himself on his bed and grabbed a book from his rucksack.

"You might be okay." Milo hovered in the doorway, smiling like a bear with a toothache. "The tower will be set up as different rooms with different puzzles or time-trials you have to escape."

Taz huffed, not looking up from his book. I had to admit, unless he was looking up 'chances of surviving a puzzle tower when you've got zero skills or useful fairy gifts' in those pages, he was seriously pissed off with my naivety right now and choosing to pretend I didn't exist.

"I've heard tales of the Puzzle Tower," he admitted after a moment. "None of them are good. It could be fighting magical creatures, or working your way out of a room filling with water."

"You might have to choose between two friends." Milo joined in. "Or choose which version of the same person is the real one, or fight a Hydralix. We might have a book about it somewhere."

He tried to give me a reassuring smile, which just made me feel worse.

"Got a book about it," Taz grunted, holding up the one he was reading without looking up. "Heard the Puzzle Tower was being held here a while back, but didn't think anyone I knew would be dim enough to actually enter it."

Ouch. He has a point, but still.

"Oh, that's good," Milo continued. "And you get the option to take a companion in with you."

Taz straightened up like a firework going off.

"She can take someone in with her? Why didn't you say so earlier?"

Guess that wasn't in his book then.

I glowered at him. "Oh yes, because I can't possibly survive anything on my own."

Milo's gaze darted in an anxious back and forth between us.

"Um, sorry, I should have led with that." He grimaced. "I didn't want anyone to overhear earlier, that's all. The less they know about your strategy the better."

I nodded. "Good thinking. Now, I might have been dragged into this competition-"

"Got tricked you mean," Taz grumbled. "Oh, shiny Fae dude, please let me sign anything you put in front of me!"

I ignored him despite my cheeks burning and continued where I'd left off.

"-but I can figure out a way to get through that, somehow. I'll just do my best, fail awfully or get eliminated and it'll all be fine."

Taz snorted and opened his mouth, no doubt to begin all of the reasons why my best wouldn't be anywhere close to good enough. I faced him, ready to more than fling it back.

Before either of us could start, Milo folded his broad arms across his torso as if he wanted to hug himself.

"Please don't argue," he said, speaking so quietly that I almost didn't make out the words. "I can't bear it when people shout at each other. Friese has a charm gift, so there's nothing anyone can do once he wants to get you to do something, and everyone makes mistakes."

He looked like he was about to cry, still standing in the doorway as if he was frightened to enter his own bedroom.

Both Taz and I froze. Looked at each other. Taz pulled a rueful face and I rubbed the back of my neck.

What has Milo been through to make him this upset at a couple of friends flinging irritation at each other?

With pity tickling my insides, I vowed to myself that I'd do whatever it took to get Milo away from this hellhole if I could.

"I don't think it's as easy as just going in and getting eliminated unfortunately," Taz said in a much softer tone. "Some are lucky but many are traumatised or changed, hurt or lost."

I sat back down, subdued. "But it's like a game, isn't it? Surely they can't allow people to get hurt?"

Taz looked up from his book again, his expression dark.

"This is a Fae club," he reminded me. "They see it as character building, like future life lessons. Sink or swim, learn or die."

Milo nodded. "They even do a mini lottery to make up numbers if they don't have enough people taking part."

"That's awful," I said.

"Yeah." Milo sighed. "Friese promised that my name would get chosen, so maybe that's why you're here? You said you didn't know what your FDP assignment was, right?"

"You think I've maybe been sent here to take your place in this tower competition?" I asked.

A cold chill splashed right into my bones. In my bewilderment, I'd almost forgotten about the actual reason I was stuck here. I had to find out about the elite Forgotten 24 club and report back.

Instead, I've spent most of my first day moving cutlery, screwing up and worrying.

"It's the only thing I can think of," Milo agreed. "But I still can't imagine anyone who would have done such a thing for me. I don't know anyone who would care."

He looked like he was going to cry again, his bottom lip wobbling. Taz started to get up, but I moved faster. I patted Milo's bulky shoulders and found a tissue in my satchel. Luckily, Leo was fairly discerning about what he chomped on, so the tissue was still mostly clean.

"We care," I insisted. "You didn't have to help us when you found us, but you did. Now we're going to help you if we can."

Milo smiled and dabbed his eyes. "Thanks, Demi. I'm really lucky you've shown up. And you as well, Taz."

"No worries." Taz shrugged.

He abandoned his book and got up to use the bathroom, while I sat back down on my bed and placed my hands over my eyes.

I needed to think and for some reason the pressured darkness seemed to help.

First, I need to get through this tower event and also find this stupid club. Once I know that, I can ask Petra how we're going to get back home.

"So, do you know who you'd want to take into the Puzzle Tower tomorrow?" Milo asked. "I'll help you in any way I can, but I'm not sure how useful I'd be."

I shook my head. "No, but Taz will likely insist I take him. He has the Fae experience. But then, you know the school better than any of us, like the kind of things they might come up with if you've seen it before."

I settled down on my bed, thankful that the blankets felt so clean and soft. At least I'd be comfortable if I was going to be up most of the night worrying.

Then I sat up with a jolt.

"Wait a minute, tomorrow?!"

CHAPTER SEVEN
TUNNELS OF SILVER, GOLD AND SECRETS

"Um, yes, didn't I say that?" Milo chewed his lip. "Actually, with that in mind, we should probably get an early night. I'll pop down for cocoa. There might even be some cookies left over."

Taz appeared as I rubbed my eyes with one hand, the other supporting my weary weight on the bed. Taz grinned so suddenly it startled me.

"Cookies are definitely the way to my heart," he said. "Don't worry, Dem, you can have the bathroom first again tomorrow morning."

Thoughts of the cocoa I was about to receive danced through my head as Milo left the room, lulling me for the couple of seconds it took for Taz to loom in front of me. I flinched as he sat on my bed and leaned unnervingly close.

"I slept really well last night," he muttered.

We'd already discussed this when we woke up, but perhaps he wanted to find a subject that didn't involve him berating me.

"Um, great, me too. Actually, I did, which is weird considering I should have been up all night worrying."

"Yeah, and I'm a really light sleeper," Taz insisted. "I rarely get more than four or five hours a night, sometimes less, and hardly any when I'm in a place I don't know or don't feel safe."

I had to grudgingly admire his honesty. When I didn't answer, Taz got closer, his voice even lower.

"Did you eat much yesterday?" he asked.

I shook my head. "No, I skipped breakfast, we didn't end up

having any lunch, then only what Milo brought up when we got here. I think actually, the only thing I really remember having was the cocoa- Oh."

Taz rewarded me with space as the cogs whirred into place in my brain.

"You think the cocoa was drugged?" I asked. "Why would Milo do that?"

Taz nodded. "Let's just say, don't eat or drink anything he gives you just in case. Did you notice that he was a bit eager to get away last night when we mentioned secret societies?"

"I think so, but I just passed it off to be honest. Do you think he knows about the 24 club?"

"It's got to be possible, right?" Taz folded his arms and glanced over his shoulder at the door. "Why else would he be so twitchy? A secret society would meet at night most likely, hence him having to sneak out without us knowing. Then again, it could be nothing."

I sighed. "It's the only lead we've got. Also, if the club is for the Forgotten and the Old King is visiting, we might be in luck for once and find them having an actual meeting. We can't accuse Milo though, just in case. Perhaps if we pretend to sleep and he does sneak out then we can follow him."

"That's an idea. I'm generally quite a suspicious person and I'm not always right, but I trust my instinct. Right now, it's saying don't drink the cocoa."

I opened my mouth to commend him for his sneaky ingenuity but gulped the words back with a splutter as the door swung open. When I saw the two mugs in Milo's hand, each with a large cookie balanced on top, a tremble of foreboding trickled over my skin.

"That looks wickedly decadent." Taz grinned like nothing in the world could be wrong. "None for you, or is Demi on rations again?"

I ignored the teasing, hoping it wasn't a conveniently timed opportunity for a legitimate dig.

Milo's cheeks flushed. "Oh, no, I'm um, I didn't feel like one."

I took the mug Milo held out and rescued the cookie. They both looked so delicious my mouth began to water.

Get this done, get back to Arcanium and the Braunees will give you as many cookies and cups of cocoa as you can stomach.

Milo hovered in between the beds. When his glance turned to Taz, I put my mug on the bedside table, broke off a bit of the cookie and dropped it onto the floor just before he turned back to me. Pretending to chew wasn't something I was used to, but I held up the cookie as evidence.

"Bliss." I pretended to mumble with my mouth full.

Taz went one better. He held the cookie and somehow knocked a bite-sized chunk off while still holding the mug in the other hand.

Show off.

I opened my mouth wide and faked a yawning noise, glad I could at least provide something useful to the situation. My single skill for mimicking noises was pretty much the only thing I had to contribute, and Milo's shoulders slumped a small amount at the sound.

"Why don't you-" Taz paused for what sounded scarily like a real yawn. "-use the bathroom first, Milo. No sense in letting the cocoa get cold."

Milo smiled then, his face brightening with heartrending gratitude.

"That's really kind, thank you. I think I will, if that's okay?"

I nodded my agreement when Milo looked at me, almost tempted to admit we were fooling him and just ask about the society outright. Only the knowledge that Taz would think I was utterly hopeless and the fear we'd chase Milo off for good held my tongue.

Milo hurried off to the bathroom, shutting the door behind him. Without a single sign of tiredness, Taz leapt up and eased open the window nearest his side of the room.

"There's a gutter," he whispered. "Give me your mug."

I hurried over to join him and tipped the contents of my mug into the drain.

"It feels like such a waste," I grumbled, still emotionally attached to the thought of the extravagant drink.

Taz laughed. "Spending tonight asleep would be a waste."

I couldn't bring myself to agree, but I couldn't exactly argue either without looking petulant so I said nothing. Taz tiptoed back to his bed and I did the same, my nerves jangling.

"You were out like a light almost immediately last night," he said. "I reckon we do a couple of sleepy mumbles when Milo comes back, but pretend to be mostly asleep."

I nodded and clambered into bed. I didn't have any pyjamas to change into so at least that was a good excuse for staying in my uniform, and if anyone questioned the socks I could say I was cold. After a quick peek to make sure my shoes were right by my bed ready to be jumped into, I closed my eyes.

There are so many potential faults in this plan. With nothing else to occupy my brain, I assessed them one by one. *Milo might lock the door behind him. If he does that, Taz will insist on climbing out the window or something and I'll break a leg. Milo might not go anywhere at all. It's likely the club doesn't meet every night anyway, so we've probably missed it knowing my luck. Even if he does lead us somewhere, there will most probably be a secret password, which we don't know. They'll discover us and we'll never be seen again.*

I sank so deep into my anxieties that I jumped when the door opened. Aware I was meant to be drugged and mostly asleep, I fidgeted as if getting comfortable and kept my eyes closed.

The sound of Taz yawning seemed realistic but, given how he'd leapt up the moment Milo went to the bathroom, I had doubts about his lack of acting ability now.

"Sorry, Milo," he mumbled. "Must be all the excitement. I'll get a shower in the morning quick, if there's time?"

Seconds passed. I held my breath, then remembered I was supposed to be asleep and tried to breathe deeply instead.

"Of course." Milo kept his voice quiet. "You've both had a really hard time today. Get some proper rest."

Taz mumbled thanks and almost immediately, the realistic snoring of a young man filled the room. I tried to copy him, finding it easier to accompany than it was to snore solo.

"Demi?" Milo's voice floated over. "Are you awake?"

I kept breathing.

Relax face, breathe in, Relax face, breathe out.

"Taz?" Milo tried again.

The silence was excruciating. A muscle in my calf started threatening to twitch. I fought every instinct I had that wanted to shuffle in my 'sleep' and find a way of peeking. I started counting upwards, anything to keep my mind off the tension.

CLICK.

I kept still despite hearing the door shut. This was more Taz's plan than mine. If Taz wanted to-

"Okay, he's gone."

I opened my eyes and sat up.

"Come on, quick." Taz already had his shoes on and was headed toward the door.

I shoved my feet into my trainers and hopped after Taz, trying to pull the backs up over my heels with my satchel swinging against my knees. The quickest of peeks in the main compartment made me roll my eyes.

Trust Leo to sleep right through all of this.

Taz pressed a finger to his lips and peered out into the hall. He beckoned and I followed, wincing at every single creak in the floorboards as we peered around the corner of the wall into the stairwell.

Milo had almost reached the bottom of the stairs. He looked both ways along the hall and set off to the right. We inched down the stairs in time to see him disappear through one of the doors.

"I'll keep look out," I whispered. "You see what he's up to."

I stood behind Taz and flicked my gaze back and forth, determined not to miss a thing.

"Whoa." Taz's low gasp drew my attention. "Look at this."

I eyed the hall one more time and craned my neck around Taz's arm to see through the gap in the door. Taz swung it open a moment later and elbowed me in the ribs for my trouble.

"Oof."

I stepped back as he hurried through the door, which gave me a full view.

"Whoa." I echoed, stepping into the room.

No Milo in sight, but a bathroom unlike any I'd ever seen. Aqua blue tiles covered every inch of wall, the white ceiling sparkled and the floor had been laid with dark grey marble, except for a rectangular space the size of a door in the middle. Inside that rectangle, mosaic tiles had been laid to show various mythical creatures.

I scanned the images, looking for clues as I dropped to one knee.

"There are fifty in total," I said. "Look, this one here, if you count the images, this one is the twenty fourth."

Taz leaned over my shoulder. "And that one there, it has an

outstretched hand pointing toward the twenty fourth one, and the bit around the tile looks worn away compared to the others."

I stared up at him. He stared down.

"Press it?" I asked.

Taz grinned. "Press it."

I pressed it and scrunched my eyes shut. A grinding noise grated as a waft of air breathed against my face, like a long-held, dusty exhale. I opened my eyes and scrambled to my feet.

Stone steps descended into a tunnel beneath the floor, but far from leading into darkness, I could see a dim white glow flickering.

"Do we go down?" Taz asked. "Or do we report it back to Petra?"

I eyed the bathroom door, convinced I could hear mumbling in the hall.

"It might not be anything relevant," I decided. "We should take a look first, but be careful and keep a good eye out."

Taz nodded and closed the hall door behind us. I gripped my satchel strap with both hands and started down into the tunnel made of stone. Taz was right behind me as I searched for a way to close and re-open the hatch.

"It'll close automatically no doubt," he said. "Come on. I can smell fresh air ahead so this will likely lead us outside somewhere."

"Protection wardings up," I added.

I found my fairy connection lurking near my left elbow and encouraged it to grow. Protection wardings were something I could do now as easily as breathing thanks to relentless practice, and my warding domed around me like an invisible safety net.

I flinched when something brushed against it.

"If you imagine yours knitting with mine, we can share one," Taz said.

I frowned. We'd not tried this before, but I did as he suggested. I visualised his warding as a soft golden haze merging into mine, which I always saw as rainbow-coloured. Whether from my imagination or because it was actually manifesting, Taz's warding sank through mine and I could sense them merging, mixing our combined strength together.

"You're getting scarily good at wardings," Taz admitted as we started walking.

An actual compliment? Wow.

"Thanks."

We continued along the stone tunnel, heading toward a white glow growing brighter at the end. I jumped as Taz's fingers brushed mine. For a mad second, I thought he was going to take my hand, but he didn't as we stepped side-by-side into the dazzling white light.

I eyed the walls behind the flaming torches set in brackets, painted with sparkles and set with delicate carvings of leaves inlaid with what looked like real silver.

"Wow," Taz muttered.

"The craft work is amazingly detailed," I conceded. "But I imagine it cost a fortune and barely ever gets seen."

His quiet chuckle whispered along the corridor, but he didn't disagree. Our path curved to the right and we emerged from pale silver into riotous, eye-burning yellow.

Although the hall continued on, the leaves fixed on the walls were made from pure gold. I peered at the nearest leaf on a vine and a stab of homesickness hit my gut as I thought of the golden lift gate back at Arcanium. Compared to that, this display, while impressively skilled, was pure ostentatious vulgarity.

"Double wow," Taz gasped.

I frowned. "Double cost a fortune. You could probably buy a country for the same price this lot would fetch."

Aware I was exaggerating, probably, I strode on ahead. If this was the sort of entrance the fabled 24 club for the Forgotten were used to, then Taz and I would stick out a mile if we found the club itself.

"We didn't think there might be passwords or ID or something to enter," I muttered.

The golden hall came to an abrupt end before Taz could answer. He opened his mouth but I pre-empted the next sentence.

"Don't say triple wow."

The dazzling white walls were back, but this time without any silver. This time, I realised, the leaves were made out of crystals.

"Actual diamonds," Taz said in quiet awe. "My oldest sister is a jeweller in the Faerie citadel, and she'd kill to get even one of these. Might make up for her abdicating her claim to the throne if she gave Mother one."

"Well, we can't risk taking anything, even as proof. I bet they'd take great pleasure in packing us off with a petty theft accusation."

The dazzle was starting to give me a headache, so I set off toward the black square at the end of the hall.

Knowing my luck, instead of a doorway it'll just be a bottomless pit.

I took a hesitant step into the dark, but my vision focused almost straight away. Chilly night air cooled my cheeks and, in the distance on the other side of a lake, lights flickered in the ruins of an old building.

"We need to get closer," I whispered. "Can you keep watch while I have a look in?"

Taz pointed to the crumbling wall nearest the bank of the lake.

"That broken window looks best hidden. Come on, we don't want to be found hanging around."

Keeping close together, we crept through the grass around the edge of the lake.

Each time one of us stepped on a stick or scuffed up a pebble, I flinched. The sound of jovial voices floated across the water and soon enough we reached the old stone wall. A quick peek through the wide gap that would have once held a window, and I recognised Friese and Penelope nearby amid a crowd of thirty or so people.

The Fae were all lounging on expensive looking armchairs, their outfits and accessories dripping wealth. I glanced up to see a sturdy canopy hanging to keep the area dry. Another peek and this time, I almost forgot to dodge back out of sight.

The Old King sat on the biggest chair, a golden throne no less, next to a wooden table overflowing with trinkets and shiny items. There seemed to be no common element to them either, other than wealth and general grandeur.

"Bring me another tankard of *Beast*," the Old King hollered, so suddenly I almost yelped in alarm.

I risked looking a bit longer as Milo broke through the crowd carrying a silver tray with a large, bronzed mug on it. The crowd continued their conversations but I recognised their split attention, exactly like my sisters did when one found a juicy excuse to pick on me and the other watched.

Anticipation filled the air. Would there be a chance to join in, they wondered. I shuddered, recognising my own regular stance in Milo's rounded shoulders and bowed head, resigned to whatever came next.

The Old King nodded to Penelope and I remembered what Milo had said about her being from one of the most influential families. Penelope grabbed the mug Milo carried by its handle.

"If only your 'fancy' new friends could see you now," she crowed. "Pathetic."

Something brushed my elbow. I almost fainted in alarm, but Taz had no intention of backing away. Eying the clenched jaw and balled fists, I decided I wouldn't unleash him on unsuspecting enemies too often.

"We've seen enough," I whispered. "We need to sneak back and speak to Petra. I'm sure she won't mind being woken up for this. The Old King is here, so this must be the 24 club."

Taz shook his head and stepped back. "Sorry, you're right. I just hate seeing entitled people taking advantage of kinder ones, even if Milo did dope us. I doubt he would have done it by choice. We should take something back as proof though."

We dodged out of sight behind the wall, and I tried to think of what we could take without being caught.

"I've only got my pen-knife," I said. "It wouldn't be strong enough to hack any of the gold off, and I bet the diamonds are fixed tight."

Taz looked back and forth, but I recalled the layout of the ruin and had a less than advisable idea.

With a deep breath, I faced him.

"I'm going to do something dim."

CHAPTER EIGHT
A CLOSE CALL AND A NARROW ESCAPE

Taz eyed me, doubt scrawled across his face. He was definitely thinking about all the dim things I'd done to date in the relatively short time we'd known each other.

"Don't tell Petra," I said. "At least, not unless I'm successful. Or if I get caught, but I'll try not to."

His lips twitched. "What are you planning?"

I peeked into the ruin and veered behind the wall again.

"Something dim. You start heading back to the tunnel. If you can, get the way out open in case they see me." I reached into my pocket and held my hand up. "I'm no runner so if I get caught, orb Petra. I'm hoping it should just work for you as well."

Taz closed his fingers around my orb and snared my hand along with it.

"Are you sure about this?" he asked. "I could give it a go, I'm a faster runner, no offense."

I nodded. "That's why it has to be me. If we need to escape, you need to be furthest away to raise the alarm."

Taz said nothing for a long moment, his gaze sweeping over my face.

"Okay." He dropped my hand and gave me a thumbs up. "But if there's *any* chance you're likely to get caught, or you get into trouble, just shout and I'll run back, I mean it. Good luck then, Sparky."

I pulled a face. "This is me we're talking about. Luck doesn't tend to get involved much."

I took comfort from his quiet chuckle, then turned my attention to sneaking along the wall. As I rounded the corner, I could just make out Taz's silhouette creeping around the water's edge back to the glowing beacon of the tunnel in the hill.

I inched toward the gap in the wall, which was right behind the Old King's chair. For once, I was glad that the Fae had such delusions of grandeur, to make the chair an enormous one with a great winged back. His two bodyguards stood facing his chair, their eyes fixed on him. That would make what I planned to do more dangerous, but thankfully they weren't flanking the table behind him or I'd have no chance. The entire tabletop glittered, but I saw immediately what trinket I intended to take.

A pale gold pocket watch sat on the edge, face down, the nearest and smallest thing within my reach. On the back of it three familiar letters were engraved.

A.R.C.

The same initials I'd seen embroidered on Director Cornelius' cloak.

It could be a coincidence, not his watch at all, but either way it's the closest thing I can grab.

I pressed a delicate hand against the edge of the wall, but it showed no signs of breaking easily. With my stomach threatening to boil over from anxiety, I reached my free hand forward.

"Sagar, Eldrich, go about your business," the Old King bellowed.

I almost toppled over onto the table from shock, but managed to keep my balance. The Old King's two bodyguards exchanged a doubtful look. They both stood with feet planted wide and hands clasped in front of them, but as they relaxed their stance, the red-headed one's gaze swept my way. I flinched my hand back, heart pounding, and tried to angle myself to peek while staying hidden behind the chair.

"As you wish, your majesty." The dark-haired one bowed his head.

The Old King leaned forward in his chair. I thought about making a grab for something from the table, but kept still.

"Eldrich, a moment."

The red-headed one, Eldrich, stepped forward. I watched the other one, Sagar, stomp through the crowd of assembled Fae and take a guarded stance at the wide entrance to the ruin. Then I dodged behind the chair again, checking my route back to the tunnel was still clear and out of the guard's line of sight if I had to run.

"There is something I'd like to acquire." The Old King lowered his voice for only Eldrich to hear. Little did he know I was right behind him with no intention of giving him any privacy. "One of the Queen's children is in our midst here, we've had confirmation. We need to find out who it is. They may not have been here long."

Fiery ants of fear tapped over my skin and I shuddered.

So the King knows Taz is here. How? Only Arcanium should have known, Emil, Petra, Queenie- unless Milo told.

I shook my head. I couldn't accuse him, or even question him, not without any proof. For now, keeping safe and getting back to the room with some proof of this meeting would be a start. Maybe Queenie would even let us come home if I told Petra I'd found the 24 club.

Eldrich joined Sagar at the entrance, but neither of them made any motion to go anywhere. I hoped they would keep their search for the Queen's child until the morning at least. Perhaps if we were quick, we wouldn't even have to go into the Puzzle Tower.

I found my balance against the wall again and leaned toward the trinket table. Just out of reach, I took a slow breath and strained that little bit further. The Old King stood and thumped his tankard on the arm of his chair.

I froze as silence fell.

"Welcome," the Old King announced. "To this very special gathering of the Forgotten 24 club. It is my pleasure to welcome to our latest member, Eloise Grantly, who I'm sure will prove herself a valuable asset."

My arm muscles burned as I hovered with one arm toward the table.

"Eloise is also from the noble family line of Belarin," The King continued. "My family line. *Make her welcome.*"

A smattering of applause filled the air.

"Now, we are all Forgotten-sworn here, so I will begin. Our intention to overthrow the Queen continues at a steady pace, and we now have a plan."

"Tell us, your Majesty!" Someone called out.

A round of cheering echoed. My fingers snagged the gold pocket-watch, the end of the chain still curled on the table. Link by agonising link, the chain started to slide. I almost let go of the wall to catch it with my other hand, but that would send me sprawling face first into the table. And into the back of the Old King's chair.

"We move to eliminate the Queen's children," he continued. "We must lessen her hold on Faerie further, and soon she will be nothing more than a memory."

Another cheer went up. I winced as the chain gathered weight and slithered free of the table. I heaved against the wall to push myself back as the crowd noise died away. The chain whipped sideways and thwacked into the wall.

"What was that?" The Old King's voice bounced through the

air. "I heard a noise."

I lifted the chain and fumbled to curl it into my fingers.

"Maybe the Director has finally found us?" someone asked. "He's been dying to join for years but never found the skip-way."

A slight round of nervous laughter.

So the tunnel has a skip-way, that explains a lot.

"Impossible," someone shouted.

"Well, we need to go out and look then."

"I don't see you charging forward."

"Well, it was my idea. You're always boasting about your gifts, now's your chance to perform."

I thanked my lucky stars for argumentative Fae.

I can't risk them coming out looking and finding me here.

I took a deep breath and huffed out two low notes with my best mimicking voice.

"*HOO-HOO.*"

"Oh, false alarm." I couldn't be sure, but that sounded like Penelope. "That was an owl, we get them all the time at home. They're probably nesting in the higher gaps."

The Old King sat back down.

"Filthy animals," he said. "Boy, what are you gawping at? You don't belong here. Serve everyone and then leave."

I inched along the wall, my heart still hammering. My stomach churned like after eating too much candy as I peered around the corner of the ruin.

The boy the Old King had referred to might be right behind me at any moment. Sagar and Eldrich wouldn't be so willing to let me go on my way this time if they decided to patrol the perimeter. I took the risk and set off at a speedy jog toward the glowing tunnel.

Just a bit further.

I panted onward, the edge of the lake seeming to drag on forever. Each time I heard a noise, I was convinced someone would grab me from behind, but now I could see Taz waiting by the mouth of the tunnel.

Almost there, I stumbled over a rut of grass. My hand opened on instinct, ready to stop my fall, and the watch sailed out of it into the darkness.

"Crud," I muttered, looking over my shoulder.

A shadowed figure was moving away from the ruin walls now. I'd run out of time. Cursing myself for not being more careful, I had to leave the watch and run the rest of the way toward Taz with my satchel swinging against my hip. I mumbled an apology to Leo that he probably couldn't hear, but he never usually grumbled when I had to run with him in my bag. Perhaps he thought it was like some kind of lizard rollercoaster. Either way, if I needed the watch as proof, I'd have to come back and search in the light of morning.

Assuming I make it that long.

"Did you get anything?" Taz asked.

I shook my head, coming to a ragged halt in front of him.

"Almost, but someone might be right behind us soon," I puffed. "They confirmed it was the club though, and that this tunnel is a skip-way, and that the Director has been trying to find it or join the club for years."

Without warning me first, Taz grabbed my hand in his and set off into the blinding dazzle of the tunnel. I stumbled alongside him, unnerved by the feel of his fingers threaded between mine and his thumb firm against the back of my hand.

"We still have the information though," I babbled. "With any luck, Petra can get us a special permission to go back home before I have to go through with this Tower Puzzle thing. I'll get up early and orb her, but it might even be Milo on his way back behind us so for now we just need to get into bed."

Taz grinned, apparently not bothered about my failure.

"First time anyone's asked me to get into bed, Sparky."

If my face hadn't been already burning from the running, I would have blushed. Or shoved him. I shook my hand free of his.

"You know what I mean." I tried to glare at him while trotting along the dazzling tunnel. "If we can prove we've done the assignment and that we're about to be in mortal peril, maybe Queenie will let us come home."

I ignored the doubtful quirk on Taz's face as we reached the steps up into the bathroom.

"Do you know how to get-" I hesitated as Taz pulled a lever on the wall. "I guess you do. Do we need to shut it again after?"

He led the way up and opened the bathroom door, peeking out into the hall. I hurried after him and eyed the gaping hole in the floor. Taz pushed the door wider.

"Don't worry about it," he said. "I bet it's on a time-lock, so it'll close itself. If not, not our problem as we've been sweetly sleeping all this time."

I decided not to mention the Old King's plan involving the Queen's children just yet. Taz might take matters into his own hands, and I couldn't let him do anything dim or dangerous. So I said nothing as we hurried through the silent corridors.

Only when we reached Milo's floor did I feel it was safe enough to stop jogging and open the flap of my satchel to get Leo out. He could do his thing in the bathroom before bed and Milo would never know the difference if I emerged sleepy-eyed and said I woke in the night to use the loo.

"Oh, hell." I stopped dead.

Taz turned back, beside me in a second. "What?"

"Leo's gone."

Fear lit my connection inside me, the tingle spreading through my skin. Taz caught my wrist and I half expected him to flinch away with a jolt, but my new gift wasn't quite ready to shock him yet apparently.

"You can't get caught racing around the grounds," he insisted.

I grimaced in anguish. "I can't just leave him. Why would he jump out, he never has before. It's not like I was swinging the bag around my head or anything."

"Demi-"

"I'm serious, I have to go out and find him."

"No, look."

Taz pointed past me. I looked down the hall just in time to see a fleeting shiver over the floorboards. When the ripple of colour reached my feet, I realised that while my lizard was camouflaged, the pale gold pocket watch clamped in his jaws along with a massive chunk of the chain was not.

"Leo!" I huffed. "You don't escape like that! Even if it is to apparently do me a huge favour."

Taz frowned at me in query.

"What's that?" he asked.

"I lifted this watch from their trinket table, but I stumbled on my way back and dropped it. Didn't have time to hunt in the dark, but apparently Leo had other ideas." I held Leo up in front of my face and ignored his satisfied crooning. "You are a horror."

I eased the watch out of his jaws and followed Taz into our room, my heart still pounding with ebbing relief. I pressed the watch deep into the satchel while toeing off my trainers and settled Leo back on top of it like a dragon guarding his plunder.

"You won't be in there forever, don't worry," I murmured to him, not caring if Taz could hear. "You'll be back home before you know it, and I'll get you a huge log or something to hang around on,"

Taz grinned, clearly still buoyed up with adrenalin.

"I'll get him his own room next to yours if we have to. Okay, off to sleep. Well done though, that was some really stealthy stealing."

I shrugged and clambered into bed fully-clothed. I put my satchel just under the covers beside me, enough to hide Leo but also keep a hold on him if he tried to escape again.

I attempted to sleep, but each creak of the floorboards or noise outside made me flinch. When Milo finally came back, I couldn't be sure if five minutes or five hours had passed. I kept my eyes shut tight and let my mind go over and over the same plan.

Wake up. Orb Petra. Wake up. Orb Petra.

By the time I finally drifted into a restless slumber, the sky was already dawning an ominous, thundery grey.

CHAPTER NINE
THE ONE WITH ALL THE KEYS

The morning dawned bright and cold, with the crisp scent of frost in the air. I couldn't bring myself to eat, or to lie convincingly to Milo that I slept well. I kept the watch buried deep in my satchel, along with Leo, who seemed to have taken offense to it overnight and now kept trying to chew on it.

My attempts to orb Petra in the bathroom came to nothing. I even tried Emil, on the pretext of Petra not answering and me having completed my assignment, but Taz insisted we stop short of trying Queenie. Now I stood outside in front of an ancient, crumbling stone tower without a coat, shivering in just my hoodie. Crowds swarmed around, and I could see a golden platform near the tower, no doubt for the Old King to watch the proceedings from.

Someone shoved past me and I staggered forward, almost colliding with Taz.

"Hey, watch where you're going!" he growled.

I righted myself, about to bite back before I realised he was talking to my assailant. Penelope smirked back at me, looking every inch the dashing young Fae in a smart pair of black jeans and a peacock green coat, her auburn hair set without a strand out of place despite the wind. She gave Taz a mocking bow.

"My apologies, but your friend should really watch where she stands. All sorts of mishaps happen to people just lolling about like that."

Penelope powered off through the crowd toward the tower before I could find a suitably cutting retort.

At least she looks like she fits in.

I glanced down over my baggy jeans, mucky trainers and shapeless hoodie. I'd decided against wearing the Gallows Oak uniform in the end, determined to carry some essence of myself, even if it was just in the fabric. Milo had thought to bring his big duffel coat and put his hands in his pockets, rocking back and forth on the balls of his feet.

"A bit chilly, isn't it?" he said.

"Yes, the weather is lovely," Taz huffed. "Now Demi has to decide who she's taking in with her."

Milo immediately tucked his chin to his chest

"I, um, I can help, if you really need me to," he said.

He didn't exactly seem keen, and Taz inched closer to me.

"You'll need as much knowledge and wit as possible to complete any of these puzzles," he murmured. "Your choice, but you know I've got your back, always."

I hadn't thought about it yet, but I didn't need to, not really. I thought back to the previous evening and the sleepy-night cocoa, and Milo's part in the Forgotten-24 club. I couldn't hold it against him, but at the same time, I couldn't risk trusting him. Either way, Taz could be a total pain in the ego, but I'd trust him to the death.

"Go on then." I shot Taz a quick glance. "You look like you could do with taking down a couple of pegs anyway."

"Cheers!" He grinned like I'd just told him he won the lottery.

"You don't have to if you don't want to." I was so full of jittering nerves I couldn't stop baiting him now. "There's no chivalry or sexism needed here. You can stay out here in relative safety and I can just meet you on the other side, assuming I survive."

Taz swung an arm around my shoulder. I flinched, but he

wasn't about to get me in a headlock and try to throw me into anything or onto anything like my sisters would do. He squeezed for a moment then let go, still smiling.

"Assuming *we* survive. Come on, it'll be fun."

Milo looked at us like we were both crazy, but I noticed several of the Fae nearby were also watching Taz's behaviour.

He's making a show of it, putting on a brave front.

Milo pointed to the crowd swelling around the tower.

"The first person is going in," he said. "There are thirteen entries in total. I checked the sheet at breakfast and you're going in fourth."

I took a breath and started to panic quietly to myself. I didn't want anyone else to see how nervous I was, but I couldn't quite unclench my fingers from around my satchel strap. I'd agonized over leaving Leo behind in the room to keep him safe, but couldn't bring myself to risk it in case someone went snooping while we were busy.

"Watch the VC," Taz said.

"VC?"

"Vision-cast, up there."

I looked up to find a sharp image projected onto the side of the tower in front of the expectant crowd. It showed a dark room and a young man wading through what looked like a pool of water.

The murmurs of the crowd grew louder as he stumbled and fell. The water was only knee-deep, but moments later the projection disappeared and a loud bonging noise filled the air.

"Oh, that's the first over," Milo announced.

I stared at the unconscious young man now being carried out of the tower on a stretcher. Deep purple blotches were blooming over his face and it looked like his throat was swelling.

"That must mean they have Hurdroxi in one of the rooms."

Milo started a continuous muttering. "If I'm right, then that means they'll also have the time-trial water room puzzle. Hurdroxi will need somewhere to stay and it's easier for them to flood a whole room rather than bring in tanks."

I had no idea what he was talking about, but Taz started rubbing his forehead.

"Hurdroxi are vicious," he said. "They're like water bees, huge blue creatures with suckers on their bellies that break the skin and spill poison into the wound, but they won't bother you if you don't bother them. I'd say if you see them, it means the puzzle is to find a way around them rather than actually tackle them."

I stared at the stretcher being sprinted up the hill to the club. "Will he be okay?"

Taz shrugged. "If they have the antidote he will, eventually. I imagine they would have thought of that."

I glanced at the Old King now sitting on the raised platform painted gold with a matching awning over it. The two bodyguards flanked him, but I could see Eldrich's gaze wandering. His eyes locked on us and his russet beard twitched into a smile. He stared for a moment longer than I was comfortable with before his attention moved on.

He's looking for Taz. Oh hell.

My attention froze, every hair on my body rising like hackles as someone stepped out from behind the Old King's chair to stand at his side. I nudged Taz and he followed the flick of my chin to the woman now standing on the golden platform.

"It's her," I hissed. "Elvira, she's here, with *him*. We should have guessed she'd be lurking somewhere near the pit of evil."

Only a month ago Elvira had been tormenting us, one of the Forgotten who'd tried to invade Arcanium. She'd locked me in a box knowing that my biggest fear was being trapped in small spaces, and had given Taz a bloody face.

I clenched my fists and took a step forward, to do what I had no idea. Something snared around my waist and stopped me going any further. I looked down, then over my shoulder.

Taz withdrew his arm from around my middle, not quite able to keep the amused smile from the corners of his mouth.

"Calm down," he said. "You're telling me not to do anything about the Old King, even though he's an enemy of my family, and she's what sets you spitting? Fair enough, but there's nothing we can do about her now. Focus on getting out of this alive first, then you can get all defensive, Sparky."

I huffed but knew he was right.

"Well she's an enemy of my family now," I shot back. "Well, me at least, I guess."

My fury ebbed. After we'd beaten her and her Forgotten minions, she would no doubt be out for our blood. Except Taz was glamoured as someone else. The only enemy here she would recognise was me.

I forced myself to focus back on the VC and the issue of my immediate future. The second competitor, a young woman with a multitude of blades strapped across her back, charged into the tower. I started wondering how many people would truly judge me if I orbed Petra and begged her to just illegally realm-skip me home somehow.

"The rooms are mostly underground," Milo explained. "The actual tower structure is merely symbolic. Oh, she didn't even get past the first room it looks like."

A few of the girl's friends rushed forward to support her, but she seemed to be crying so hard she couldn't speak.

"Oh, and there's the walking toilet brush." Taz pointed. "Careful he doesn't ask you to carry his gloves, Dem, you might say yes again."

I squinted through the crowds and recognised Friese striding forward. He rushed straight into the tower, throwing the door open without waiting for the official to do it for him first. I didn't hold out any hopes of beating anyone, but a thought occurred to me.

"What's the point of this?" I asked. "I mean, torture young people into surviving anything, but what do we have to do to win?"

Milo scratched the back of his head.

"You need to come out with your token. Actually, we should go and see what token they've chosen for you. Usually you have to give them something personal to up the stakes, but obviously you didn't have time."

Taz and I followed Milo through the crowds. I'd not managed much of my breakfast so the sickness crept up my throat like acid. Fear flipped up and down in my chest like a cannonball on a trampoline, and I sought for any way to get out of going inside. We came to a stop at the base of the tower, right in front of the Director Cornelius.

"Miss Darcy." Cornelius eyed me up and down. "Glad to see you entertaining our traditions. We weren't able to ask you for a token, so we saved you the trouble and asked the cleaners to pick something up."

He held up his hand between us. A small pearlescent orb hung from his finger on a delicate silver keychain.

I tried to speak and choked over my breath instead. I searched my pocket frantically but of course the orb wasn't there.

I definitely put it in the pocket of my jeans before leaving the bedroom, so someone must have lifted it in this crowd. I bet that's why Penelope shoved me.

Taz jostled at my side, his cheeks pink with fury.

"You can't just take stuff without asking," he insisted. "Even in a twisted morality hub like this, you can't just take her stuff."

Cornelius raised one eyebrow, the rest of his face entirely still.

"Well, Miss Darcy entered the contest, did she not? She would have taken due care and attention when reading the rules first, wouldn't she? And of course, we will overlook the fact that she didn't bother to come and present her choice of token after entering."

I tried to think of some way of getting my orb back, but my mind tangled on the one thing that I couldn't escape: I had entered the contest, even though I hadn't bothered to ask to see any rules first.

"What happens to it?" Milo asked.

Cornelius gave the orb to someone else who spirited it off around the outside of the tower. I watched it go, my heart sinking.

"Either Miss Darcy finds it in the tower, or she doesn't. When the latter happens, she can apply to have it returned to her through the normal school Lost and Found procedure. I believe the current process time is three weeks. Now, if you're quite ready?"

I found myself nodding. There was no getting out of this, not now. The strap of my satchel dug into my clenched fists and I took a step forward.

"Wait!" Taz's arm shot out to stop me.

Oh thank Faerie, he has a plan. Or he's going to make a last minute sacrifice. But I can't let him do that.

I froze as he reached toward me, arms outstretched. I tried not to breathe as his hands moved behind my head, but ended up huffing a ragged breath out as he stepped back. I looked down at the small white crystal pendant he'd fixed around my neck.

"It might bring you good luck," he explained. "Trust me."

My cheeks burned and I did what my sister Mary called my constipated tortoise face. I thought it was more of a smile but then, Mary was usually right about the brutally honest things. All I knew was that when Taz said to trust him, I did.

"Um, thanks," I said. "I'll give it back, I promise. If I don't get the keychain my life is over anyway so I've got to give it my best shot."

A young man opened the tower door and, with Taz right beside me, I walked through the doorway into murky gloom.

CRASH.

I flinched as the slammed shut behind us.

The corridor ahead, stone-walled and narrow, was lit by flaming torches with several doors on both sides I took a deep breath and turned to Taz.

"I guess do we just try the first door, or is the corridor itself a puzzle?"

Taz shrugged. "Some of the doors will lead to dead ends. We need to get your orb back so we should try to save time if we can."

I pressed my hands to my eyes so I could think and resurfaced moments later.

"We just need to be sensible," I decided. "The boy came out dripping wet, so we need to be careful of any rooms with water. The girl came out crying which could mean anything."

I tried the first door to my left. A square space appeared behind it, more of a roomy cell than a small room, looked empty. I couldn't see any other door or exit.

"This one has nothing. Do you think it's a hidden door or something?"

"I don't think so." Taz shook his head. "Look up."

I lifted my head to gaze upwards. Clinging to the ceiling were what looked like several dark green bats the size of Koalas.

"They drop down and feed on people's faces," he explained helpfully. "Even the organisers wouldn't dare make that the only route. At least, the event wouldn't last long if they did, and they'll want to make it as tortuously drawn out as possible."

I nodded and shut the door fast. Taz tried the next one but only came up against a brick wall right behind it. He shut the door and noticed my expression.

"You'd be surprised how many people that will distract," he said. "They'd be convinced it's put there to hide something and look for secret moving bricks and things."

I decided not to dwell on that and tried a third door.

"This could be something," I called. "A room full of keys."

Taz poked his head over my shoulder and peered up, down and all around. Aside from another door in the opposite wall and a pile of keys, the room was entirely bare.

"I can't see anything dangerous," he agreed. "Let me go in first."

I stepped aside obligingly before I remembered that I was the FDP and should have insisted I take the risks. Taz shuffled into the room and rotated, but nothing jumped out to get him.

"There's a small notice on that other door," he said. "Find the key to go one step further."

I frowned. "Is that a trick? Like you'll go one step through the door and there'll be another brick wall?"

Taz sighed. "Who knows? You could start sorting these keys and I'll check the other doors in the hall just in case."

As he left the room, I peered at the lock in the closed door opposite.

"Wrought iron," I muttered.

I remembered the legends that Fae hated solid iron, something they couldn't manipulate or pass through. It didn't hurt us like the myths suggested, but it was immune to our trickery. The specifics were something I might have considered confirming with Taz, but after my recent blunders I was surprised he was even still associating with me.

I eyed the huge pile of keys. There must have been hundreds, so I sank to my knees to begin sorting them.

Taz reappeared, slamming the door shut behind him. I almost threw a small key at him in alarm. Then I saw one side of his face was cut and his hair was messy.

"Don't worry, I checked all the doors and I think this is the way forward," he insisted.

He crouched beside me as I frowned back at him.

"But are you okay? Is that going to swell or, I don't know, poison you?"

Taz touched his cheek and shrugged with a wry smile.

"It'll be fine. They just have a few of the guard dogs chained up down here. I tried to reassure one of them but it thought I was going to hurt it so it lunged."

I shook my head and started sorting keys again.

"As long as you're okay. We're looking probably for a black iron key, one of the old-fashioned ones with the teeth and the big loop at the end."

Taz eyed the pile for several seconds before diving into it like a lucky dip. Keys flew left and right as I gawped in amazement.

"The ones on my right are possibilities," Taz said.

I took a handful from the mound and started trying each one. A pile of discarded keys built quickly at my feet. We worked for several minutes until Taz sat back on his heels.

"I can't believe I've missed one," he grumbled. "I was so careful."

I turned back to look at him and something caught my eye.

"There's a key in the back of the door to the hall, look."

Taz looked. Moments later he sent discarded keys flying as he rushed across the room.

"Try it!" He held it out.

I took the key and slid it into the lock. It almost didn't turn, almost, but I gave it my strongest effort and the lock mechanism clicked.

"Good thinking, Dem!"

I flushed. "I looked at a door, it was nothing. Come on, carefully."

I led us into the next room and stumbled to a halt, my arms flying out as I braced myself in the doorway. A shallow pool of water covered the entire floor. Not even a tiny lip existed around the edges, only wall. Inside the water, I could make out darting flickers of blue. I flinched as Taz's head loomed up beside mine as he peered over my shoulder.

"Okay, those are Hurdroxi," he said. "And the door is in the opposite wall. We could try walking through slowly and hope they don't notice us, but there are so many of them."

"How are we going to get across then? Do you know what these Hurdroxi like, or don't like?"

"Let me have a think." He sighed. "Either way, there's a key hanging from the ceiling so we'll have to grab that I'd guess."

I felt in my pocket but remembered I'd lost my orb, so calling Petra for advice wasn't an option. Cursing myself for not being more careful, I wracked my brain. I recalled something from one of the books in Beasts and Baronies class and closed my eyes to picture the text.

"Hurdroxi," I recited aloud. "Winged water creatures with poisonous suckers on their underbellies. Antidotes are known but costly to produce. Advice is to avoid but, if unavoidable, Hurdroxi can be hypnotised by a naked flame."

I opened my eyes to find Taz blinking in amazement.

"Wow. How did you know all that? Do you have a knowledge or learning gift I don't know about? Come to think of it, you usually remember things quite easily, don't you, why is that?"

I shrugged. "Just memory really. I can visualise things I've seen if I find them interesting."

"Double wow." He rubbed his chin, turning back to the problem in front of us. "Okay, we can't take the torches from the hall. They're welded to the wall believe it or not. Oh, here I have matches though, but we can't exactly put those in the water."

I looked around, hoping to find some sort of answer. Adrenalin pounded, keeping my mind sharp as I stared up at the key hanging from the ceiling.

"That key looks different to the door lock." I distracted us from the obvious issue. "See, that one is brass and the door lock is the same as the previous one. I reckon that hanging key is a decoy."

Taz nodded. "That's clever. But how are we going to get across without getting stung?"

"We need to find something that will float. We can put a flame on it. Even if it starts to burn up the float, we only need less than a minute to run across and open the door."

Taz patted his pockets. I looked at the keys in the previous room, but even if we had some way of tying them together, they'd just sink and take the match with them.

I smacked a hand to my forehead and made Taz jump.

"I've got it! We just light the rope somehow."

Taz grinned. "How's your hand-eye coordination?"

"Awful. Can you maybe try throwing one match, just to see? If not we won't waste them. Or we could try fashion some kind of whip out of keys to bring it closer- but no, that's just ridiculous."

Taz pulled a box of matches out of his pocket and struck one. The water in the room shivered and I eyed the growing mass of blue floating toward the flame.

With great confidence, Taz lifted his hand back to his shoulder and threw the match like a dart. I gasped as the match spun and the flame quivered. The blue mass seemed to spin a circle, gathering underneath the light.

It hit the rope and the fire caught, gobbling at the fibres.

"Go!" Taz gave my shoulder a push and shoved me into the water.

I stumbled and dodged one of the Hurdroxi, kicking up water as I waded with high-stepping legs to the door. I pushed the key into the lock, almost fainting when my fingers fumbled.

The lock clicked. Taz hauled the door open and pushed. I fell forward, crashing to my hands and knees with a yelp as Taz stepped right over me.

I peered behind me to see the rope had burned out completely and that there was now a swarm of blue only inches from my toes. I scrambled forward as Taz pulled the door shut.

"That was close," he huffed.

I looked around the new room, an empty hallway stretching ahead in front of us. Even as I peered into the gloom, I saw yet another door with a keyhole at the far end.

"Why is it always keys?" I asked. "Like, couldn't they have a code to decipher or something as well?"

Taz managed a smile as I pocketed the key we'd used twice now, but he looked uneasy as he surveyed the hallway ahead of us.

"Fae love keys," he said. "It probably goes back to the days of little doors in trees leading to Faerie gardens and realms. Back then Fae had to keep making themselves tiny to avoid humans instead of learning to blend in as they do now."

I didn't answer. My focus got stuck on a figure striding toward us, one I recognised.

One I really didn't want to see right now.

"Um, Demi?" Taz lowered his voice. "Why is there a scary girl in a bandana coming towards us with a hockey stick?"

CHAPTER TEN
TAZ COCKS UP FOR ONCE

Of both my sisters, Jenny was the scariest. Mary could strip paint with her taunts, but Jenny loved dishing out physical torment.

None of that explained why she was walking toward us, waving a hockey stick back and forth.

"Um, that appears to be my sister," I told Taz. "They can't have possibly brought her all the way here. How could they know she's the worst thing to put in front of me?"

Jenny stopped a few metres away, blocking our path.

"There you are." Even her voice was identical to the original. "Still wasting time with this fairy crap? Would have thought we'd knocked it out of you by now, but no."

I took a step back.

"You're not my sister," I mumbled. "Not really."

Jenny brandished the hockey stick again. "Don't be dim. You always were the worst of us."

My stomach clenched like a vice. A choked breath escaped and I felt Taz's hand on my shoulder.

"It's not her, just a glamour or a Reflectator, they can read your fears," he said.

I let Taz propel me forward but Reflecto-Jenny side-stepped to block our way.

"Oh no, you're not going anywhere." She smiled, wide and cruel. "It's about time you grew up and took a few home truths."

She lunged out and whacked the side of my arm with the hockey stick, like she did at home whenever I dared pass her.

The pain was real enough, and I winced.

"You're not my sister," I repeated, my voice shaking. "Go away!"

Taz gripped my shoulder tighter.

"Don't listen to it," he insisted. "I've seen this trick done before. She isn't really your sister, it's just meant to distract you. Don't let her distract you."

I fought the urge to retaliate. I hated that part of me, the irrepressible urge to take the hockey stick and show her how it felt to be on the other end for once. As I faced the Reflecto-Jenny, I knew deep down that it was picking out exactly what my real sister thought of me.

I stepped right and, as it followed to block me, I dodged back left and around. Strong hands grabbed the strap of my satchel, clutching at handfuls of my hoodie with it. The Reflecto-Jenny pulled me backwards but let go just as quickly with a loud yelp.

I spun round in time to see Leo retreating back into my satchel as the Reflecto-Jenny clutched its hand to its chest. Taz took the opportunity to shove it out of the way.

"Go, get to the door!" he shouted.

I set off with the sound of pounding feet behind me. I heard another scuffle but didn't dare look back. With adrenalin thundering, the fear of my sister swelling to hugely irrational levels, I reached the door.

My hand shook as I tried to get the key in the lock.

"You always were a disappointment." Reflecto-Jenny sounded breathless, desperate to hurt me even if it was just with words. "Mum wanted a boy and she got you, an abomination. She should have thrown you out when you were born."

I shoved the key in the lock and twisted, but it wouldn't turn. I jammed my hand on the handle to try and get some strength behind the key. The door crept open and I cursed myself for assuming it would be locked. I threw it wide and dashed through, Taz jostling right behind me.

The door slammed shut and the sound of the Reflecto-Jenny's shrieking faded. I doubled over with my hands on my thighs, gasping for breath.

"Are you okay?" Taz asked. "Sorry, that's a stupid question. Leo's got some skills as well."

Distracted by my familial woes, I shook my head.

"I'm not sure what that was about. His teeth are tiny and don't really hurt at all if he does bite. It must have been her panicking. Although, last time the real Jenny tried to grab him he did the same thing and she screamed like anything."

Taz shrugged. "Who cares, he gave us a handy bit of time just now. Do you want to go on, or we can try and figure out another plan?"

I straightened up, my cheeks burning with shame.

"You're not going to say how sure you are that my real sister wouldn't say things like that?"

Taz shook his head. "Lots of families suck in my opinion. Besides, the tower organisers would want to figure out the most tormenting way to distract you. They have their ways of finding these things. Your sister sounds awful anyway so who cares what she or something imitating her thinks?"

"Thanks." I rubbed sweat from my forehead. "What do you think this room is all about?"

We looked around the small square room and at the banks of sand underfoot. I could reach up and with a small jump I'd be touching the ceiling. The only thing of note was a door in the wall opposite the one we'd entered through. Taz tried the handle, but it was locked.

"Do you reckon there are sand snakes or anything?" I asked.

Taz approached a paper sign on the far wall.

"I doubt it," he said. "This says to dig until we find the box with the code. There's a padlock on the door that has individual letters, but we've got this helpful arrow here pointing downwards. There you go, you wanted a code instead of a key."

"Er, yeah, great."

Taz sank to his knees and started to part sand with his hands. I flinched back as an ominous rumble echoed around us. A wave of sand dropped from above, spilling down over Taz's back and shoulders.

"Are you okay?" I rushed forward.

Taz shook himself, sending grains of sand flying everywhere, and wiped his face several times.

"I think so, I might have accidentally eaten some. This will be the trickery no doubt, when you dig it refills itself."

"Like a huge hourglass. Maybe we can sweep some of the sand out."

I went back to the door and opened it without thinking. The sight of the Reflecto-Jenny flying toward me down the hall, with furious bulging eyes and hockey stick aloft, would stay in my nightmares for a long time. I slammed the door shut again, realising that each nightmare was at least apparently confined to its individual room considering Reflecto-Jenny wasn't trying to get in this one with us.

Taz had resumed digging and another load of sand fell over his head and shoulders. I kneeled beside him. As he kept going, I started to divert the sand threatening to bury him into the far corner of the room.

It seemed to be working but Taz had to stop and ride out the wave every time more sand fell.

"Do you want to swap?" I asked.

Taz shook his head. Needing to do something, I took off my satchel and wriggled out of my hoodie.

"Here, wear this over your head," I suggested. "Put the hood up."

Taz grabbed the hoodie and hung the hood over his head like a cape. The rest didn't exactly stay in place, but he started digging and didn't stop when the sand fell.

"Much better, great idea, thanks."

I kept sweeping the sand back, creating a bank behind us. I worked with an almost vengeful fury, ignoring the skin on my hands growing dry and sensitive. My brow dripped sweat. My arm muscles burned from the effort and my back ached from crouching.

"I've found a gap!" Taz shouted.

I tried to get to my feet and tumbled backwards instead, crashing into my sand pile. I clambered over to Taz's side on my hands and knees to assess the small gap he was so excited about. It was nothing more than a missing floorboard, no wider than the width of a tennis ball.

"Finally," I tried to joke. "There's a benefit to being scrawny."

I rolled up my sleeve and took a deep breath.

"There's going to be something very bitey-stingy in here, isn't there?" I asked.

Taz bit his lip. "Maybe not, you never know, they might have decided enough is enough."

Both of us knew that was one step away from an outright fib more than naive optimism, but I had no other choice.

I plunged my hand through the gap and closed my eyes tight.

The gap stretched on, morphing into a cavity. I could feel the smooth brush of dust under my fingertips and tried not to flinch as softness brushed my knuckles. If a spider crawled up my arm right now, I would scream. It didn't matter how many times I re-read my battered copy of *Milton the Mighty* when nobody was looking; every time I tried to convince myself the arachnophobia was all in my head, but my head just didn't seem to agree with me.

My fingers touched something solid and I flinched so hard that I wrenched my arm and felt my shoulder muscle ping. Gritting my teeth, I continued to pull at the corner of something.

"Got it!"

I launched upright like a very dishevelled sand mermaid emerging from beneath the dunes. I held out my hand so Taz could see the small wooden box.

"If something jumps out," I hesitated. "Smack it with something."

Taz nodded. "Smack jumping things, got it."

I opened the box.

Nothing jumped out, but I almost dropped the box all the same from sheer pent-up anxiety.

I really hope what I said about stingy-bitey things hasn't given them ideas...

Inside the box was a thin piece of paper. I picked it up and read aloud.

"The path leading out lies back the way you came. But first you must face the fear again. The code you need will be two short of three, removing the other third and me. Then out back the way you came, but keep moving fast as sand pours the same."

As if I'd summoned it, the sand started to pour from above in a continuous stream.

"Do we have a plan?" Taz asked.

I bit my lip and handed him the paper. "Read the code bit again for me?"

"The code you need will be two short of three, removing the other third and me."

I dodged the streams of sand falling down, hurried across to the padlock on the door and peered at the notches with letters printed on.

"Once more please?"

Taz read the code out again and I frowned, spinning the notches.

"Two short of three, either one or minus one, but this has four notches on it. Removing the other third and me. Any ideas?"

Taz appeared beside me. "Nope. Baffled."

"Removing the other third and me." I frowned deeper. "Me implies a person or maybe like a sentient object. If there are three, and one is me, then the other third would be not you."

Taz scratched his head. "Eh?"

"Two short of three is one, I think, one person. Remove the other third person and me, what do you have left?"

"Me?"

"No, you."

"Er… that's what I said." Taz sounded so frustrated, but I kept my gaze fixed on the spinning notches.

"No, the answer is the word you. But that's only three letters. The riddle likes rhyming."

"Oh that I could understand thee," Taz quoted, from what I had no idea.

He froze. I span the notches faster.

T – H – E –

We both leaned in as I turned the last one into place.

– E

The padlock clicked as I pulled down hard on it, determined it would open whether we were correct or we broke it by force.

"You did it!" Taz grinned as the door swung open.

I smiled back, relieved. "We did it."

We peered through the doorway together and my elation dropped like a cannon ball.

"Always more bloody doors," I muttered, stepping into the room.

I eyed the three doors in front of us and turned back as Taz followed me through.

"Wait don't let the-" I shouted as the door slammed shut behind him. "-door shut. Does it still open?"

Taz's mouth dropped open and he twisted round. A sharp tug on the door handle later, and I sagged in disbelief.

"I didn't think," Taz groaned. "Sorry. Looks like we can only go onwards."

I bit down on the retorts swimming up to the tip of my tongue and focused on the likely problem instead.

"What's the chance that one of these leads to eternal happiness?"

Taz shook his head. "Zero."

He strode forward to the middle door, but it wouldn't open. I followed his example and went left, while he veered right. I pushed the curling iron handle down and the door creaked open, like every single horror movie ever filmed. Darkness spilled out and I took a hesitant step back. A quick look sideways and Taz's door had opened too.

"Which one?" I asked.

He crossed to stand beside me. "Mine's pitch black. Oh, yours is too."

"You first then," I suggested. "It could be a portal or skip-way somewhere, or some kind of bottomless pit if we choose the wrong one."

Taz held out a hand, palm up. "Together?"

I nodded. With a disconcerting leaping in my insides, I curled my fingers around his. We stepped forward, pressing close to squeeze through.

A dragging sensation gripped me as I entered the darkness, like someone had grabbed my t-shirt to haul me in, but it was all of me instead of my t-shirt they were holding onto. Every part of me lurched and my fingers slid from Taz's grip.

Taz yelled behind me. I turned my head just in time to see him propelled back toward the light as the door slammed shut.

CHAPTER ELEVEN
FEARS IN THE DARK

Even before I could panic about being stuck in total darkness, light appeared from nowhere, casting the room in a dingy glow. The door was still behind me, and locked when I tried to open it. The only other thing I could see was a small square cut into the wall, no bigger than a ventilation hatch.

"Demi?"

I let out a ragged breath. *I can still hear him.*

"Yeah, I'm here. What happened?"

"The room rejected me."

"I think we're only supposed to go on alone."

I could hear every note of the air around me, including Taz's indignant scoffing on the other side of the wall.

"Not bloody likely!"

"Well I'm stuck here until I do," I retorted. "Unless you go through the other room and we just make sure we don't lose hearing with each other? This is designed to test us, to make us go forward, so we have to go on."

"Alright, but if something awful happens to me, I'm blaming you!"

I rolled my eyes and bent down to peer into the hole. It stretched on beyond my line of sight, a seemingly endless tunnel. My blood began to rush, the pounding in my chest tightening.

I can't go through there.

My fear of small spaces, caused by my sisters tormenting me as a child, put this as my worst possible thing to face. That or being buried alive.

A loud slam echoed and I jumped, hitting my hand on the top of the gap.

"Oh, I know what these are." Taz's voice sounded closer now, loud enough for me to hear the hitch in his tone. "Trial chambers. They make you face your worst nightmares. I'm not sure I can do this."

"Like *I'm a Celebrity*?" I asked, hysteria beginning to rise.

"What's that?"

He can sing every word of the Demolition Ducks theme tune, including the Hallow's Eve Special episode, but he's never heard of I'm A Celebrity.

I flinched as a loud gurgling noise started from the depths of the tunnel. After spending hours locked in a dark airing cupboard with what my sisters told me was a tentacle monster, I grew up and realised that the gurgling noise it made was just the old boiler. Even so, I still woke from nightmares about it and the gurgling never failed to send chills racing over my skin.

Focus on facts. I coached myself like I had done many times before. *This is an illusion. Whatever happens in there isn't real.*

A thought occurred to me then.

"Taz? What's in your room?" Silence. I waited a few beats. "Taz? You don't have to tell me, but just let me know you're still with me."

"Yeah. Um, let's just say there's a room full of spiders. I know it's not a very original fear, I just can't help it. I see the legs move and I just, can't."

I frowned. "Can you see the end of the room, a way out?"

I stuck my hand into the crawl space, testing it. My sisters had told me the monster would stick a tentacle out one day and pull me forever into the darkness, but if this was my fear playing out, no monster had come yet.

"I can see the door but there's- it's huge, Dem. I'm not sure I can."

I sank into a crouch. "Got anything you can whack it out of the way with? Can you look at them long enough to see if you need to find a key?"

"I can't, I just can't."

The sound of a frightened Taz scared me more than anything else. I pulled my satchel around to my front so it would hang underneath me with Leo safe inside, and ducked into the crawl space.

"Mine's a crawl tunnel," I shouted back. "All I need you to do is keep talking to me, okay? I'm going to crawl through, find the other end and see if I can open your door that way. If not, I'll tear the bloody tower down."

I started forward, my clammy hands brushing the cold stone underneath. The others competing would have trained themselves to be fearless. I was afraid of lots of things, but if Taz needed my help then I had to do something.

Stupid Fae bastards.

"Taz? You still there?" I stopped, just in case I'd lost him.

"Yeah, there's a huge one getting really close."

"Okay, just dodge them if you can. What part of them are you afraid of?"

At that point, I was asking as much to keep my brain focused on something other than the fear that the walls were closing in on me. I crawled a few paces further forward until my feet were in the tunnel.

SLAM.

Darkness engulfed me. In the small space I could barely twist to look behind me, but I managed it just enough to see nothing. The small amount of light the entrance had given me was gone, blocked.

"Taz, I'm stuck in this tunnel now and it's pitch black. I really need you to keep talking to me, please," I pleaded.

"Um, it's the legs. I don't know why. I just- they move and I can't help it. I shudder and then the fear crashes in. Oh orbs alive, it's so close."

I pushed on through the darkness, unable to comfort him with my mind beginning to tear in terror. Something brushed against my hand. I squealed.

Just the satchel. Keep going. If you can do this, you can do anything.

I wouldn't be too crazy about the spider room either, but now that I wasn't shouting to Taz, he'd stopped talking back.

The gurgling noise echoed through the tunnel and, in that brief moment, rationality descended like phoenix song.

It's meant to be the old boiler, which isn't a monster and can't possibly be here even if it was. So this is just part of the puzzle tower, the illusion.

The gurgling stopped as something solid brushed my face. My insides cramped from tensing so much, but I refused to scream.

Not giving them the satisfaction. I gritted my teeth and pressed on. *I'll deal with sorting Taz out after.*

Another brush against my head, and this time my shoulder as well. Against my better judgement, I reached out to the side and felt the stone wall right beside me. I touched the other side, top, and the floor. The tunnel was getting smaller.

What if it's shut at the end? What if the point is Taz has to face his fear to free me from mine? What if I die here?

I started clawing forward in the dark, but the ceiling pressed down on me until I had to go onto my elbows, and the sides were squeezing my shoulders. I pushed my satchel out from underneath me and in front so I could keep Leo safe from getting squished.

I didn't even think about him. He's stuck in here too.

"Demi?"

Taz's voice echoed in my visionless, coffinous hell. I clung to it and the satchel strap cutting into my clenched fingers.

"The tunnel's really small now." I all but screamed it. "If it gets any smaller, I won't be able to move at all. I think I'm going to die here."

I couldn't even dwell on how dramatic I sounded. Because of course the Fae wouldn't let anyone actually die.

Would they?

"Oh god, Demi, I'm sorry. Look I, just hang on okay? Sod it."

The following bellow that ricocheted through my tunnel prison sounded more like a constipated donkey than a warrior chant. I couldn't bend my arm in the tight space to wipe my eyes, so the tears of relief fell down my face instead.

A loud bang made me jump, the movement pressing all four sides against me. Also, what sounded oddly like stamp-dancing.

"Urgh, that's disgusting." Taz's horrified voice had never sounded so heavenly. "It's okay, I'm through. Orbs alive. Demi, you just need to keep crawling. The length of the room can't be that much longer than mine. It'll feel like it's impossible but you just have to keep doing what you're doing."

Easy for him to say.

"I can't." I choked over the words. "It's literally not enough room, I'm stuck. I can't even see an exit, it's pitch back."

I heard footsteps ahead, then a loud pop.

"Ouch. Okay, it won't let me come in this way to get you. Do you trust me?"

I nodded, even though he couldn't see. "Of course."

"Then even if it feels like you're reaching through solid

matter, you have to keep going. It's trickery, it's playing with your mind. I know you can do this."

Something warm slithered across my hand. I screamed, but the responding sound was a familiar crooning noise.

"Leo," I sobbed.

Again he waved his tail across my fingers, as if he wanted me to grab on. Whether it was intentional or random, he was giving me a lifeline that I desperately needed. I wrapped my fingers around his tail and inched forward with each pull.

The walls strained against me, the stone threatening to crack my bones. I couldn't breathe, each gasp taking nothing in.

A flash of light blinded me.

Something snared around my arms, pulling me forward until I collapsed onto the hard stone floor.

"You're okay." Taz's voice was right by my ear but my body hadn't caught up enough for me to even raise my head. "Shh, you're safe now, breathe."

I huffed in lungfuls of air that didn't quite hit, then lurched up onto my hands and knees because I could. Finally, I had space.

I staggered to my feet, clinging to Taz's arms as my eyesight adjusted. Another blank room with no doors, and no sign of a hatch or hole where I'd entered.

"You faced the spiders," I croaked.

Taz laughed shakily. "Barely. Couldn't let you have all the fun. Can you see if there are any left on me?"

I let go of him and wiped my eyes with my sleeve, wincing when I saw after how grimy it was. I checked him over for any remaining spiders, but couldn't see so much as a speck of web anywhere.

Needing time to get myself together, I opened my satchel flap to find Leo safe inside, almost as though he knew he shouldn't be seen by anyone who might be watching our progress. True, if they were watching the scene with the Reflecto-Jenny, they would have seen him bite, but I couldn't worry about that now. I let the flap drop and peered around the room.

Walls painted cream, a ceiling in the same colour, and no sign of ways in or out. The tunnel exit was completely gone now, and I couldn't see any sign of where Taz would have entered through.

"You okay?" Taz asked after a long moment.

I nodded. "Yeah, but I want the hell out of this place now."

"Agreed. So, the only thing we have is that sign up there."

I peered up at the wall. I wasn't even sure which wall was which now, but on one to my left was a wooden sign painted with gold lettering.

"Forget the map, all you need is right here for the asking." I scowled. "What map?"

I inched toward the wall beneath the sign, tapping it with tentative fingertips as if it might suck me back into the tunnel again. My head was still swimming, but I just wanted to get this done. I needed my orb, then I needed to speak to Fetra and find a way out of this hellish place.

Taz appeared beside me and stood on his tiptoes to inspect the sign.

"I can't see any invisible writing, no sign of secret codes, the lettering isn't distinctive," he murmured. "Maybe there's something in the wording. Or maybe we need to somehow get them to lift the lid."

I frowned as he pointed to the ceiling. "Unless there's a secret map in the floorboards, it's not like we can just ask the room. Hi, room. Could you give us the way out please?"

Taz faced me, his eyes wide.

"Um, Dem? Turn around."

I didn't want to, expecting the next wave of Fae torture, but I did. In the far wall, a door stood demurely as though it had been there the whole time. I blinked.

"It literally did mean 'ask for directions'," I said.

Taz threw an arm around my shoulders, his face breaking into a broad grin.

"Fae don't do too well with literal, they're too naturally suspicious for it. Even then, demanding is more their style. Well done!"

I sighed. "Doesn't get me any further to the goal though, unless- Hi room, could you give me my puzzle tower token please, the real one, not a fake or a decoy?"

I eyed the walls without much hope, knowing the likelihood of a shelf appearing with my orb on it was ridiculous.

A loud rumbling echoed. A second later, a small cloth bag bounced inches from my nose. I scrambled backwards, almost knocking Taz off his feet. The bag hung there, suspended from a bit of gold ribbon.

Taz didn't hesitate. He grabbed the bag, pulled it open and emptied the contents onto his palm. I stared at the small sphere with familiar pale grey swirls, and the short keychain curled beside it.

"How do I know it's real?" I asked, reaching forward to take it. "I can't um, use it, not- people could be watching."

I held it up in front of my face, trying to see any familiar nicks and marks. Taz scrunched up his nose and loomed right in front of me.

"It's definitely real. I'm guessing it'll be yours rather than them trying to procure a real one for a decoy. They're difficult to get outside of home, there are enchantments and all sorts to make them unduplicatable and things. Remember how much effort the enemy went to in order to get those orbs last time, even to the point of having someone infiltrate Arcanium itself?"

That was good enough for me. I secured the keyring on my belt loop and tucked the orb into my pocket. I was never going to be parted from it ever again.

"Right, through the door?" I asked.

Taz nodded and strode across to fling it open.

A wave of sand cascaded in, and I could just see the box we'd found the riddle for the code in lying open on one of the mounds, the ceiling still dumping more sand in with every passing second.

"At least we don't have to face the trial chambers again, but this shortcut is probably too good to be true. Come on."

Taz waited by the door for me to join him, clearly not willing to step through unless we were together. I reached his side but hesitated just a moment longer.

"Thanks, room."

Taz rolled his eyes and hustled me through the doorway, his hands firm on my upper arms. He swung the door closed behind us and turned to face me.

"We can't guarantee everything will be the same on our journey back," he said. "But we need to plan in case it is. We need a way to get past your fake sister, through the Hurdroxi and out."

I rubbed my thumb over the cool orb in my pocket. Taz and I had come this far, further than two of the people who'd entered the tower before us. With adrenalin pumping, I set to work.

I pulled out both of my shoelaces and grabbed my hoodie.

"Have you got many matches left?" I asked.

Taz checked his box and nodded, holding it out. I struck a match and let the flame begin to burn the seam of my hoodie. I shook the match out almost immediately and shoved the shirt into the sand to quash the burning.

With the stitching weakened, I tore the hoodie in two. I reached into the hidden side pocket of my satchel and took out my penknife. It had been my gift from Xavio last summer when I left for Arcanium, and it had come in handy since.

"See the torch there?" I held the knife out to Taz. "Do you think you could get two long strips out of the wood? We need to make two poles."

Taz took the knife as I tied one shoelace to one half of the torn shirt, and the second to the other half.

"Here you go." Taz appeared a moment later, holding two long pieces of splintered wood.

I looked over to find the rest of the torch in pieces.

"Brilliant." I grinned. "Okay, now I just need to make a hole in the wood."

I set to work and chiselled a hole in one end of each pole.

"I see what you're doing," Taz said, a note of admiration in his tone. "So you tie the string to the end of the pole, then the flaming rag hangs from the string?"

"Yeah like the cartoons where they hang a carrot in front of the donkey. Only we're going to light the cloth and use it to guide the Hurdroxi out of our way."

I handed both sticks to Taz and took two handfuls of sand.

"Okay." I took a deep breath. "When I say go, swing the door open. No matter what happens, shove and run. At the other end we'll need to light the cloth quick and just hope for the best."

"Hang on," Taz said. "I'll douse these cloths in the oil that keeps the torches burning. It might give us more time."

I nodded and waited for him to do his thing. When he was in place to open the door, I clutched my handfuls of sand and faced the door.

"Okay, now!"

Taz pulled the door open and held it steady. The Reflecto-Jenny turned to face us and started running. I lifted a hand in front of my face.

"You," it cried. "Ungrateful, unwanted, useless-aaaah!"

I took all my buried anguish and blew the sand into its face. It stumbled to a halt and raised a hand to its eyes, but I wasn't waiting around. I pushed past it and ran down the hall as fast as my aching legs could carry me.

"Light the cloth," I shouted back. "I'll open the door."

"Lighting the cloth!"

I threw the door open. Responding to the motion, or possibly the torches in the hall, the Hurdroxi swarmed toward the edge of the water pool.

"Here." Taz handed me one of the poles.

I took it from him and hovered the flaming cloth over the water. The Hurdroxi only moved two feet away from the edge, floating underneath the fire, but it was enough.

Behind Taz, the Reflecto-Jenny seemed to be confused now that I was out of its hallway. It blinked at Taz, and I wondered then if it might start tormenting him instead.

I stepped into the water and walked as fast as I dared. Each step might swirl one of the Hurdroxi into my path, but I couldn't risk the fire snuffing out.

I twisted in a slow circle and backed up until my calves bumped the step on the far wall. Aware of Taz lighting his own Hurdroxi lure on the other side, I clambered up onto safe ground.

"Okay, my turn." Taz's voice shook.

He made his way the same as I had, keeping his steps slow and smooth. When he reached the wall he spun around.

A loud, incandescent shrieking echoed a moment before the Reflecto-Jenny appeared in the opposite doorway. I hadn't told

Taz to close the door and he clearly hadn't thought of it either.

Taz's fire flickered and his hand fumbled around the end of his pole. The cloth teetered and dropped into the water.

"Get out!" I screamed.

I leaned forward as far as I dared and held out my own lure, the cloth almost eaten and the fire nearly out. The Hurdroxi froze as my flame died. In those vital few seconds, Taz leapt with all his might through the doorway.

The sheer weight of him crashed against me. I flew backwards, bouncing against the unforgiving stone floor. My shoulders took the brunt of the impact and even though I could feel Taz's hand firm around the back of my head, the thumping sensation of the rebound made me feel queasy. He stumbled up, grabbed my hands and hauled me to my feet.

"I'm sorry," he gabbled. "I panicked, are you okay?"

I nodded and quickly wished I hadn't. Taz ran a hand over my forehead, brushing my hair back as if the injury of impact might have bounced to the front of my head instead. I took a shaky step back.

"Let's just get through the rest," I said. "They'll probably put something in our way still, right?"

Taz peered into the key room and shook his head.

"This room looks as we left it. Let's get through and see."

He eyed me up and down and, after a pause, held out his hand. I conceded with a nod and let him wrap a surprisingly strong arm around my waist. The elephants danced clumsily on my brain and I wondered if the subtle bubbling of nausea in my gut was from lack of food or if I'd simply pass out in the tower, never to be seen again.

Even for me that's melodramatic. Just focus on the next step. Get out of here. Orb Petra. Get Trevor to come and get us. Or just getting out of here would be a start.

"They'll have released those dogs that cut up your face," I suggested.

Taz didn't reply as he marched me around the piles of keys and into the empty hallway beyond. I stumbled over my own feet but Taz powered us forward to the exit. He pushed the door handle and rattled it a couple of times.

"The door's locked," he groaned. "It looks like a brass keyhole as well. Do they really expect us to go and sort through the rest of the keys again?"

I heard the frustration in his voice, but with my head still spinning and my eyes squinting from the pain, I saw the air around the keyhole shiver.

"No, wait. I think it's another glamour. The keyhole looks like brass, but it's too dark."

I pulled the original iron key from my pocket and slid it past the vision of the keyhole. It shouldn't have fit, but the key kept sliding in. Iron keyholes that couldn't be charmed to open or change form, but apparently could be glamoured to look different. I turned the key and heard the most blessed sound.

CLICK.

The door swung outwards. I blinked and lifted an arm to shade against the blinding sunlight.

"That's a typically mean Fae trick." Taz's voice echoed beside me, dripping with fury. "Most of the students would have just thrown the key away after the first door and have to keep going back for it."

I might have answered, or burst into relieved tears, but something blocked most of the sunlight before I could decide.

A pair of forceful arms slammed around my neck. I froze in horror as Taz hugged the life out of me.

"We did it," he murmured against my head. "Now don't you ever get us signed up for anything like that ever again."

"I can't believe you did it!" Milo's voice echoed somewhere right by my left shoulder, but Taz didn't seem to be letting me go any time soon. "Friese is still in there and several have failed already, including Penelope."

"Thanks to Ta- Roger. He was brilliant."

I tried to remember if I'd used Taz's name in the tower, my mind lumbering through the rooms. If anyone here knew the nickname he'd given himself, if they knew the Prince of Faerie called himself Taz, then I'd given him away to the Old King and his guards and everyone else watching.

Taz stepped back but kept a firm arm around me.

"I'm just glad to be out of there," he said. "We had to find a key then cross a Hurdroxi pool, but Demi was amazing at figuring out how to distract them. It was mostly distraction but I still have sand in my mouth from one of the rooms."

"We'll get you some water," Milo promised. "It was amazing, we were all watching on the VC. I mean, I won't lie and say people were cheering you on, but I think a few bets may have changed hands midway through as your odds went up."

"Well, that's something then," I muttered.

I closed my eyes, not caring that Taz was left supporting me. He stood beside me with his arm still anchored around my waist, but I was too exhausted and frazzle-headed to care about feeling awkward. If he let go now, I'd likely fall over, and the worst thing we could do now with a whole host of Fae around was get separated.

"All the other entrants have gone in already," Milo continued. "Out of thirteen, eleven have come out including you. Seven of them had bad injuries. One girl came out a while back and thought she'd won, but turned out she'd picked up a decoy token."

I reached into my pocket, paranoid my orb would have

morphed into something useless, but didn't dare take it out for people to see. I knew I'd be worrying either way until I could find somewhere quiet to orb Petra and prove it worked.

"We didn't see anyone." I said, mainly to distract myself. "Maybe the tower has a separate path for each person somehow."

Everyone fell silent as the door swung open. Two adult Fae trotted out with a man on a stretcher, unconscious with cuts across his face and arms. A collective groan passed through the crowd.

"That means Friese is the only one left in there." Milo gawped at me. "That makes you the winner."

I gulped, my dizziness stepping up a gear.

"You mean we're the winners. Taz was with me the whole way. But maybe we forfeited somehow. I can't be a winner, that's nuts."

Taz's perturbed frown made it look like he silently agreed with me, but Milo gave my arm a diffident nudge.

"You did amazing," he insisted. "But even assuming Friese finds his true token, you'll likely win based on timing. Don't worry about it until they announce it for sure, then we can go find somewhere you can relax for a while."

Relaxing did sound so good. I wanted to sidle into the crowd, blend in, be invisible, but I didn't have any time.

The tower door smashed open in a shower of fiery sparks. Friese strode out, his shoulders puffed and his nose in the air. He had dirt across his cheeks that looked like it had been applied with his fingers and his hair looked artfully messed. Given the lack of injuries and general all-over grime, I'd have put all my money on him being the chosen pet champion given an easy route to make the bets swing a certain way.

Which paints an even bigger target on our backs.

Friese glanced around the crowd, victorious. Then he saw us. He blinked, his eyes wide to the point of bursting. His mouth twisted in a disgusted snarl, like he'd just sucked a Hurdroxi belly, as Director Cornelius appeared on the golden platform.

"All entrants have exited the tower," he announced. "Of the three that completed the puzzles, only two have obtained their true tokens. This means we need to base our winner on time, which means the winner of the two-hundred and sixty-fifth Puzzle Tower event is Demerara Darcy."

I tried to shrink behind Taz, but Milo seemed intent on pushing us forward. I managed a couple of steps before I noticed the ominous silence. The only sound might have been the furious grinding of Friese's teeth nearby.

"The celebratory feast will be held," Cornelius continued, his amplified voice highlighting the lack of crowd noise. "It is now time for fun, frivolity and, as is tradition, a blind eye will be turned to any mischief for tonight only, for our staff and for clientele alike."

I tried to see some aspect of disappointment in Cornelius' face, but he seemed amused rather than anything else. As the crowd began to buzz with low fervour, Taz and Milo stepped closer to me like bodyguards. I glanced up at the Old King's platform in time to see him mutter something to Cornelius, who then stalked off. As the Old King's cold gaze focused on me, both Sagar and Eldrich looked over at us, and this time there were no smiles in sight.

"Well," Taz muttered, sizing up the crowd. "If that hasn't singled us out as Forgotten enemy number one, I don't know what will."

CHAPTER TWELVE
OF COURSE TAZ HAS A PERFECT AIM

"You have to shake hands with the King."

Milo's words sounded in my head, but it took me a moment to catch on.

"I- what? Why? I'm part-human, he'll probably slaughter me."

Taz's arm tightened around my waist. In the sudden panic, I'd barely noticed him holding onto me like I was about to collapse. Even though I'd gathered control of my legs now, I took comfort from his unerring protectiveness.

The crowd was buzzing, low conversations flying, but on the platform I could see the Old King waiting with Elvira glowering beside him. He had a trophy hanging from one hand, and I knew I couldn't risk snubbing him by not going to receive it.

"Um, Taz, you'll have to let her go," Milo whispered.

Taz grunted, not moving an inch.

"I have to go up there," I told him. "Be ready though. Put a warding around me if you have to, but keep it discreet."

He scowled but released me so quick I almost fell over. It was only as I picked my way through the watchful crowd alone that I realised this was likely a ploy to separate us.

If they know who Taz is already, perhaps they'll snatch him now. I should have told him to put the warding over himself.

I looked back as I reached the platform, flinching to find Taz right behind me.

"I'll wait here," he promised. "Don't do anything mad."

That gave me the strength to square my shoulders and take

those dangerous steps up to stand a respectful, and somewhat safe, distance from the Old King.

"This is the one I was telling you about," Elvira hissed.

I gave her my best dismissive look, despite the fact every particle of my body was quaking with nerves and I couldn't meet her eyes. But I noticed her expression when the Old King dismissed her with a flick of his head; disgust and absolute hatred for me burned in her dark eyes.

"A fairy masquerading as Fae," the Old King sneered, not projecting his voice to the crowd but not bothering to keep it down either. "I am surprised. I would shake your hand, but you'll forgive me if I do not. We sometimes have these anomalies happen, a reminder for us to renew our efforts toward the *rightful* way of things."

I felt a wave of heat prickle over me, like sitting in the sun for too long. I recognised it as the subtle sensation that came from someone trying to attack with Fae magic and wondered what he was trying to achieve. Given that it was a Fae regent casting against me, even a deposed outcast one, something awful should have happened.

The Old King's eyes narrowed. "You aren't responding."

"Am I meant to?" I tried to copy the Fae-like, wide-eyed innocence I'd seen so many of them toy with. "I didn't mean to offend, but I have a habit of not doing what I'm supposed to."

I had no idea what he'd been trying to do to me, or why I wasn't responding as he expected. He opened his mouth to reply, the snarl getting stuck on his face as a tinkling voice interrupted us.

"Demerara Darcy! Cynthia Meadows from *The Faerie Net*. Such a scoop for a *fairy* to win the Puzzle Tower! Would you allow us a few words with her your highness, for your fans?"

The Old King nodded, not taking his narrowed gold eyes off

me.

"Yes, of course. The quicker it's out of my sight, the better."

Perhaps being dismissed so rudely by a person of power should have upset me, but I was belligerent, sore and exhausted. Knowing it was overkill, and likely me-kill, I gave the Old King a wicked smile and swept my arms out wide, dipping as low into a mocking bow as my shaking limbs would allow.

As I turned my back on him, I saw Taz with his expression clenched tight in concentration, one hand ever so slightly raised.

Of course, whatever the Old King was trying to do to me had hit against Taz's protection.

Apparently outcast royalty couldn't compete against legitimate royalty, even a half-blooded one.

Taz sagged the moment I was beside him.

"I would say that was rash," he muttered. "But you've got guts, I'll give you that."

I could only imagine how much effort protecting against the powers of a king would take, even for a prince. Taz slid an arm around my shoulders this time and I forced myself past the awkward fluttering in my chest to secure mine around his waist to steady him. As we faced Cynthia Meadows together, it was me supporting his weight this time.

"Well now, that was quite an event!" Cynthia Meadows seemed determined to adorn herself in exclamations. "How did you manage it?"

I froze as she appeared right in front of me, holding a large orb in the palm of her hand.

I hope that's not recording visual, I probably look like an extra from a horror film.

"Um, it was team work."

Cynthia blinked, momentarily thrown. "Yes, but what I mean is, how did *you* manage it? By all accounts you have mostly human blood."

Shocker.

I tried to restrain myself from saying exactly what I thought and give an interview that Arcanium would at least be proud of.

"I do, half human and half fairy at least, that we know of. But many of those rooms were testing ingenuity. I'm sure you must have noticed the skill in passing them was less to do with gifts than it was effort. Perhaps that was the point of this exercise, to show that gifts aren't always what carry you through?"

I knew I was pushing it, baiting the Fae tigers by belittling what they prized the most, but I couldn't help it. Taz choked on a hysterical laugh beside me.

"Interesting view." Cynthia recovered fast from her shock. "So, there was no advantage before you went in? No, shall we say, stacking of the decks?"

She wants to know if I cheated.

I refused to let the realisation deflate me, and forced my face into what I hoped was baffled surprise.

"Why, is that common around here? I'm not in a position to stack any decks I don't think, I don't have influential family to pull strings and make things easier for me like some around here do, that's been made abundantly clear. Still, I should probably go and get freshened up. Nice to meet you, love the show."

I'd watched *The Faerie Net* a handful of times, kind of like if *OK! Magazine* did a reality news TV show. Love might have been a bit of a strong way to put it, but Ace and I did love laughing at all the famous Faerie dramas so it technically wasn't a lie.

Taz was still pinning his lips together with his teeth, but as we turned around still arm in arm and left a horrified Cynthia Meadows behind, he let the laughter spill out.

"I will never backchat you again, Sparky. That was genius."

I wasn't so sure. I'd no doubt signed off on my fate now, not just with the Old King and the Fae at Gallows Oak, but probably most of *The Faerie Net*'s viewing public as well.

The crowds were still milling as we reached Milo, and I noticed a scary amount of them watching us.

"We need to get a move on," Taz said, his laughter long gone.

We set off toward the building, and I forced my legs to pick up the pace as I eyed the grumbling crowd. It was either that or have Taz pull me off my feet.

We only made it halfway across the grass of the quadrangle at the back of the club building.

"Running off so soon?" Friese's snide tone brought us to a stop. "We haven't yet celebrated your triumph. How did you manage it anyway?"

Taz and I threw up protection wardings at the same time, the essence of both merging as they had down in the tunnel, but this time without any intervention from me.

"Don't answer that," Taz growled.

Friese chuckled and ignored him. I tensed as the confident boy appeared in front of me, his dark hair falling without a strand out of place, and the marks from the Puzzle Tower vanished from his perfectly angular cheeks. He pressed against our shared warding and had to take a step back. Several others swamped behind him, nudging each other and exchanging gleeful glances.

"So hostile," he mocked. "We will need to host an initiation for you soon, Demerara. It will be a real welcome to our Fae ranks. You won't know when it's coming, but soon."

Taz barged forward to stand in front of me, his icy scowl sending waves of hostility through the already chilly air. The effect was still marred by his Roger disguise, but I could still remember what pissed off Taz looked like normally.

"Play-acting at being a grown-up, are you?" he taunted. "Run along with your little buddies and leave her alone. She's with me, and you *really* don't want me to be your problem."

The rest of us froze in confusion, but none more so than I did. Moments of silence passed until realisation dawned.

He doesn't mean 'with him' like that, idiot. He means part of his group. He's forgotten his glamour and he thinks he's saying I'm part of his royal entourage or something, get a grip.

Friese glanced over his shoulder at his group. There were nine other Fae flanking him, all stunning in their appearance and hungry with their wide eyes and eager smiles. On the surface, I couldn't see any noticeable difference, but then I looked deeper, past the perfections they cloaked themselves in. The features were all too perfect, the noses too pert or too delicately freckled, the eyes larger than they should be and the skin flawless without any visible pores. They were more like the fairies of horror stories, all treacherously smooth spite and sharp edges.

I flinched when Friese stood as close to Taz as he could get, challenging him with a look. If he and his friends decided to fight with gifts, our warding wouldn't hold long against so many of them.

"Even if that were true, Milo belongs here," he sneered. "You don't get to decide what happens to him, the school does. Isn't that right, Milo?"

Friese caught Milo's eye. Milo lowered his chin to his chest, his shoulders slumping as he said nothing. Friese chuckled and turned back to Taz.

"See? He came here a worthless loser and he'll remain here the same. Not everyone is meant to shine. Some are meant to serve. Sure Demerara will appreciate that too in time."

I bit my lip, aware of Taz's fists bunching and his eyes

whirling a storm. I wouldn't put automatic money on him in a flat fist fight against Friese, but I knew enough to guess he would give it one hell of a go anyway. I grabbed his wrist.

"He's not worth it," I hissed. "He wants you to get angry."

Taz's fingers unfurled and I let out a tumbling breath of relief. He took a step back, his forearms flexing with residual anger.

Friese brushed past us, almost knocking Taz to the ground. The gathered posse surged after their leader and I stumbled back to get out of the way.

"I hate Fae-folk," Taz muttered.

I dipped my forefinger into my pocket to check the orb was still there as we let our warding fade.

I almost missed Taz summoning an object from somewhere, whether his pocket or thin air I couldn't tell. As he weighed it in his palm, I saw it was a strange lump of paper, half-round, half-square, like the paper balls my sisters used to make and fill with shaving cream. I'd always been their favourite target, but I knew they could have filled the balls with much worse stuff.

"Hey, idiot," Taz shouted.

I groaned under my breath, powerless to stop him. I wasn't even sure I wanted to stop him. Only five or so metres away, Friese turned as Taz wound his arm back. He took aim and let go.

The paper ball sailed through the air. Milo gasped softly beside me. Taz grinned.

The ball struck Friese on his right cheek. A gloopy explosion of dark red spattered over his face, splashed into his hair and dribbled down his neck.

"Is that blood?" I had to ask.

"Of course not." Taz snorted gleefully. "Where would I get blood from? It's just ground up Kimpta berries from one of the realms. My last lot unfortunately but so worth it. They um, have an unfortunate smell that seeps into most things."

Friese stood swiping furiously at his face and hair. The other Fae begin to turn up their noses and back away from him.

"What kind of things?" I asked.

Milo gawped. "What do you mean by 'seeps'?"

Taz beamed wide. "Remember when you showed us that human film, Dem, *Labyrinth*? Well, you know the bog of eternal stench? It's like a semi-permanent version of that."

"That's genius," I admitted.

Taz shot me a spirited grin. The Fae were scattering, their desire not to be seen around such an embarrassing situation overriding any loyalty. Only Penelope remained, although she hovered at a safe distance with an anxious grimace as Friese managed to clear his face. I wondered if we should take the furious glint in his eyes as a warning.

"Ah." Taz nodded gravely. "Now might be a really good time for us to vanish."

We picked up the pace and dashed past Friese before he could gather his senses and chase after us. I gasped for air, still worn out from the Puzzle Tower with what felt like acid pumping through my legs.

I followed the other two through the halls toward the laundry room.

"They won't look in here I don't think," Milo panted.

We slipped behind the piled up laundry bags and I pressed my back to the wall, sliding down to sit on the floor. My head spinning had taken a brief break what with all the excess adrenalin, but now it started a slow, lumbering thump with a vengeance. Taz collapsed beside me, his brown Roger hair ruffled and his cheeks pink. He flicked a glance at me, his smile fading.

"Are you okay? You hit the floor really hard earlier. Sorry about that."

I lifted tentative fingers to the back of my head but couldn't feel a bump.

"It might be whiplash," he added. "Can you turn your head? Maybe we should get the healers."

I turned my head slowly from side to side, up and down.

"My shoulder blades feel a bit tender, like they're going to bruise. Same with my back a bit, but I think my head's okay. I'll be fine."

Milo balanced back on one of the laundry bag piles, his wide eyes stuck on my satchel. I looked down to find Leo had stuck his head out and was blinking at me.

"He wants to make sure you're okay too," Taz said with a small smile. "He cares."

I ran my finger over Leo's head and eyed Milo.

"You're not going to tell anyone he's here, are you? He's harmless."

I chose to ignore the flash of memory where Leo bit the Reflecto-Jenny. And also the real Jenny.

He was just defending me.

Milo shook his head, still staring as Leo squeezed out of the satchel fully and turned himself the same colour as my jeans. As he curled up, I knew he wouldn't be instantly visible if anyone burst in and found us.

"So, what are the chances this initiation is a really bad idea?" I had to ask.

Milo's face shadowed with something indescribably dark and he focused on his hands wringing in his lap.

"It's, um, bad. It's all built around hierarchy and somewhat on family ties. If you come from a known family or you make friends here early on, they go easy on you."

I nodded. "I don't have family ties, or friends."

I ignored Taz's indignant scoffing beside me. I could feel my eyelids beginning to weaken in the cosy warmth of the laundry room with the whirr of the washing machines, but I tried not to let my head drop onto Taz's shoulder or anything embarrassing.

"Um, not really no," Milo agreed. "Except me, I hope, but I'm no good either. Like Friese said, I don't matter, worthless really."

Taz's face crunched into a scowl. I blinked. I kept expecting the familiar Taz with his freckles and stormy blue-green eyes to reappear, but now I was getting used to his Roger disguise.

"Nobody is worthless, that's a horrid thing for him to say," I tried. "The knee jerk reaction for people like him is to get defensive and condemn. They lash out because of fear."

Milo shook his head. "I don't think Friese is afraid of me."

I soldiered on, mainly because they were both looking at me and I had no ability to stop my mouth speaking once my mind had started feeding it words.

"No, but I'll bet he is afraid of something. It could be fear of not fitting in, of failing, of not being good enough. They would be things he can't admit to because it would ruin who he's trying to be, like it's a weakness to the people he's trying to impress."

"You've got a point," Taz admitted. "People like him are always bullies because they're afraid if something deep down. But that doesn't make it okay."

I let my head drop back against the wall. "Of course it doesn't. And there are bad people out there, but most of us just want to turn a blind eye and pretend humanity isn't as bad as it's got, because how is there any hope of coming back from all the bad stuff otherwise?"

Milo blinked around at us with big eyes, making him look like an anime teddy bear.

"I still say we should kick him from behind and leave him hanging from a flag pole," Taz grumbled.

I rolled my eyes and stuck my tongue out at him, slouching down with my arms clamped over my stomach to avoid dislodging Leo.

"Until people side-line their egos, nobody will listen or learn anything," I said. "We won't make things any better. Fae, human, it's all the same. It's all to do with ego, and Fae are clearly *really* big on ego."

Taz threw up his hands. "Okay, we get it."

"No, I don't think you do."

His bottom lip dropped at the vehemence in my voice. After being run ragged through the Puzzle Tower and tormented by Fae and seeing Elvira again, I couldn't shake the irrepressible fear that things were going to get a lot worse and fast.

Even Milo stared at me in surprise, and I softened my tone when I remembered how much he hated arguments.

"Think of everything going on in the human world," I continued. "When people speak, other people don't listen. When people explain, nobody wants to learn. Everybody just shouts louder. When people are different, people like Friese are threatened so they shout, and bait and bully, because they're afraid."

"Okay, okay," Taz eyed my face as if he expected me to start sprouting devil horns and spitting acid. "Calm down."

Milo raised a hesitant hand like he was in a classroom.

"Um, I think you're right, Demi. Friese is from a really important Fae family, so there must be a lot of pressure on him to be perfect. I've always known that, and I get he's very important too, unlike me. It makes sense that he's lording it over me."

"What- no!" I ignored Taz returning to glaring. "None of this makes what he does okay. It's not acceptable. I'm just saying there's a cause, not an excuse. You know what is important? You were kind to us. You didn't have to help us but you did it anyway. Why?"

"Because you were lost." Milo grimaced, confused. "What else could I do?"

I pressed my forefinger and thumb to the bridge of my nose, my mind lurching with dizziness.

I should be better at explaining these things.

"She means you could have left us there," Taz tried. "You didn't have to trouble yourself with us."

I nodded. "You could have run to Friese or Director Cornelius and turned us in. Or left us the moment we got through the school gates."

"But why would I do that?" Milo continued. "You don't know anyone here. I couldn't just leave you."

Taz and I exchanged bewildered looks. I could almost see the apology bubbling up Milo's windpipe and charged back in.

"Some people put themselves first, and they're cruel about it, like Friese does when he picks on us. That's bad. Others help people when they need it without being asked, even if it's going to mean bad things for them as a result, because they're kind, like you. That's good. Well, not good about the whole bad things happening but helping people without expecting anything in return is."

Milo tilted his head. "Oh. So, you're saying that you think I'm a kind person, and that makes me a good one?"

"Yes!" I all but shouted it. Then I lowered my voice again in case someone appeared to lynch us or worse, kick us out to play with all the Fae. "I mean, it gets a bit more complex than that, but yeah kindness equals good."

Milo started to smile. "You're a good person too."

"Um, thanks." I wasn't sure how to cope with that.

Taz folded his arms with a loud huff.

"Yes, very touching," he grumbled. "Everyone loves everyone else. Now the question is, what are we supposed to do with all this fluffy philosophy? I don't think kindness is going to get us out of a hostile Fae club where they see it as a debilitating disease."

"Are you seriously saying all Fae are ruthless psychopaths?" I demanded. "Every single one in Faerie?"

"Don't be dim, just the high elite ones from well-off families all linked to the grand circle of power. So yeah, pretty much most of them, and definitely the ones here. They won't let us off easy, especially since Demi has effectively humiliated their pet champion and made a total mockery of their social hierarchy."

I buried my head in my hands. "Yay me."

"Look, we know that we're public enemy number one now," Taz continued. "How bad exactly are these initiations they mentioned, Milo? If that's coming next, we might need to think of a plan sooner rather than later."

I lifted my head. A plan sounded good. The problem was that Taz would probably insist I thought of one, as the official FDP, and I had absolutely nothing in mind beyond a strong urge for something edible that involved melted cheese and a long sleep. Milo hunched his chin further into his chest.

"The last really bad one was about three months ago. They hunted one boy into the forest until he disappeared. Then he turned up a few days later babbling about monsters. His family had to come and take him home."

"They allow that to happen?" I asked.

Taz gave me one of his withering looks.

"You know how bad the human world outside Arcanium is meant to be these days, right?" he asked. I nodded. "How people feel they're entitled to everything just by way of being born? Well, it's much the same with the Fae. They have zero compassion and see fairies and humans as commodities. It's typical behaviour."

"Okay, okay," I copied his words from earlier. "Calm down."

He pulled a face at me, but there wasn't any effort in it.

Milo sighed. "You're right, of course. The club still insisted that the family pay the boy's tab he'd run up. I always dreamed about getting away from this place. My uncle never wanted me. He took me to a huge market once and tried to lose me in the crowd soon after my parents died. I haven't heard from him since I've been in here, but the Director takes great enjoyment from telling me that I belong to him now."

I sat up, bristling with anger. Milo gave me a wan smile, as if he knew.

"I have nowhere to go and no future," he continued. "I thought perhaps if I worked hard enough here, I could apprentice with Mrs. Paget, but when she retires someone awful will no doubt take over and Penelope and Friese will make my life hell. They're probably counting on it, assuming they don't move on before then. I bet if they do, someone worse will take their place."

I thought back to what I'd seen at the Forgotten 24 club last night, Penelope bullying Milo in front of all her Fae friends. I knew I'd have to get up and orb Petra asap, but Milo's dejected, defeated tone needed my focus first.

"I won't let that happen," I insisted. "I can't promise anything, but I can ask at Arcanium if there's any available jobs there or something. I'm not sure what would happen after that, but I'd do everything I can to speak up for you. They might find you a role to do."

Taz shot me a resigned frown. "There is meant to be a

position vacant to help the new librarian, who apparently hasn't been hired yet, so we could talk you up and say you have experience, but it's not like we're the ones that can decide to hire people or anything."

I ignored Taz's dubious tone. "Yeah, we'd definitely make sure you were given something if we could. The food's okay too, and you get your own room."

Milo's jaw dropped. He stared at us.

"You'd put in a word for me? Even though you don't really know me?"

I nodded. "Yep, pretty much, but as I said, no promises. They might not agree to anything. But there's no pressure if you want to stay her-"

"No! Please, take me with you," he begged. "Anything is better than this."

I slid my fingers into my pocket, reassured to feel the orb still there.

"I need to make a call," I said.

Taz's fingers settled on my wrist. Leo snapped open one eye with a warning grumble, but no teeth made a reappearance. The open-mouthed indignation on Taz's face at least made me smile.

"You're sure you're okay?" he asked.

I nodded. "I'll be fine, don't fuss. If I feel like keeling over, I'll warn you so you can get your fingers out of the way before I hit the floor this time."

It was a mean jab, especially considering he'd saved me from dashing my head on the floor back at the Puzzle Tower. He rolled his eyes and jumped to his feet, holding out a hand to me. I took it, warm and dry whereas mine was cold and clammy, and he hauled me up. I put Leo back in my satchel and hurried into the hall.

The daylight was waning outside, casting pale pink hues

through the glass windows and turning the walls purple. I made sure nobody was anywhere nearby and held up the orb, standing with my back against the laundry room door, just in case.

"Petra?"

Her face loomed in front of me in very irate hues of grey.

"Just what the hell is going on?" she raged, her voice echoing along the hall. "I've been watching your screen non-stop but all I've seen is a load of cheering Fae, some huge tower, and what looked like a desert?"

I winced. "Um, can you just keep your voice down please? You're coming through very loud."

The responding silence only lasted a few seconds.

"No I cannot keep my voice down! You're there to keep *your head* down and get the information, not go gallivanting!"

I knew Petra was just being cautious, worried for my safety. Until that moment, I'd not really considered either that this was my mission and I was essentially responsible for fate of the prince of Faerie. Unsure of how to deal with such unerring responsibility, I scowled and started pacing down the hall.

"Well I've got Fae threatening to initiate me and they might still be lurking around corners. I don't know what an initiation involves, but experience of this place tells me it's nothing good."

Petra disappeared for a moment before reappearing with a chastened, somewhat disgruntled expression.

"Okay, this is my normal volume. Better?"

I nodded. "Yes, thanks. Look, I told you about the Puzzle Tower but I didn't realise it would be today. First they stole my orb to use as a token."

I would have ticked the injustices off on my fingers but I had to keep holding the orb up. My muscles ached from my ordeals earlier but my indignation gave me a final shot of strength.

"Then I had to go through these huge po sonous water creatures, face something glamouring as my sister, who hates me by the way, and sort through a bunch of keys. I beat this boy called Friese who almost won, he also hates me, and I'm trying very hard not to panic here."

Petra huffed out a short breath of surprise and then her eyebrows shot up.

"You mean you won?"

I rolled my eyes. "Yes, I did, or Taz and I did technically. I know it's the most unbelievable thing ever, but-"

"That is seriously impressive."

I fell silent. Petra couldn't lie. There was a small chance that this was another trick, but Petra was safe in Arcanium so I doubted it. Nobody here would know that she was my mentor either, at least it was unlikely, so this was further proof that the orb in my hand was the real thing.

When I didn't respond, Petra's surprised face enlarged as she leaned closer to the orb.

"Seriously, Demi, the Puzzle Towers are one of the most prestigious events in the outcast Fae calendar. Technically they're not allowed anymore, but blind eyes seem to be being turned everywhere these days. You'll no doubt have ruthless Fae training most of their lives for the honour of winning. I am so proud of you. I'm furious, like I'm never letting them send you into a realm ever again, but I'm so proud!"

I had no idea how to process that. The small, sensible part of my emotions told me Petra was being genuine, but so many instinctive defences clouded that thought.

"Um, thanks."

Petra shook her head in resignation. "Right, we'll celebrate later. Do you have any further movement on the actual assignment?"

"Oh, yes! I almost forgot. We found it, you know, the actual thing we were meant to find. Oh, and Milo wants to come to Arcanium, like really would do anything to come with us. So, mission accomplished but I can't really talk now just in case I don't think, it might not be safe?"

Petra grinned. "That is good news! I'm still trying to sort something out to get you home, but if you run into serious trouble, I'll pull you out illegally if I have to. I can take the consequences later."

I would have thanked her, but the sound of distant voices striding ever closer stopped me.

"People coming," I hissed. "I have to hang up now."

Petra leaned close enough for me to see a small spot under her nose.

"Keep the orb handy, and the moment I can extract you I'll let you know."

"Oh, trust me." I managed a brief smile. "I'm never letting it out of my sight. Thanks, Petra."

I put the orb in my pocket and eyed the hall. Voices echoed along the corridor, almost turning the corner. I couldn't hear their words yet, but they would see me any moment now and I'd stupidly strayed further from the laundry room than I intended.

The toilets.

I found the right door and darted inside, pulling it shut quietly. A blast of something floral almost choked me and I eyed the huge, gold bowl of dried flowers with distaste. The toilet had gold piping around the edges of the sinks and silver-plated taps, with huge mirrors above and thick towels hung underneath. I stared at what I assumed were two bidets alongside a row of urinals.

Boys' toilets.

The voices echoed outside. They might well be on their way

to the bathroom, so I hid myself in a stall and sat on the toilet with my knees pinned to my chest.

The door swung open. I held my breath. I just had to sit here and not make a single movement. As my already exhausted limbs started to shake from holding myself still, I hoped whatever boys tended to do in here didn't take too long.

CHAPTER THIRTEEN
DEMI IS EITHER RECKLESS OR BOLD – THE JURY IS STILL OUT

"It's a long, dangerous game to be playing," an unfamiliar male voice said.

"True, but it's a lucrative one."

The second belonged to Director Cornelius, I was almost certain about that.

"The Queen will not go easily as she's held her crown for so long now. The defences are impenetrable as long as she holds sway over her subjects. You really think your contact can provide enough leverage?"

Cornelius laughed. I closed my eyes as both men did what they'd come to do and silence fell temporarily. After two flushes and the rush of tap water, I just wanted them to get out.

"I have no doubt," Cornelius said. "Never underestimate the lure of what greedy people don't have. Elvira will do anything to regain her status, to re-establish herself. She will support us for that all the way to toppling the Queen's nonsensical reign, especially after her tragic defeat at Arcanium. Besides, she still has the ear of the King."

Both men laughed and I breathed a ragged sigh of relief as the door slammed shut. I listened for a while, just in case, but the only sound was the quiet hiss of the plumbing.

I pushed open the stall door and stepped out.

"Whoa." I flinched back against the door. "You startled me!"

My heart started pounding and I stared at Director Cornelius, who was sitting on the counter next to one of the sinks. All I could think was that the green waistcoat and swept back hair, albeit light brown, reminded me very much of Friese.

"I must congratulate you personally on your triumph earlier today," Cornelius said.

I shrugged. "Thanks, Ta- Roger did a lot of it."

I wondered what my chances would be if I just tried to walk out of the bathroom.

He hasn't said anything about me being in the boys' loos yet either.

"Ah, yes." Cornelius slid off of the counter. "I have wondered about that. I also wonder why you continue to associate with Milo, even after seeing his current living quarters and his clear lack of social status."

He crossed the room and blocked my path to the door in two strides. Even though he gave me the jitters, my indignation overrode the anxiety and I shoved my hands in my pockets. The feel of the orb, safe there even though he had tried to take it from me, gave me courage.

"Milo's been kind to me and that's something I've learned to value."

I forced myself to meet his eye for a few excruciating seconds.

"Hmm," Cornelius held my gaze, unwavering. "Why have you been sent to Fae club, I also wonder, when you clearly have human blood."

I heard the implied slur attached to the word 'human' and saw the tiniest curl of his lip, hidden behind suspiciously wide eyes.

"I've been sent to work," I said glibly. "So here I am, working."

I had no clue where my sudden bravado was coming from and wondered if it was something I could bottle for future use.

Cornelius accepted the vague answer with an amused nod.

"Very well," he said. "I would remind you however, Miss Darcy, that alliances can make or break a future. Perhaps you would want to give some thought to *your* future choices."

He walked to the door and my gut twisted as he turned back.

"Do you know why Friese is so well thought of here, Penelope too?" he asked.

Because they're psycho?

"Because they have rich families?"

Cornelius shook his head. "It is because they have *influential* families. Anyone can have riches, but power is another currency entirely. Penelope, for example, belongs to the Belarin clan, one of the two most important families in the history of Faerie."

I remembered what Cornelius had said before about the Queen. Given that the man seemed to be in the mood for talking, I decided to ask.

"The other family would be the Queen's?"

Cornelius raised an eyebrow then, his confident expression frozen for a miniscule moment.

"It would," he agreed. "Their line is one of the oldest, but she has long been losing her grasp on the title. Her hold over it weakens and more allegiances change daily. It appears her time is near its long overdue end. I would suggest again that you heed your own alliances and choose more suitable companions."

I couldn't understand why he would even bother speaking to me, let alone advising me on choice of allegiance. I wondered if it was just because I'd won the Puzzle Tower, if I was now worth noticing because of that. Then I saw my reflection in the mirror, all messy hair, dull skin and scraggy, unfashionable clothing. Cornelius was more than likely tormenting me in a way I couldn't comprehend yet. He knew I'd heard him talking to his companion, and he wanted to find out who I might know, who I might tell.

Cornelius opened the door, but I decided to spring for a dangerous move, knowing without a doubt, Petra, Queenie and most definitely Taz would kill me when they found out.

"I believe there's an elite society whispered about in this school," I suggested. "It's something called the Forgotten 24 Club?"

The Director halted. Paused. Turned back. A small smile brewed on his face.

"I did wonder which of you was the FDP," he said. "I thought perhaps the boy, but he doesn't appear to be a leader, not like you."

My ego preened for all of two blissful seconds before my brain caught up.

Don't be an idiot. Someone like him would only ever praise to manipulate. He might even know the Old King is looking for the Queen's children, and if he knows we're from Arcanium, then he'll guess it's Taz.

When I didn't answer, Cornelius closed the door again.

"Well?"

I dug into my satchel and pulled out the pocket watch. If I wanted to get us all out of here safe, I had to play my hand now. He knew we were from Arcanium as well, which meant he may have even been the one to hire our services. The fact that I had what I hoped was his pocket watch, given the initials engraved on the back, could tip this situation in my favour. Either that or he'd accuse me of stealing it instead.

"Does this mean anything to you?"

His eyes widened. "That's mine! It disappeared three months ago from my study."

"Here." I lifted my hand. "Take it."

I threw the watch, gently because I had zero hand-eye

coordination. Cornelius reached out and caught it with deft fingers.

"I found it in a crumbling old ruin, the other side of a lake. There are boats to carry you across, but you can also walk around. The way to the lake is through three tunnels, one of silver, one of gold and one jewelled with diamonds, but I believe part of that tunnel is a skip-way."

His eyes narrowed, his mouth pressing thin.

"How do you know this?" he asked.

"I followed someone through to the ruin, then took that watch from their trinket table. They were having quite the party, elite invitation only."

"And where is the entrance to this tunnel?"

I heard the bite in his tone, the urgency. I could perhaps bribe him for something, a way home for us. *Not all of us.*

His face contorted as I hesitated, then flattened into a roguish smile. If I hadn't known better, I would have found him utterly charming.

"I believe I should give you an accolade for performing so well in the Puzzle Tower today," he suggested. "It is custom although, admittedly not enforced. I will extend this honour to you."

My insides started knitting themselves. "Um, thanks?"

"To make it a little more interesting, I will let you choose. You may decide the fate of one of the party-goers you spied on. You may choose any of them and what happens to them."

I swallowed, my mind racing. Cornelius wanted his information, so he'd try to rush me for a decision. I pressed the back of my hand to my forehead to cool my face down.

I can turn this to my advantage still somehow. Think, idiot!

The idea sprung into my head, and it was all I had. It was a mad one perhaps, but I had to play it carefully, like one of the

Fae.

"You're saying I can choose one person in attendance at that party I witnessed last night, the one I took that pocket watch I gave you from, and decide what happens to them? No caveats?"

"I will add the condition that there will be no death, and no permanent injuries, but other than that yes, that is what I'm promising."

I hurried through the loopholes, my head dizzy with possibilities like a game of chess. He expected me to use it to punish someone. Thoughts of having the Old King struck with some kind of embarrassing infliction occurred to me. That might be what Taz would go for, but I had a longer plan in mind. I couldn't find a single issue with what I intended to do, but that didn't mean it wasn't still riddled with holes.

Worth a shot.

"Milo was serving them," I said. "So technically he was in attendance. He will be allowed to leave here and come with us to Arcanium when we go, permanently if he wants. If he doesn't want to come to Arcanium, then he will always be free to leave here and go anywhere he chooses, when he chooses, without any kick-back or punishment."

I waited, heart hammering inside my chest. Cornelius stood, frozen in time, lips ever so slightly slack with shock.

"I'm sure you can pull some strings," I prompted. "Important as you are, you can probably speak to Queenie or whoever at Arcanium and say you're sending them a transfer trainee to help in the library. I'm sure they would be glad of an extra pair of hands. If not, I bet Milo would like to know he has freedom if he wants it."

A scraping noise filled the room. My first thought was that Cornelius might just have me swallowed by some kind of magic Fae plumbing. Then I realised it was his teeth steadily grinding back and forth.

"I have to agree." He barely unclenched his teeth in time. "Where is the entrance?"

I wasn't quite that dumb. "You swear it?"

"I swear it, now where is the entrance?"

"There's a boy's bathroom on the ground floor with a mosaic. One of the floor tiles is worn, the twenty-fourth one. You press that and the tunnel appears in the floor."

"Finally."

Cornelius' eyes lit up with a savage glow of vengeance and I think he forgot about me for that moment. I flinched when he glanced at me, his lip curled in disgust.

"You've done Milo no favour, you impudent girl. You are meddling in dangers you have absolutely no comprehension of. Our deal is done, and I'll show you and yours no more hospitality. You may have earned a few secrets to take back to your superiors, but Faerie still thinks of us as the most prestigious club to gain membership to, and what the people of Faerie think, is *everything*. We are untouchable by the likes of fairy scum like you."

With that ominous threat hanging in the air, Cornelius slammed out of the room and left me swilling in bewildered confusion.

"I need to remember the facts, just in case," I muttered to myself. "I've effectively been warned that I'm choosing the wrong side friendship-wise. Oh and Elvira wants to regain her status, nothing new there, and will topple the Queen to do it. I've also exposed the 24 Club and made a deal for Milo's freedom as my reward. Without asking him first. Or anyone at Arcanium. Or checking it was a good idea. Either way, Taz is going to slaughter me."

I crept out into the hall. Before I could race back to the

laundry room and tell the others, a loud holler held me still.
   "There you are, Demerara!"

CHAPTER FOURTEEN
DEMI GETS POLITICAL

I turned to see Friese and his crowd of groupie Fae at the other end of the hall.

Friese started toward me, but I didn't wait to brazen it out. I dashed as fast as I could toward the laundry room door. My fingers slipped on the doorknob but I managed to wrench the door open and close it behind me.

"You were gone ages," Taz said accusingly, his face pouty and his arms folded.

I ignored his temper. "I was speaking to Petra, but then Friese cornered me in the hall, he's out there now with a gang of Fae. Oh and I kind of ran into the Director and exposed the 24 club's location, and he gave me the chance to choose what happens to one of them, so I told him he had to sort it so Milo can come back to Arcanium with us if he wants to."

"You *WHAT?*" Taz's voice almost shattered machines.

I gave Milo what I hoped was an apologetic look.

"I added caveats, so if you don't want to come back with us you don't have to, you are free to go anywhere you like, not just Arcanium, but only if you choose to."

I didn't think about making sure he could stay here if he wanted to though, did I? What if the Director throws him out as he's 'free' to go? What if Queenie refuses to let him stay with us?

What Cornelius had said about the club being untouchable because the people of Faerie thought it was also rankled in my mind. I'd been tormented, forced to go through a barbaric trial mostly against my will, and faced with the hatred of a supposed regent simply for having human blood. Even thinking about him and Elvira made my insides boil.

I can't let him be right. Somehow, I'm going to prove this place isn't any kind of wonderland.

A loud, mocking knock echoed three times on the door.

"There's no time for this," Taz said. "We have to hide, or run, or something."

We both looked at Milo. He bit his lip and glanced over his shoulder.

"There is an exit of sorts," he said.

I nodded. "Lead the way."

Milo set off toward the back of the vast laundry room, dodging around the sacks. Taz looked me up and down before grabbing my hand in his and pulling me along.

"Why do you smell sickening, like a funeral parlour?" he asked.

Bewildered by the impromptu hand-holding, although I noticed myself stumbling over my own feet as we hurried along, I returned his sarcastic look narrowed brow for narrowed brow.

"You've clearly never been inside the boys' toilets here."

We hurtled along side by side. Up ahead, Milo slowed down in front of a painting of the club in earlier years. I wanted to be kind, but unless the painting morphed into a magic fairy door pretty quick, we'd just get tripped up by the wall or smack into the frame.

"I know how it looks." Milo pre-empted my doubt. "I have to take you through. Taz, Demi, take my hands."

Milo held his hands out. I shook Taz off and took Milo's left. I thought Taz would hesitate or argue, but then he was too busy looking at Milo with bemused curiosity as he took Milo's free hand.

"Okay." Milo shuffled me in front of him. "Close your eyes, keep walking forward and don't let go of my hand."

I did as I was told. With tentative steps, fully expecting to squash my nose on some ancient Fae art, I started walking. A whooshing sensation shot around me, almost similar to the feeling I got when realm-skipping in Trevor's rickshaw.

I opened my eyes to find the semi-darkness of the kitchen around me, lit by lamps with all the hatches closed and quiet. It wouldn't keep us hidden for long, but the Fae might search the laundry room for a few minutes thinking we'd hidden ourselves.

I let go of Milo's hand as he doubled over.

"You can skip at will?" Taz asked, a sharp edge now lacing his tone. "And where's this exit?"

I wondered if he was also thinking of the spiked cocoa as we faced Milo, who bit his lip and glanced around the room as if for eavesdropping ears.

"I won't be able to do that again for a while," he panted. "Director Cornelius allows me the ability to realm-skip through the facility wherever I need to, but that painting is a secret skip-way. I've never tried skipping anyone other than myself before though. Ouch."

I frowned as sounds echoed louder in the hall beyond the kitchen door.

"Okay, we can unpack that later. The exit?"

Milo pointed to the hatch on the far wall.

Director Cornelius' personal hatch.

"There's a secret emergency exit out of the building through his office," he said. "I've only seen it once, but he makes me wait for things at the bottom sometimes that he drops down if the hatch is busy, or if he doesn't want anyone to know what he's dealing with."

"He uses you like a servant," Taz muttered.

Milo shrugged his burly shoulders.

"Sometimes he makes me do things I'd rather not do, like embarrass myself in front of his private guests or serve at parties. Sometimes, when he's had a hard day, he throws things at me for fun."

I clenched my fists at my sides, then slid my arms behind my back. My sisters had done much the same to me growing up, at least in terms of throwing things. But they were spiteful kids ganging up. While that didn't make it any better, this was a grown man manipulating and harming someone he should have protected.

My connection flickered and the tingle of tiny sparks raced toward my fingertips.

"So we have to go up in the hatch," I confirmed, my jaw tight. Milo nodded. "Does he have an orb in there?"

Potentially lethal idea.

I ignored Taz who was back to glaring at me again.

Milo nodded. "Yes, his private connection. He's very paranoid about things. There's not even a normal door to the room itself, just the hatch and a skip-way that only he can pass through, plus the emergency exit."

"Right, up we go then." I eyed the hatch as the ridiculous plan borne of indignant fury bloomed in my head. "One by one, and I'll go first. I only need a couple of minutes for what I need to do."

"You're not thinking what I think you're thinking," Taz warned.

I strode to the hatch and pressed the big red button to wake it up, giving him a look.

"How can I possibly know what you think I'm thinking, to tell you whether I'm thinking it or not?"

The hatch rumbled and the door slid up. I pressed the floor

of the service lift inside with both hands and hopped, balancing my weight on it.

"Do you reckon it'll hold?" I asked.

My momentary determination faded as I stared at the narrow shaft. I would fit inside, assuming I kept my legs and elbows pinned tight to my body, but it was in no way guaranteed to be safe. I poked my head through the hatch and looked up to find faint yellow light glimmering somewhere above.

As I backed out again, Milo blinked at me, nerves creasing his face.

"Um, it will definitely take your weight," he said. "If that's what you mean. We send laundry and furniture and all sorts up in it."

Before my anxiety could tear holes in my plan, I hopped up onto the counter beneath the hatch and wriggled into the lift. The darkness closed around me but I forced my breathing to keep going in and out.

Taz's scowl appeared framed in the hatch.

"I'll be right behind you," he insisted. "If Cornelius is in there, reach out and hit the button to send you back down. If you can't reach it, shout down. If he isn't there, send the lift back down anyway and I'll follow you up."

I hadn't thought that Cornelius might have returned to his office by now. With a nervous gulp against the dryness of my throat, I nodded and clenched my arms tight around my knees.

"Okay. Press the button."

I winced as the hatch clanged shut and focused on staying as still as possible as the service lift shot upwards.

It's just like the lifts at home. The golden ones where you can see through to the brickwork. Air rushing past, it's fine.

None of my frantic placating did any good, my limbs shaking and my breathing not quite hitting my lungs. But the yellow glow above grew brighter until it engulfed me. I blinked against it as the lift shuddered to a halt and almost sent the contents of my gut plummeting back downward.

I peered into the room beyond and clutched at the edges of the hatch.

Empty.

I squeezed out with a huge sigh of relief and surveyed the room. Decorated in various shades of grey with the odd swathe of dark blue, it was smaller than I'd expected given the size of Queenie's office back at Arcanium.

I almost forgot to press the button to send the lift back down for Taz and tapped it before venturing further into the room. Towering cabinets lined the walls, separated only by hanging frames that held various maps of Faerie. A desk dominated the centre of the room, but I only had eyes for the large grey orb nestled on top.

I flinched as the lift clanked behind me. Taz scrambled out of the hatch and stood staring around with wide eyes, bashing the button to send the lift down for Milo without even looking at it.

"Some of these maps are ancient!" he said.

I ignored that. "Okay. I'm going to do something ill-advised, and I need you not to stop me."

"What's that then?" He folded his arms.

"I'm going to contact that woman from *The Faerie Net* and give her an exclusive. Tell her everything that's happened, especially the secret bits. I may be only a fairy, but they'll know I still can't lie."

Taz blinked, his bottom lip dropping. "What do you think that'll achieve?"

I stepped up to the orb and took a deep breath as the lift appeared with Milo inside.

"Clarity, I hope, at least enough to turn a few minds back to your mother's rule. Humiliating Director Cornelius is just a huge bonus."

I lifted a hand to the orb, but froze as Taz hurried forward. He swiped a strand of hair behind my ear with a frown before plucking at the top of my head.

"There. Good luck."

I blinked, baffled by the idea that he was trying to somehow neaten me up. I checked quickly down, but both my grubby clothes and my reflection in the orb told me he hadn't glamoured me or anything.

"Cynthia Meadows," I told the orb.

Moments later, the woman who'd interviewed me after the Puzzle Tower appeared magnified in the middle of the office as a vision in pearlescent grey.

"Oh, it's you," she frowned, patting down her hair. "Did we have a follow-up booked? I'm sure I would have remembered."

I gripped the edge of the desk. *Here goes.*

"I thought you might want an exclusive, some of the insider gossip as it were. Gallows Oak is a prestigious place, one that I'm sure loads of people would love a glimpse into."

Cynthia's eyes took on a gleam despite the colourless projection, her lips curving.

"Well now, I could of course get my own exposé…"

"Of course you could, you seem extremely resourceful." I hurried on, quickly realising flattery would do every job here. "I'm sure your viewers trust your word completely, but a fairy outing the secrets of a Fae society has a certain shock value."

I clung to the desk, the wood biting into my fingers. I hated saying it like that, using the fact I was a fairy, or 'only a fairy' as many would see it, as a cheap sales trick. But I only had a couple of minutes before we had to scram. Once Cornelius found out, I'd either be going back to Arcanium under my own steam, or never again in one piece.

"True, true…" Cynthia straightened up. "Very well then, and your terms are?"

With a click of her fingers, her appearance smartened up to vision-cast-ready. I tried not to think shallow thoughts about how ghastly I must look right now.

Focus on the point of all this.

"You have to swear to broadcast this live, right now, and to not edit my feed or interrupt," I insisted. "I'll only need a few minutes. I'm sure with your reputation you can hijack the current stream with a live feed."

Cynthia preened with a satisfied smile.

"Well, yes. Alright, I swear to the terms you've laid out. Be ready, I'll introduce you and then you have your few minutes. After that I'd love to do a Q&A."

I didn't answer, relieved that she was already focused elsewhere so I didn't have to actually agree to anything past my speech. Not that I had a speech. Or knew exactly what I intended to say.

Oh, hell. What am I even doing this for? What do I say?

My hands shook around the edge of the desk as Cynthia's voice filled the office.

"My darling Fae companions, I interrupt to bring you a juicy live interview from none other than today's Puzzle Tower champion herself! Demerara Darcy, self-confessed fairy and rebel against all things traditional, has approached me *personally* to offer an insight into what she's learned at the exclusive Gallows Oak club! Demerara, you have the VC."

Silence.

I stared at her with my shoulders quaking. I looked at Taz, waiting for him to roll his eyes or give me one of his traditional death-glares.

"Go on," he mouthed. "You've got this."

I cleared my throat.

"Many of you know Gallows Oak as a prestigious club for elite Fae, many with more money than sense, if what I've seen over the last few days is to go by."

I thought of the jewel-encrusted tunnels, my indignation rising right to where my voice needed it most. I looked at Milo and thought of what he'd just told us about how he'd been treated here. Anger burned inside my chest, powering me on.

"There are secret tunnels in ground floor bathrooms, societies full of thieves that meet in the dark of night, illicit clubs that even the Old King himself is rumoured to frequent. I know many watching this will think that's as it should be, but actually, I'm less of a traditionalist. Ask yourself how many of them have actually earned that privilege, or is it by right of simply being born? The Director of this facility would probably wish me to keep this a secret, but of course, in his own words, this place is untouchable because the people of Faerie think it is. Well, I'm a fairy. Many of you think I'm scum because of my blood. But I'm right here, broadcasting to you from inside the Director's office. Question is, if they let me in, why not you?"

I took a step back and eyed Taz, who stood with his hands over his face, his eyes just about peeking out over the fingertips.

"Well, that is certainly a bold statement!" Cynthia smiled, the projection of her face enlarging as she leaned forward. "Why not indeed? And Demerara, I must ask, why *did* they let you in?"

I smiled then, thinking of the vast amounts of wealth downstairs, and the money exchange that Milo had said was used for laundering human money.

I leaned closer to the orb, just a little, and grinned.

"Security problem."

I strode around the desk and toward the others without looking back, Cynthia's determined questions flurrying in my ears.

"Lead the way, Milo," I croaked, ignoring the sensation of my legs feeling like they were about to buckle under me.

Milo stared at me in what could have been devoted awe for a moment before rushing across and pulling aside a hefty wooden filing cabinet like it was made of paper.

"Just step through and you'll be in the store-room on the ground floor," he said.

I only took one step forward before something snared my fingers. Taz stepped beside me, his face set in stubborn determination.

"Together." It wasn't a request.

I nodded and we moved as one unit into the darkness. I closed my eyes as the sensation of air brushed my face, and opened them again a second later.

Old desks and what looked like picture frames were piled against the walls, but Taz was already dragging me toward the door before I could get a proper look.

I glanced over my shoulder to see Milo behind us, pink-cheeked as we disappeared into one of the familiar halls of the main building.

"I've pulled the cabinet back into place," Milo puffed along beside us. "But he'll know that's how we got out."

I nodded as the realisation of what I'd just done caught up with me. I started shaking all over.

If I ever get out of here alive and unharmed, Petra is going to kill me. Queenie is going to kill me for endangering Arcanium-Fae relations or something. Taz is probably going to get over his shock by time we stop running and he'll kill me.

"We need to get to the forest," Taz said, heading for the main exit to the quad outside. "Then we're going to hide in the trees while you orb Petra. Queenie will have to call us home after this."

At least he seemed to have the same idea as I had initially. Queenie had to summon us back now, even if just to punish us and refuse to let us ever step foot inside Arcanium again. Or to release me from Arcanium forever. The mere thought almost slayed me, but I focused on keeping up with Taz's relentless pounding speed along the hall.

Milo squeaked in alarm as the tell-tale sound of a mob echoed behind us, and Taz wrenched open the door, flinging me through ahead of him.

A blast of cold hit, biting my face and whistling through to my bones as though my t-shirt was made of lace. Taz and I slowed, disorientated, but Milo surged ahead to guide us across the quad. I could see the dark outline of the forest against the dancing glow of firelight that lit up the club grounds.

"There they are!"

I turned my head in time to see faces flickering at the open windows as we raced past.

"How did they get out there?"

"Who cares, get them!"

Taz growled under his breath. "Time to go."

I couldn't help but glance back as we turned left to get to the archway leading out of the quad. I counted Friese, Penelope and about sixteen other Fae in the crowd that swelled out of the building. Taz's fingers tightened around my hand as he pulled me on toward the shadowed trees.

"We might be safe if we get right into the forest," Milo shouted back. "But there's no guarantee."

I nodded, even though Milo was already barrelling ahead of us with a surprising turn of speed.

"If you'd just given Petra the message and come back, they'd never have seen you," Taz grunted. "There wouldn't have been any opportunity for mass declarations of anti-traditionalism and we'd have been able to seal away somewhere with minimal fuss."

He always assumes it's my fault, that I'm just being hopeless.

I'd only been in the realm two days and I'd been tormented, put through a sadistic competition, and I was being chased by hostile Fae. I didn't need Taz belittling me as well right now.

"I did just give Petra the message," I grunted. "Cornelius came down the hall to use the toilet so I had to hide in the stall, but he caught me. He said something about unseating the Queen, I'll go out on a limb and assume that still means your mother, and that Elvira would do anything to get her status back. He said she had the ear of the Old King and that the Queen's rule had gone on too long. Then he suggested I choose my friends more carefully. That's when I told him about Club 24 and everything."

Taz's step faltered, but he plunged forward again before I could slow down. His expression looked so grim in the dusky darkness between the trees, that I didn't dare question him.

"There they are," a gleeful voice shouted behind us. "They're heading into the forest, toward the training gauntlet."

"Let's give them a refresher course then!"

They didn't sound far away. We ran after Milo, my face burning and my satchel bashing against my hip. I had to hope Leo liked a bit of a rollercoaster ride.

"We can't run forever," I panted.

Something flitted in the trees to our right. I couldn't turn my head for more than a moment as briars and twigs snagged at my feet, but I guessed some of the students would have been gifted with speed by indulgent Fae relatives.

"Through here," Taz pointed to a gap in a large hedge. "Milo, this way, quick!"

My mind gave me a furtive nudge, the sensible part not liking how neat and well-maintained the particular stretch of hedge was. It reminded me of something, but I was too exhausted and battered to think straight. I tumbled through the gap in the hedge, Taz cannoning into the back of me a moment later. I took a couple of steps, but Taz had an arm around me before I fell.

"Thanks," I muttered.

Taz didn't take any notice of me, or his arm still anchored around my hips, already scoping out the next stretch.

"It's a maze," Milo announced.

I bit my lip and glanced back at the growing sound of voices.

"What do we do, wait it out? Keep running?"

Taz grimaced. "With any luck, the Fae will expect us to perish here and they'll get bored."

I heard the doubtful catch in his tone and gave him a look.

"You of all people should know they'll want to watch the show if we're due to meet a sticky end."

For once, he didn't have some kind of dismissive retort. He released me finally and strode forward with his shoulders square and his head held in high defiance. I decided not to mention that I could see his fists now shaking at his sides.

As we ventured further along the hedge corridor, I jostled alongside him, not wanting us to get separated.

"What if they come in after us?" I asked. "What is this place anyway?"

"I don't think they will come in here." Milo piped up behind us. "Friese will have them block the exits instead and wait us out as this maze hasn't been approved yet. Actually, it was never supposed to be built. It failed the application for approval from the Official Fae Societies and Training Establishments

Department. It looks like they built it anyway, so who knows what traps lurk inside."

I stared at the hedges blocking our way in most directions. Taz made a low growling noise in his throat, but I was growing more worried about a subtle rumbling sound that had nothing to do with him.

CHAPTER FIFTEEN
MAGIC MAZES ARE MAYHEM

"What's that sound?" Taz asked.

I frowned, trying to listen. "It sounds like, a cappella purring."

"Don't be ridiculous. Although, whatever it is, that's our only way forward."

With a communal look of doubt exchanged, the three of us crunched over the gravel underfoot to the end of the path.

Small lanterns lit around the edge of a large square space. In the far corner there were five or six bundles of silvery grey and a really frosty chill to the air.

"Whoa." Even Taz seemed struck by surprise.

Milo grabbed one of the lanterns and held it higher so the beam of light travelled over the nearest misshapen lump. The lump looked every inch a cat, except for the puffball silver fur and the fact it was the size of a calf.

"Frost cats," Taz muttered.

I recalled one errand he and I had done for Emil where we'd rescued a Shrieker bat and brought it back to the Arcanium quarantine facility shortly after the Forgotten's attempted invasion. Simone, the head handler, had mentioned frost cats being stolen from them during the battle.

"What if these are the frost cats that got taken from Arcanium?" I wondered aloud.

Taz frowned. "May well be, they're rare nowadays and if it was the Forgotten that nicked them this would be a likely place they'd be sold to. Exotic creatures. Not our biggest problem right now though."

The nearest frost cat started to uncurl, its tail flicking with warning slowness. The eyes, which I'd expected to be electric blue for some reason, were inky black, but its fur was covered with a fine dusting of frost. I shivered and decided I would carry a coat in my satchel every day for the rest of my FDP career.

Taz started walking toward a wide gap in the opposite hedge, but the animal grumbled a warning and slunk toward him, driving him back.

"How does one get past a frost cat?" Milo asked.

The others were starting to wake up now, elongating onto their paws with innate, lethal grace. A low meow came from near the back, sending an extra chill rippling over my shoulder blades.

"I don't suppose anyone has any Dreamies handy?" I suggested.

I could almost telepathically hear the word 'idiot' screaming around in Taz's mind, but luckily for me, I actually had the answer.

"I remember," I whispered. "Xavio was talking ages ago about frost animals from realm- I can't remember which one actually, but it was one of the bigger ones-"

"Dem, just the answer, please," Taz begged.

"Yes, sorry. Frost animals can't go near fire. It doesn't hurt them or anything, no more than it would us, it doesn't make them melt, but they can't bear being near it."

Taz caught on and pulled out his matches. As if the frost cats could sense the fire power, they arched their backs and started to hiss. Taz gulped.

"Somehow, I doubt six of them are going to be too worried about us having a couple of tiny matches each," he said.

I hunted in my satchel, hoping for something flammable, and

pulled out the red Gallows Oak t-shirt I'd stashed in there as a bit of softness for Leo. At least burning a Gallows Oak t-shirt would send a message, even if nobody else was around to see it.

"I guess you could light this and we could wave it as we go past?" I suggested.

Taz seemed to be thinking. I waited with an unsettling feeling in my gut that whatever he said next would not end well for me.

"Can you try and talk to them instead?" he asked. "Last time you spoke to those furry creatures, didn't you?"

I shook my head and waved the t-shirt at him in case he magically changed his mind.

"I can't talk to animals, it doesn't work like that. I can make the noises, but I don't know what they mean. I can't communicate meaning or intention."

"You could at least try, we won't judge if you can't."

I closed my eyes in torment. I could try of course, but it was pointless wasting time while a multitude of irate Fae were closing in on us. Then again, an irate Taz wasn't exactly something I had the energy to face right now either. I threw him the t-shirt and turned to the nearest cat.

"*Meow*." I introduced myself, or so I desperately hoped. "*Mrow, meow, mauw*."

The frost cat blinked and its tail stopped flicking. When it tilted its head to one side, I copied it. I could hear Taz and Milo taking not so subtle sneak-steps toward the exit, but I kept my gaze on the frost cat in front of me.

I saw the eyes widen and the jaw open just in time, and was already halfway across the square when the cat snarled and pounced forward.

"Negotiations did not go well," I shouted, managing to refrain from adding 'I told you so'.

A scraping noise and a tiny flicker turned the cats' heads away from me. Taz held a flaming match to my t-shirt and waved it between me and the cat.

The cats hissed and darted away from the fire. I hurried toward the exit with Milo while Taz held the t-shirt in front of him as a defensive weapon. I hovered in the next hedge corridor as Taz dropped the fast disintegrating fabric onto the gravel and we set off at a run.

"Do you think they'll follow us once the fire burns out?" Milo asked.

Taz shook his head. "I doubt it. We're more likely to have the maze burn down around us."

I could easily visualise the headline running underneath Cynthia Meadows on the next vision cast of *The Faerie Net*:

'Winner of the Puzzle Tower and Self-Confessed Anarchist Burns Entire Club to Celebrate'.

I decided not to dwell on that until it happened.

The gravel disappeared underfoot, leaving us walking on bare dirt. We came to a fork in the path almost immediately, as if the people building the maze had simply given up.

"Left or right?" Milo peered down both turnings. "I can't see anything on either route. Should we split up?"

Taz gave him a withering look. "That's exactly what they want you to do. We stay together no matter what happens. Demi, orb Petra. Tell her if she's got a way to get us out, it has to be now or never."

I ignored the fact he was issuing demands and focused on the facts.

"What do you mean, never?"

"Just do it!"

I pulled out my orb.

"Petra?" I hoped she wasn't asleep or busy. "Please if you're there, if you can hear me, we're in deep-"

Petra's face blossomed into magnified view in front of us. I knew better than to comment on the curling rags tangled in her hair, but she did look sort of demented, all wide-eyed and angry. Through her pearlescent image, I could see Taz and Milo staring at her in awe.

"Seriously, you're going to be the end of me if you can't handle these things on your own," Petra huffed. "What's going on now?"

I bit my lip, ignoring Taz as he started to glare at her. Apparently in his head, he was the only one allowed to insult or belittle me.

"The Fae were chasing us, and we ended up in some maze, an illegal one apparently. We need to get out of here now. I gave the location of the 24 club to the Director so the assignment is done. I also kind of made a deal for Milo's freedom, so if we have room for an extra body as well that'd be great."

I twisted around so that Milo was next to me and Petra could see his emphatic nodding.

"Demi, I can't haul you out," she groaned. "Queenie's still refusing to let any FDPs return, although for some reason she's still happily sending them out. As soon as I can get some kind of permission, I'll get you back, I promise. I am trying my hardest but you just need to be patient."

I nodded slowly, a tiny spark of curiosity igniting.

"I understand. So, the trolls are still going into realms and back, they're just not allowed to bring anyone back into Arcanium? They still physically can if they have to?"

Petra scowled. "Yes, dubious if you ask me. Focus on keeping yourselves safe and I'm sure the ban will be lifted in a day or two, okay?"

We didn't have a day or two. We probably didn't have an

hour or two considering Cornelius had said we weren't welcome here anymore.

I stepped away from Milo and Taz, a plan forming.

"Of course, thanks Petra, I know you're doing everything you can."

Petra's face disappeared and I clipped the key-ring back through my belt loop with the orb safe in my pocket. I looked around at the narrow passage between the hedges, the idea blossoming.

It won't work here, not enough room. At least I know what I need to do now, although I don't imagine I'll get applauded for it.

I eyed the others, both looking at me expectantly. I opened my mouth, determined to tell them the whole plan, but a familiar rumbling filled the air.

"More frost cats?" Milo asked warily.

I turned my head and saw a soft icy blue sheen further down the path to the left. One frost cat, a young one given the size, had been trapped in a cage far too small for it and was curled up in an uncomfortable ball.

I started toward it, ignoring Taz groaning at me to come back. The cat hissed as I drew closer, but I could feel the heat coming off of its cage before I reached it.

"Oh you poor thing," I murmured. "Who's caged you in hot metal like some kind of torture, huh?"

I tapped a finger against the bar, seething through my teeth as it burned my skin. I couldn't leave the cat inside and looked around for a lock. Instead, I found the lid was weighted down with a rock.

"The monsters have trapped the poor thing inside a heated cage," I called back.

Taz appeared beside me and tapped both hands on the rock.

"Can you lift this, and I'll open the lid?" he asked.

"You'll burn yourself."

He rolled his eyes. "I'm a big boy, I'll cope. Can you lift the rock or not?"

I nodded and wrapped my hands around it. The cat hissed again, but the dark eyes were watching us intently.

"Be ready to spring out," I told the cat as if it could understand me.

Taz held my gaze. "Three, two, one…"

I hauled the rock up and sideways, letting it drop to the ground. Taz yelped as he dragged the lid of the cage open and flinched free to blow on his hands. The frost cat leapt out, the subtle scent of steam filling the air.

Taz froze as the cat prowled toward him, no bigger than a medium-sized dog but with shards of fur puffing a warning.

I watched the cat with a frown. The tail wasn't flicking and the eyes were docile enough, not that I knew much about cats.

"Let it sniff your hands," I murmured. "It'll know you're not a threat then."

Taz looked at me like I was crazy but lowered his hands down until they were level with the cat's head. The cat sniffed the burnt skin and Taz yowled as it lashed a silver-blue tongue against his injuries. Heedless of him huffing in pain, the cat turned its head to me next.

"I'm not injured, or anything, I'm good." I took a step back. "But you're free. Your cat friends are that way."

It stared at me as I pointed back the way we'd come. With a soft purr, the cat winked and darted away into the darkness.

Milo sidled up beside me as Taz stood staring at his hands in wonder.

"It's gone," Taz said, holding up his palms for us to see.

The surface of both palms were unmarked, with no sign of

any burn marks on his skin.

"Okay, so frost-cat saliva good for burns." I sighed. "We should remember that. Not that we'll probably ever see one or be in a position to save one again. Good deed done but we're still in trouble. We need to get a move on."

I turned to set off again, but a voice near my knee echoed before I could take so much as a step.

"Humour a fellow with a story, would you?"

I stared down to see the top of a ragged mossy green hat and a lot of brown beard spouting out from beneath it.

"Oh, hi." I frowned. "Um, sorry, we're in a bit of a hurry."

The hat, a long one like the cheap Santa hats that did the rounds at Christmas, wobbled as a weather-beaten face turned upward to look at me.

"Then you'll need to know the way out," the man countered. "I'll tell you, if you'll listen to an old man's tale. It's only a short one."

I looked to Taz and Milo, hoping they'd have the solution. Taz folded his arms and Milo shrugged.

"Are you a gnome?" I asked.

The gnome nodded. "I am that, and I don't see folk often. I want to tell someone this story before I forget it. Have a listen. It's really short and if you do, I'll tell you the short way out of this maze."

"We can figure it out for ourselves," Taz muttered.

I ignored him. "Okay, a quick story in exchange for the way out, but we've only got a couple of minutes, like two at the most. Is your story any longer than that?"

The Gnome shook his head and pulled a long piece of wood out from a bag slung over his back. He folded the wood out until it formed a little stool and sat down.

"You are too kind," he said. "This story begins in a realm

such as this, where three children played games all day long. The woodland liked to hear the children laugh, but wished it could join in the games."

I tried not to look at Taz as he fidgeted to make his irritation clear, but his jitteriness was catching. I wrapped my hands around the strap of my satchel and reassured myself the story would be over soon.

"But the children didn't want the trees to join in, so the wood appealed to a spirit of the forest. The spirit told the trees to show the children how to play nice, and include everyone."

I flinched as something touched my ankle. In the darkness, with only the maze lamps to see by, I guessed it was a stray leaf or twig moving in the wind.

"The trees took the spirit's advice." The gnome's voice dipped lower. "They found the children playing and decided to join in anyway."

I flinched again as something slid past my leg. This was no leaf in the wind. For one thing, there was no wind.

"The trees called the vines and brambles to help them teach the children how to play," the gnome continued.

"Ouch!" Milo tried to step away from a bramble snaring his wrist.

Taz was quickest and managed to untangle himself from a reaching branch, but he stumbled straight back into the hedge.

"The trees caught the children and told them that they would not let the children go, until they had played all the games the trees wanted to play."

I squeaked as a particularly affectionate vine caught me around the middle and started to squeeze. Leo's head popped out and he started chomping through it with enthusiasm, but more strands were arriving to snatch at him like a reverse whack-a-mole game. Taz tried to reach into his pocket for his matches but the bushes now literally had his hands tied behind his back.

"The trees said to the children-"

"How?" I interrupted.

The gnome looked up, his eyes glazed with confusion. I felt the tightening vine around my middle freeze, as if it was also confused.

"What do you mean, how?"

I sensed the temporary ceasing of all woodland activity from the surrounding silence and ploughed on before the gnome could get his rhythm back.

"Well, how do the trees say things? Do they have mouths?"

The gnome scratched his forehead, almost dislodging his hat.

"No," he said, unsure. "They don't have mouths, they're trees. But anyway, they said-"

"But how do they say?" I interrupted again. "Do they have some kind of woodland telepathy? Because that would suggest the children have to be magic. And why do the children not want to play with the woods anyway?"

The gnome gawped at me.

"Trees don't have whatever you said, and the children are just nasty little things, going around freeing caged cats being kept as sacrifices to the water-beast, and never wanting to listen to a man's story!"

A-ha.

"I thought you said the children just didn't want to play? Nothing was said about a man's story, are you sure you're remembering this right?"

Taz closed his eyes in torment nearby. Milo's gaze dashed from the gnome to me and back again like we were a tennis match on fast-forward.

"Of course I'm remembering it right!"

The gnome leapt up from his stool and knocked it over. I wondered if I'd potentially be losing my kneecaps in the next few seconds, but if it got the others free then that was something.

"Well it just doesn't make any sense, where did you even hear such a story?"

The gnome raised his fists, his cheeks burning red just visible above the beard as the hat fell down over his eyes.

"It was in my book," he shouted.

I folded my arms as best I could over the thick vine around my middle.

"I don't believe you. Prove it."

The gnome made a strange yipping noise. I stumbled back and fell on my butt as he launched into the air, managed a one-eighty somersault and drilled straight into the ground, leaving a dark hole behind.

Panicking and high on adrenalin, I tore at the vine around my waist, relieved when it didn't try to fight me.

"We should get going before he comes back," I said.

I clambered to my feet and started forward, stopping again when I realised nobody was following me.

"What?"

I noticed the stunned expressions on the other two faces, none more so than Taz.

"That was-" He seemed to be struggling to give me an actual compliment, his mouth flapping words that his brain wouldn't help with.

"That was awesome!" Milo beamed.

I flushed, unsettled by the praise. Luckily, Taz had recovered from his shock.

"Well there'll be time for the prize-giving later, if we all survive," he said as he strode past us. "We still have a whole maze to contend with yet."

I followed him along the path until he swung around a left turn and stumbled to a halt. I almost walked into the back of him but grabbed the side of the hedge to stop myself just in time. Milo didn't get the memo though and ploughed straight into the back of me.

At least I provided a nice buffer.

In front of us, the maze opened out into a wide area the size of a car-park.

"That's the exit look." Taz pointed. "Over there."

I squinted through the gloom to see a gap in the hedge and forest stretching beyond.

"Okay, so we just have all these weird little water pools to step around," I added.

The weird little water pools were no wider in circumference than a kid's hula-hoop, the surface still and dark. Taz started forward.

"This doesn't seem so bad," Milo said.

Taz skirted around one of the small pools of water before I could announce I still had a plan. Here would be more than enough space to call Trevor illegally and have his rickshaw land. No doubt I'd have to face Queenie straight after, but we weren't safe here.

I opened my mouth to call Taz back, but stopped as the surface of the nearest pool shivered.

Something pointy emerged and kept emerging, getting longer and longer, reaching for Taz's back.

"Watch out!" I shouted.

CHAPTER SIXTEEN
TAZ ENRAGES AN ANCIENT BEAST
AND DEMI ENRAGES EVERYONE ELSE

Taz looked to the left and darted out of the way. A long tentacle lashed onto the ground right where he'd been standing. If he'd looked to the right first, he'd have gone splat. I couldn't find my breath, my chest hammering.

Taz feinted toward another pool and back again as the tentacle shot out from that one and whipped through the air at him. It retreated back into the water, but I'd been able to make out the dark red scales, more like a lizard tail than a tentacle.

"Okay, this maybe seems quite bad," Milo said.

I tried to think, but I couldn't remember a single mention of scaly red water lizards, except-

"Oh, hang on," I said, perking up. "We were doing a trip to Glastonbury and we were mucking about by the well- actually, I wasn't invited to the mucking about part." I hesitated as Taz grimaced meaningfully at me. "Right, babbling, sorry. My mentor told us about these creatures, like water dragons that emerge from bottomless pools to feed on people passing, a Knocker he called it I think."

Milo wrung his hands together. "You mean a Knucker? I've read about those. We have to call it out and then, um, I don't know what, but I remember hearing that they're always hungry."

"Neither do I," I admitted. "I think there was something about a kid who poisoned it somehow, but that seems a bit barbaric considering it's just trying to protect its water holes."

"Does anyone have anything that we might be able to feed it?" Milo asked.

He gave Taz and me a meaningful look, as if unsure whether water-dragons could understand enough human language to recognise the suggestion that by 'feed' he meant 'poison'.

"Knucker." Taz's voice booming right beside me made me jump. "We're calling you out. Show yourself, or the bit of you that we can talk with at least."

For several moments, nothing happened. No tail, no ripples on the water and no sound at all. Then one of the pools erupted in a spray of water and we came face to snout with the Knucker.

Despite the sheer pounding of panic in my chest, I tried to take mental notes. It may have been the hysteria of facing a fifteen-foot high scaly monster with fangs the length of a man's forearm, but I tried to assess everything I could scribble down later for study purposes.

"I cannot let you pass," the Knucker hissed, its voice like the rushing of a river. "It has been long since I have eaten human."

"Um, we're Fae, some of us, kind of, sorry," I tried.

The rhythmic hissing suggested laughter. "Fae-folk or human, it makes no difference. I am always hungry."

I eyed the exit behind us. We'd taken one path at the fork, so we could go back and still try the other. If we ran fast enough we might make it past the gnome and his branches.

When Taz sauntered forward to approach the Knucker, I almost whimpered in frustration.

"Hey, mate." He beamed up at it. "I get the whole forever hungry thing, I've played sports before, sort of. Works up an appetite. They've made this new tonic now though, and it's kind of like magic. Drink one of them and you'll never be hungry again. Here, have it."

Taz held his hand up. I narrowed my eyes to see better and

could just make out a can with a familiar label on it.

"I will try your tonic," the Knucker hissed. "Then I will eat you for afters."

I had to admire Taz's bravery. I also had no idea if he'd somehow summoned the drink or been carrying it in his pocket all day.

As the creature opened its jaws, Taz pulled his arm back and took aim. The can of *Beast* sailed through the air and straight onto the Knucker's tongue. It snapped the can up, tossing it into the air and piercing it on a fang before gobbling down the liquid inside.

Almost immediately, the Knucker's head began to sway. I hadn't ever tried *Beast*, but I'd heard from others that it gave you a head rush and acted a bit like drinking alcohol.

"Yeah, gets you the first time," Taz said with a grin.

He beckoned to us and set off at a speedy jog around the pools. Milo and I hurried after him.

"You cannot- fool- me." The Knucker faltered over its words and let out a huge bubbling belch.

Taz ducked just in time as a stream of stagnant water rushed over his head.

"Time to go," he yelled.

The Knucker gave a bellow of pure outrage. I ducked as a disorientated scaly tentacle whipped out of a pool behind me.

Taz managed to go one better and hurdled over the one that tried to catch him out. The Knucker's head popped up to my left and I yelped as one of the fangs almost grazed my side. I could see Taz screaming and jumping up and down, but I couldn't focus on his voice over the Knucker hissing very inappropriate and colourful things after us.

I cleared the final pool and tumbled past Taz with my lungs threatening to go squish like a set of bagpipes. I doubled over, hands on my knees.

"Wow." Taz didn't even sound that out of breath. "That dragon has a filthy grasp of the English language. I bet that cat was being kept caged as a sacrifice. Did it get you, Dem? Are you okay?"

I managed to stand up without my head falling off.

"I'm fine. So, do we have any idea where exactly we are? Oh, actually never mind, I had a pla-"

"There they are!" A shout echoed in the distance.

Milo groaned. Taz swore, loudly.

"We can't let them catch us," I insisted. "We can't separate either."

Lights were growing between the trees, getting closer as a horde of Fae students hurried toward us, gaining ground. Taz took a step back as I fumbled to free my orb. If I was going to call Trevor, it had to be now. I just had to hope he'd listen to my pleading rather than obey Queenie's orders, and fast.

"Milo, am I right in thinking you can travel places?" Taz asked. "Like beyond what Cornelius said he lets you do? Either you can, or he's unbelievably powerful."

Milo bit his lip. "Um, yeah, but nobody's meant to know. And I can't go to different realms, at least, they said I couldn't and I've never tried."

"Okay, good." Taz nodded. "Go hide yourself somewhere. If you need to, keep moving around from place to place. Keep hidden. When you can, get word to Queenie at Arcanium, or Petra, or Ace. Whoever you end up talking to will know them. This is important, you have to tell them that the acorn is with the oak, okay?"

"Queenie, Petra or Ace, the acorn is with the oak, got it." Milo's eyes widened and his bottom lip wobbled. "I'm really pleased I met-"

"No time." Taz cut him off with a glare. "You can't take us both with you this time so go, now."

Milo nodded and walked toward the hedge. He kept going right up to it, and through it.

"He disappeared!" I gaped.

Taz nodded. "Yeah, turns out he can translocate at will."

"But that's so rare, even *I* know that. And what did you mean about acorns and oaks?"

"That's communication in code, but doesn't matter now." Taz glanced at the horde growing closer. "There's no sense me hiding anymore either. If we're going to get out of this safe, I'm going to have to do something awful."

"Like what?"

"Use my family name."

A moment later his face narrowed and shortened, his nose dipping in ever so slightly and his skin exploding with freckles. The brown hair of his Roger disguise curled itself and lightened to honey brown, until the boy in front of me was the Taz I knew, his turquoise eyes flashing back at me. As the sounds of the approaching Fae grew louder, I almost made the fatal mistake of showing my relief at him being him again. Almost.

"It's him, the prince!"

"Get him!"

"There'll be a reward for this!"

They were almost upon us.

We just have to get somewhere else with enough time for me to call Trevor.

Taz reached out for me. "Demi, quick, take my hand."

Before I could catch his fingers, someone appeared beside him with super speed and yanked him back. I shrieked, but one second Taz was alone and the next one of Friese's lackeys was behind him with a short blade at his throat.

The mob was getting closer now, and some of the Fae were holding objects, none of them friendly-looking.

I panicked and did the first thing that came to my head as one of girls came flying toward me.

I lifted my hands and searched in frantic panic for my connection. Before I could find it, the Fae girl hit something invisible and bounced. I looked at Taz and saw the corners of his eyes pinched in concentration.

He's holding a protection warding over me.

Rather than searching for my illusive connection, I fell back on my few natural skills.

"Idiots!" I mimicked Taz's voice to perfection. "Don't you know a glamour when you see one?"

My words were so vague they wouldn't count as lies, or at least I dearly hoped they wouldn't. The words flowed out of my mouth either way, and I ran with it.

"You think Fae wouldn't let themselves be so easily swayed by trickery," I added, trying to keep Taz's tone suitably scathing. "But there you are. Useless."

It was a dangerous move, especially as I couldn't exactly change my appearance into Taz's to prove them wrong. The sheer horror on Taz's face almost made the ruse worth it. He caught on before the general confusion faded and changed his glamour once again. This time, I came face to face with myself.

Oh, my, god. Do I really look that gormless and slumpy? Is that actually what I look like, or just how he sees me?

The crowd were looking at each other, and Taz's assailant shoved him away, proving that they really did see me as worthless, expendable. I pushed the indignation aside. If they chased me, I'd not have any more time left to keep tricking them. I couldn't call Trevor yet either, not until Taz was right beside me. With sweat running from my forehead and my cheeks burning, I gave the next impression my best shot.

"Are you going to let these impudent runts get the better of you?"

I managed to keep my mouth mostly shut as Director Cornelius' voice boomed through the trees. I'd done better imitations before, but I was struggling to breathe from all the panic and the running. The crowd stopped, uncertain as they looked around for the Director. I had to hope Taz would come charging to stand with me rather than assume I was giving him a chance to escape. If we could just get into a protection together, he could hold it over both of us while I orbed Trevor.

The crowd turned like a herd to face me. They barely noticed Taz now, still looking like me. He pelted past them and I almost fainted with relief as he got closer. Given the number of them now following him, we would have one last shot at this.

Taz was almost with me, just in reaching distance, when someone tackled him. I could almost sense the protection lifting me, and realised through all his running, he'd been holding it over me still.

His whole aim has been to protect me.

The boy who tackled Taz landed a swift punch to his gut. He spluttered and doubled over. Panic-laced anger fired through me. Another punch landed on Taz's chin and he dropped to his knees, his head lolling forward. I dug deep inside.

If I don't connect, if I can't use my gift now, I'll never accept my fairy side ever.

I roared as another boy came running toward me with a long metal stick. The moment he got within reaching distance, I slammed my hand against his shoulder as he lifted his arms to attack.

My gift sizzled through me and a scream filled the air as he staggered backwards, his shirt smoking. He raised the metal weapon again but I grabbed it. The shockwaves pulsed through it and into his body, wracking him with convulsions. I focused on his contorted face.

It's so easy. Why have I been afraid of this?

I wondered what else my new power could do.

A group of three tried to attack next from all sides, but I imagined my anger white-hot and strong lashing out of my palm in one crackling whip of energy. I couldn't see it, there were no lights or bolts, but I could feel the crackle of the air as the three of them started to jolt before dropping to the ground.

My chest heaved with vindictive energy as Friese and Penelope came next. Penelope was beside me before I could blink, but I reached over and clamped my anger around her middle. I focused on leaving scorch marks in the shape of fingers, a reminder that she shouldn't have let her friends go after Taz. She shouldn't have tried me.

The others hesitated nearby, and I started smiling.

"We need to get the Director," one muttered. "The help has gone mad and he said he wants her mostly unharmed."

I wanted to laugh. I was feeling light-headed now, euphoric.

Several of them ran off through the trees as someone else approached me from behind. I sent a flick of pain out to meet them and heard a grunt, but no sound of anyone falling to the ground in agony.

I spun round.

"Demi, stop now." Taz was right in front of me, his face twisted.

Droplets of sanity ebbed in through the power-mania. I blinked at him, taking in his red chin and watering eyes.

"Oh god, did I hurt you?"

I pressed my hands to my face as the connection drained out of me, along with any remaining essence of strength. I sagged and stumbled a couple of paces sideways. Taz reached out but I lurched away from him.

"Don't touch me!" I yelped. "I don't want to hurt you."

He kept coming, his hands outstretched like a caring, sharing zombie who refused to listen. I pushed his arms away but he didn't jolt or wince, just wound them tight around my waist as the tears streamed down my face.

My gift must have exhausted itself.

Given the unsettling zap of sensitivity clogging up my limbs and raking against my skin, I probably had nothing left to attack with, which meant we were vulnerable again.

I blinked away the tears as two more figures approached. The Old King's bodyguards pounded through the shadows toward us, their faces set in determination. Taz had his back to them and I opened my mouth to warn him, but he spoke before I could find the breath.

"They'll be back any minute," he said, his tone soft. "Do you trust me? You have to trust me, and I can get us out of here."

I blinked up at him, the boy who'd risked his own skin to protect me.

"Of course." I nodded.

"Put your arms around me, your head on my shoulder and close your eyes."

Weird.

I did as I was told. It felt kind of nice, in a really excruciating, awkward way.

"Eyes closed?" he asked.

I could hear the sounds of a much larger mob almost upon us now.

"Yes."

The world shifted then, the rush of air against my face a familiar blessing.

Taz can realm-skip at will? How? Why on earth wouldn't he do it earlier? First Milo, now him?

We stumbled on landing, and Taz weighed heavy against me. I tried to stand us both up, but it was all I could do to collapse us to the ground somewhat gently.

"We're safe here," he mumbled. "Orbs alive, my head is killing me."

"How?" I had to ask, and not about his headache.

Taz still had his arms around my waist, even though I was sprawled on my back with mine above my head. It might have looked dodgy to anyone passing by, but I was too wrecked to care. I checked my satchel, but Leo seemed content enough to stay inside with his beady eyes blinking back at me.

"My mother put a warding on me so that I could always get here if I had to." He managed to balance himself up on one elbow so I could see him. "It only works to get me back to wherever her court is at the time though."

I frowned and sat up. "So you could have done that anytime, and you didn't? Why?"

"Because it only works for me."

I glared up at him. "Not buying it. You were able to bring me with you just now, so why not do that in the laundry room, or Cornelius' office, or even before we went into the Puzzle Tower? How can you even do it? Is it a gift?"

Taz lifted a struggling arm and pointed a finger at my chest.

"Remember before we went into the puzzle tower, I gave you my neck chain to wear?"

I nodded. "Yeah, for luck you said."

"That necklace is quartz, which is the only reason I was able to bring you here, like realm-skipping with Trevor through the despatch wall. I can realm-skip to my mother's court at will as part of the joy of being royalty, but you can't so the necklace did that part for you using my power."

I let that sink in for a moment, my exhaustion warring with my common sense. Whatever way I looked at it, he could have gotten us out of there before now.

"So even when we were being chased by half the elite of Faerie, you didn't think it worth at least mentioning, 'oh, by the way, Dem, I can skip us out of trouble whenever I feel like it'?"

Taz groaned and my chest squished at the thought of how much pain he must be in.

"I wasn't going to leave you," he argued. "Also, be honest, if I'd said we could leave, would you have honestly gone without Milo unless you had to?"

I knew that answer to that, and since it agreed with what he was saying I said nothing instead. He rolled his eyes.

"Exactly. I couldn't skip three of us with only one necklace and you wouldn't have left him behind. That's why I sent him away, because if it was a choice between him and you, I'd always choose you."

Because I'm the FDP, and his friend. Poor Milo.

I frowned then, an idea occurring.

"Couldn't you have skipped me here while we were in the maze then gone back for him?"

"I-" Taz hesitated as the idea sank in. "No. Bringing Milo here when he belonged to the club wouldn't make any difference. My mother would just send him back."

I bit my lip, feeling awful for hassling him. His face was pale and sweaty now, and his chin looked a tiny bit puffier than normal.

"Okay, I get that. You could have escaped those spiders in the puzzle tower easily though. You didn't sign any contracts."

He stared at me, his mouth dropping open.

"Well, technically yes, but you couldn't have left until your assignment was done, and I'd *never* leave you behind like that. Besides, even if I'd gone to my mother and begged her to intervene, she definitely wouldn't do anything to help."

I raised my eyebrows at that. "She wouldn't help her son when he was in potentially life-threatening danger?"

"Nope. She wouldn't be caught dead interfering or showing favouritism, and to her being chased by a bunch of elite Fae is nothing more than a sporting day out. Either way, I have to stand on my own two feet, or I'm supposed to."

He glanced at our surroundings and slowly heaved himself up to a seated position, his shoulders slumping as if in defeat.

It hit me then, the stark reality of what he was telling me. He could skip here at will, but he wouldn't have done it until I'd finished my assignment because that would have ruined my chances as an FDP. Then, knowing I wouldn't want to leave Milo behind, he'd waited until I found a way to bargain for Milo's freedom before bringing me to the one place I knew he hated because it was safe.

Even now he's ashamed that he's had to retreat back to the safety of his familial connections.

"I can also realm-skip from the court to Arcanium and back at will," he added. "But before you ask, I don't have the strength to skip myself at the moment, let alone both of us."

I bit my lip. "Sorry, I didn't mean to bombard you. You don't have to explain a thing to me."

He flicked a half-hearted glare at me.

"Don't do that."

I frowned back. "Do what?"

"Don't go all polite, it doesn't suit you. Look, I intended to bring us here if it all went badly wrong, but then you got yourself signed up for the Puzzle Tower and that contract is binding, unbreakable."

Another mistake of mine.

"I would have done it straight after," he continued, "but I know how important achieving these assignments are to you and the future you want, and we were mostly safe. Then one minute you're nipping to the bathroom and the next we're running with Milo and making mad declarations to the whole of Faerie."

I touched my fingers to the necklace and moved to unclasp it so I could give it back. Taz shook his head.

"No, keep it for now. I can get back home anytime I want, but if anything happens while we're at my mother's court, I need to know you can get back to Arcanium safely."

He cleared his throat as I dropped my hands back into my lap. Awkward silence drifted between us for a few moments until I couldn't keep the words in any longer.

"Thank you for sticking by me. I know I'm hopeless at most things, and I get into trouble a lot, but it means the world to me."

I couldn't tell if there was a slight reddening of Taz's cheeks, but the tiny twitch at the corner of his mouth suggested I'd at least done the gratitude part right for once.

"We should get moving," he said. "When we get to the court itself I'll show you the skip-way to Arcanium. But after taking that last beating just now and holding the warding over you, I haven't got much energy left. So yeah, um, that explains the hugging to get here as well, obviously."

I glossed over the awkwardness, unwilling to swill in it when I finally had something of Taz's past to dissect.

"So, this is your home?"

Silver birch and bluebell woods, with the hint of a tree-tunnelled lane up ahead. Daylight reigned, soft and warm, as though the outside world of Faerie couldn't touch the safe space.

"Arcanium is home," Taz grumbled. "But this is where my mother lives, where I grew up. Are we going to talk about how your gift splurged a bit back there?"

All the stress, the lack of food and sleep, the exhaustion and the agony of thinking I'd harmed him spilled out. I couldn't help it. At the mere mention of my gift, I started crying.

Taz didn't move to comfort me or anything and I couldn't blame him. I wiped my eyes and looked away, trying to take some calm from the surroundings.

"It's an embarrassing story, but you've earned the right to know I guess." I sniffed. "A whole week with my family would have been bad, except I spent the first three days hanging out at Xavio's, helping with the junior fairy classes. I got talking to a boy, and long story short, he basically tricked me into accepting this dodgy gift. I'm not sure how you weren't fried back there. I'm so sorry."

Taz reached out and took my hand. I glanced at him, but he was resolutely not looking me in the eyes. I knew I should shake him off, be strong, but he'd done it so many times over the past few days that the contact felt reassuring rather than uncomfortable, and so unnervingly welcome. I clung on to his fingers and focused my gaze on the trees instead.

"There's only one way to give a fairy gift," he murmured. "A kiss. Was it like, on the lips or- actually, it's none of my business. I don't need to know, sorry."

I froze, mortified he was even asking, but I had to clear any confusion between us.

"Forehead. Wasn't even expecting it. He just said, I have a gift for you and loomed in front of me. Didn't even say what the gift was. Afterwards, he started laughing, and said it was a gift from an old friend."

Taz squeezed my fingers and let go.

Probably thinks I'm a total idiot now. Probably right.

"You said it was Diana," he prompted.

I sighed. "Well, she overheard you calling me Sparky a while back and taunted me with it. That's what he said, "an old friend sends their regards, Sparky". I knew it couldn't be you, or Ace, so I guessed it was her. Sorry if I hurt you though back there, I didn't mean to."

Taz glowered, the effect marred by the lidded tiredness around his eyes.

"When we got back to Arcanium, when my mother asked to speak to me outside the arcade, she gifted me imperviousness to your gift. So, even if you wanted to hurt me, Sparky, you can't. Stings a tiny bit, but I'm basically Demi-proof."

I sat there for a few long moments. "I'm not sure how to process that."

Taz struggled to his feet. Even though he was swaying a bit, he held out a hand to help me up. I didn't accept it or we'd probably end up rolling down the lane instead of walking, and stood up wearily under my own effort. Taz tried to take a wobbling step but I slid my shoulder under his arm before he could fall.

"Thanks," he muttered. "Now we just need to walk down that lane and you'll be in the devil's lair. Realm-skipping always takes it out of me a bit, but this time's really knocked me sideways having to bear two of us. With any luck, I'll pass out before I have to cope with my mother."

I smiled and started to shuffle forwards. "I don't know how I feel about that either."

"It's not you that should be dreading it."

CHAPTER SEVENTEEN
THE QUEEN'S COURT

Each step took a lifetime, but it was Taz's pale, sweaty face and hooded eyes that worried me most. Next to that, meeting the Queen again became less of a panic.

We reached the end of the lane, the scent of berries wafting from somewhere nearby. I flicked the odd gaze to the bushes, but couldn't see any sign of fruit. We left the lane and emerged onto a curving driveway paved with light grey stones. The drive sloped upward, the ground falling away underneath and turning it into a stone bridge that leapt over a rushing body of water.

"What are you seeing?" Taz asked, his tone weary.

I brought us to a stop. "Is this not the right place? Is something wrong?"

He shook his head and tried to get us going forward again.

"The house takes on a glamour, so it looks different to everyone who sees it. I want to know what it looks like to you."

As we started walking again, I gave the house a closer inspection.

"A manor house. Strange, I expected a towering black castle for some reason. It's got white walls and a slate roof, with wide chimneys. There's slate porch over the door as well, and roses growing up the side of the house- no, not roses, but they're like roses just with bigger flowers in different colours. It's beautiful."

"The house changes but the grounds don't. Don't trust my sisters, at all. Take my mother exactly at her word and don't agree to anything."

BANG.

A cluster of people came rushing out of the house, two men and a brisk-looking woman wearing a white hair-net.

"Master Oakthorn!" the woman gasped.

It took me a moment to remember Taz's real name, but I didn't have time for confusion as the woman jostled me aside so she could see him clearly.

A moment later, the Queen herself came striding out. Her hair was loose about her shoulders, and she wore a simple Tudor-style dress of peach velvet. She looked more like a Fae Queen now than the last time I'd seen her, especially when I noticed the droplets of pearls nestling in her hair that didn't seem to have anything holding them in place.

She flicked a glance at me, then looked Taz up and down with a disapproving frown.

"Clean him up, Marthe. It's unseemly for a prince of Faerie to look beaten."

The woman with the hairnet, Marthe, grabbed Taz's arm and started hustling him toward the house, the two men scampering after them. Taz tried to look back at me over his shoulder, but Marthe seemed to have super-Fae strength and dragged him through the front door out of sight.

I gulped as the Queen faced me and waited. The silence lengthened, and I guessed she was expecting me to fill it.

"Our assignment went a bit awry." I tried to pick my words carefully. "Taz realm-skipped us back here, but said it took a lot out of him. Will he be okay?"

The Queen eyed me over, no doubt taking in how grubby and badly dressed I was for meeting royalty. When she sighed, I saw her shoulders sag a minute amount.

"He'll be fine after a rest. But what do you mean, our assignment?"

I hesitated. *This is the literal Queen of Faerie, it's not like there's anyone can outrank her and she's asking you a question.*

"Taz and I were sent to Gallows Oak to discover this Forgotten 24 club, and to find out information about them."

The Queen clasped her hands in front of her as if she was trying to show calm, but her eyes were a whirl of tumultuous intent.

"And did you?"

Again I hesitated. "Um, sorry, but is that something I should be reporting to Emil and Queenie? I don't mean any disrespect, honestly, but the rules we're given are clear and um, I don't want to risk getting kicked out. I mean, I probably will be anyway after just leaving like that, but still."

The Queen's cheek twitched, but I couldn't tell if it was an attempt to quell a smile or a subtle clench of her jaw.

"You're quite right," she said after an excruciating pause. "But I've heard of this club you speak of, and rumours that even the so called usurper who calls himself "King" is meant to frequent it. You can understand why such rumours are of particular interest to me."

I couldn't tell her outright what I'd seen, not until I'd reported in and Arcanium had given me permission. The rules were clear about not divulging assignment particulars. Although I guessed that didn't apply to Faerie royalty, and I doubted someone could get away with glamouring as the Queen in her own court, I wasn't taking any chances.

But I was still a fairy. I could still twist the decks.

"I've heard the same rumour," I said carefully. "And there's usually truth in rumours I've found."

A broad smile broke across the Queen's face, lightening the mood in an instant. In my weariness, I hadn't noticed the skies darkening with her arrival outside, but now the clouds cleared like magic and a gentle ray of sunlight appeared.

"Oh, apologies." The Queen smiled wider. "I am to congratulate you of course on your completion of the Puzzle Tower. They are somewhat frowned upon, if not outlawed now, but I daresay your competing was mostly against your will."

Typical. Trust it to be basically illegal.

"Completely against my will," I said. "But Taz went in with me and he was brilliant."

"I take it the reception to your winning was less than enthusiastic?"

"Yeah, just a bit." I almost forgot who I was talking to now that the Queen was smiling so charmingly. "The Old King was almost spitting acid at me and called me 'it', and that woman from *The Faerie Net* show kept hinting I'd cheated. I may have made some enemies to be honest, not least the Director. I don't know if you watch *Faerie Net*, but um, I may have done something rash involving their live vision cast stream."

The Queen started laughing, and the sunshine bloomed warm and blissful around us.

"I did see, and, as my son's mother, I commend your somewhat unorthodox bravery," she said. "As Queen of Faerie, I can tell you that this is exactly why we fought that first war. When we deposed the usurper, it was to make sure that their ideals could never hold dominance over Faerie ever again. Clearly, however, some things never change."

I couldn't argue with her there, both because she was right and also because I was treading a very precarious path already in talking with too much familiarity to the all-powerful regent of Faerie.

"You no doubt need to rest and report in to your mentor." The Queen turned toward the house. "You are welcome in our home, and none here shall harm you."

I flinched. "Why would anyone here want to harm me?"

The Queen gave me a look, so withering it was like looking at an older, female Taz. I hurried at her side as she swept toward the front door.

"Oakthorn perhaps hasn't mentioned his siblings."

I nodded. "He did, in passing."

"Well, as I'm sure he's told you, families are complicated."

"Not how he put it." The words slipped out without me thinking first.

The Queen laughed. "I can well imagine. But you are under my protection, and no doubt his, for the duration of this stay here. I'll freely admit that I have feared the usurper is trying to reclaim his power, and there are some parts of Faerie even I can't reach but others can."

I came to a halt in the doorway. The Queen continued a few paces through the entrance hall and turned back when I didn't follow.

"This is what Arcanium is really for, isn't it?" I asked, realisation dawning. "Taz said once that you designed the library yourself, and there are some parts of Arcanium Queenie can't control, like the paintings, I remember him saying that on my first day there. Arcanium is your way of seeing further into Faerie than you can on your own. The motto is even 'Watch, Listen, Learn'. We're like your spies."

She eyed me for a long moment. I thought she might dismiss me from her presence then, or even kick me out of the house entirely. Right now, if it weren't for Taz potentially passing out somewhere in the house, being punted back to Arcanium sounded like absolute bliss.

"It comes down to whether you want to work alongside the human world, or try to roll over it," the Queen said, her tone grave. "The Forgotten, the usurper, many Lords and Ladies, they want to return to the old ways, to force their will over the human world and use it as their playground. I would rather work *with* the human world. There is much they can teach us, no matter how many gifts or abilities we have."

I thought about my sisters hating on me, and people at school blanking me because of it. I thought of all the wars, and the ignorance, and the prejudice. Then, I wondered if the Queen could read my mind, given the tiny smirk at the corner of her lips.

"I guess both sides have their ups and downs," I said. "But arrogance and entitlement are the two worst traits that cause most of the evils no matter what side we're talking about."

The Queen only smiled wider. "Very wise. I'm glad Oakthorn has a *special friend* like you."

The 'special friend' was delivered in a stage whisper, and now I knew she was making fun of me. My face flushed hot.

"Oh no, we're definitely not special anything, just mates."

"Hmm." The Queen raised an eyebrow. "It is very serendipitous that you've ended up here even so, and that I have the chance to speak to you alone, because it's his birthday tomorrow."

I frowned. "He never said. Actually, I never even thought to ask him when it is. Or Ace."

"Yes, his is tomorrow. Although, he's not the most cheerful soul about having to celebrate them. When is yours?"

A tingle prickled over my skin. "August nineteenth."

I blinked as the tingle lifted, the sensation familiar. I remembered well how it felt for someone to cast a compulsion on me from practicing various attempts to ward against them in classes.

She used a compulsion on me?!

I would have told her my birthday freely, but clearly she'd

assumed I wouldn't.

Before I could find a way to suggest that compelling your visitors shouldn't be allowed without getting either kicked out or my head chopped off, the Queen clapped her hands. The sound echoed off the walls, but I could hear it reverberating through the house like a gong. A tall, thin man wearing a black suit appeared. He looked old, like ancient old, one step away from turning into cobwebs.

"Ah, Merryweather, good." The Queen nodded to him. "Oakthorn has returned home unexpectedly. He's resting now, but we will organise a little birthday party for him tomorrow. Sadly it will require a lot of obligation." She turned back to me. "If we invite one type of court Fae, it means we need to invite them all, which makes it somewhat of a parliament-style shark tank, but needs must."

"Um, I'm not sure Taz would want a fuss, let alone a party," I tried.

The Queen rolled her eyes and waved her hand, sending Merryweather scurrying at alarming speed through the nearest doorway.

"My dear, boys don't know what they want."

I watched her sweep off along a corridor which took her deeper into the bowels of the house and stood there, alone with no idea where I should go or what I should do.

Will she expect me to pitch in with the staff? Am I a guest? I pressed a clammy hand to my burning forehead. *Maybe I'll just lie down here and wait for someone to come and move me. I could stick a tag on my arm with 'Arcanium' on it and they'll just assume they need to mail me back.*

"The house won't eat you."

I jumped at the sound of Taz's voice and bashed my elbow on the doorframe. Wincing and rubbing the sore spot, I glared up at him standing on the stairs.

"Our housekeeper, Marthe, has this amazing drink that makes you feel like new," he said with a grin. "But she forced the last of it on me I'm afraid, or I'd have offered it to you."

Typical. I couldn't be mad with him for long, but in that moment he looked so rosy-cheeked, bright-eyed and well-rested that I wanted to take his stupid magic house and batter him with it.

I thought back to what the Queen had said about humans, and guessed they'd be all clamouring to dissect fairies if they thought there was some kind of 'like new' tonic they could get their hands on.

"Come on." Taz came down the steps and held out a hand. "I've asked for some food to be set out, and it'll be warm and peaceful now Mother has calmed down again."

I ignored the hand and folded my arms across my chest, waiting for him to lead the way. He took me along the corridor the Queen had disappeared down toward a vast tapestry hung on the wall.

"So, what do you see?" I asked. "You said the house looks different to everyone."

He shrugged. "I don't need much, so outside I see a cottage with white walls and those small criss-cross windows. Sometimes there's a thatch roof, sometimes it's just a tile one. My sister, Belladonna, once said she saw a hundred-roomed castle made from obsidian, which tells you all you need to know about her."

I snorted. "Joys of having staff, I guess. I wouldn't want to have to clean a hundred rooms, although an obsidian castle does sound kind of cool and edgy. If people attacked you could just chip bits off and stab them."

Taz started laughing as we came to a stop by the tapestry.

Two doorways stood on either side of us, one open to a pantry full of wonders, and another leading to what looked like a vast farmhouse kitchen. The scent of bread floated out and my stomach growled.

"Through the kitchen?" I pointed.

Taz shook his head. "Through the secret door."

He lifted the edge of the tapestry to reveal a short corridor of stone underneath with a wooden door waiting at the end. I took a step forward but he held out an arm to keep me back.

"I give you permission to come in here any time you want or need to with or without me," he announced.

I stilled. "Very formal of you. Some kind of super-secret password?"

He ushered me under the tapestry and toward the door.

So my brain is creating the stone here. I wonder what this house looks like in its natural form, if it even has one?

"This was my twelfth birthday present," Taz said. "A place only I can go, or people I give permission to. It's part of the house though so whatever you see is all you."

We emerged from the corridor into a blinding dazzle of light. I shaded my eyes, aware of Taz doing the same.

"What do you see?" He sounded almost urgent.

I took my time, drinking in whatever my brain was creating. A large conservatory spanned around us, the metal structure holding walls and a roof of glass. Plants grew everywhere, and I had no hope of knowing most of the names or types, but they were thriving.

Do they really exist, or am I just creating this?

A soft trickle of running water echoed nearby, and in the middle of the wooden floorboards was a space filled with cushions and seats, covered by a hanging canopy to create shade.

"It's beautiful," I breathed. "I told you about the house first. Now you have to tell me what you see. It's your present after all."

Taz sighed. "Okay. It's a conservatory, maybe the size of one of the Arcanium classrooms. There are seats in the middle, just like floor cushions but really comfy, and big umbrellas. There are some plants, but I don't know what ones."

A smaller version of what I'm seeing. I swallowed a lump in my throat.

"If we took the plants out, like literally picked one up and held it all the way back to Arcanium, would it still exist?" I asked. "I'm finding it hard to understand all this."

Taz hesitated. "It takes a while to wrap your head around if you've not grown up with it. So, you see plants too?"

I nodded. "A bigger conservatory space, like those old Victorian ones made of metal and glass, loads of plants, a canopy hanging over a load of seats in the middle. I wish I knew how all this worked. Like, I get it's fairy magic, but if we go and sit down right now, seeing different things, are we going to end up sitting at opposite ends because we can't see the same thing, or does the magic adjust?"

Taz started laughing. "It adjusts. Come on, we'll try it. Go sit down on your chairs and I'll sit on my cushions and we'll see."

I rolled my eyes but humoured him, determined to find out everything I could. Relief that we were safe and he was okay tumbled into guilt when I realised that I hadn't properly thought about Milo since leaving Gallows Oak. I thudded down into a seat with Taz doing the same right next to me.

"See?" He grinned. "Magic."

I bit my lip. "I wonder if Milo's okay."

"He can skip at will, so he'll have hidden himself somewhere if he's sensible, and will keep moving about. I noticed that when he took us through the laundry room wall, he recovered remarkably quickly."

I rubbed my forehead. I hadn't slept in what felt like days, hadn't eaten, completed a Puzzle Tower tournament, been chased, hounded, went on a maniac power trip with my gift and then had to speak to the Queen of Faerie. Now I just wanted to eat something, sleep a lot and go home, back to Arcanium.

When Marthe appeared in front of us, literally just materialising out of thin air, it took all my effort not to burst into tears from the surprise. She put a plate of cold meat, salad and bread slathered with butter on a coffee table in front of our knees, as well as some dark pastry things oozing purple goo.

Was there a coffee table there a minute ago? I couldn't remember now.

"Eat stuff," Taz insisted. "It'll make you feel better. Marthe makes the pastry things herself and they're amazing. She's the only one around here I'm fond of."

I blinked at him. "What about 'never eat fairy food'?"

Taz laughed and grabbed one of the pastries. He bit into it, sending the jam or whatever it was full of all over his fingers.

"See? Safe. I promise nothing will trick you, except maybe my sisters but I reckon my mother will have put a restriction on them while you're here."

I picked up meat with a slice of bread and opened my satchel for Leo. He poked his head out and his eyes bulged with delight. In a wriggle he was off, scampering across the floor and scaling the nearest tree, a weird ominous looking thing with branches striped black and russet.

"There's nothing in here that can poison him, is there?" I scanned the room as if I had any idea what plants might be poisonous or not.

Taz groaned. "He'll be fine, seriously. Relax, please, you're putting me on edge. It's safe here. Milo will be fine. Leo knows what he can and can't eat. You need to learn to stop worrying."

A spark of irritation flickered in my gut at his nagging.

"Your Mum's throwing you a birthday party tomorrow."

He sat up. "What?!"

"She said something about a political shark tank and all the court Fae."

"WHAT?!"

Okay, I'm the worst person in the world, but that made me feel so much better.

Before Taz could do anything drastic, I felt a subtle vibration. It couldn't be Leo snoring, although his snores had been getting more vocal and rumbling lately as he grew. I dug in my satchel and pulled out my mobile phone.

"It's Ace." I thumbed the screen. "I'm surprised this is the first to be honest, he was sending me messages loads of times a day while I was at home."

Taz raised one eyebrow. "I'm surprised it came through. Your human devices can't transmit through Faerie. Maybe while we were moving from one realm to another? He must have gone up to the arcade to send it. What's it say?"

"Hope you get this." I read it aloud. "Everyone going mad here. Petra's facing enquiries because you've disappeared, and some boy called Milo's turned up saying he knows you but is insisting he needs to speak to you or Taz. We can't even get through on the orb so this is my desperate shot at getting hold of you. Where are you?"

I looked at Taz and bit my lip. "I haven't orbed to Petra or anything yet."

He gasped. "Why not? People can't just orb in here, outgoing orbs only because of my mother wanting to micro-manage every aspect of her court."

That explains them not being able to get hold of me then.

I grabbed my orb and stood up, my irritation returning.

"Because I did a Puzzle Tower this morning. Because I got chased and hounded into a maze by evil Fae people, then got dragged here, and you collapsed, and I had to deal with speaking to your mother who is the Queen of freaking Faerie and I'm exhausted. Give me a break!"

Taz took a breath as if to say something, but nothing came out. He huffed and flicked his hand to my orb, wordlessly telling me to get on with it.

"Petra, um, hi?" I waited.

No answer.

"They might have taken her orb away already. if there are enquiries." Taz got to his feet.

I slid my orb back in my pocket.

"What can we do though?"

Taz held out a hand. "Go back. Sort it out."

"What about the no energy to realm-skip both of us thing?"

"Marthe fixed me. I could bounce us back and forth all day now."

"But what about your party?"

He grinned. "Hope we don't get sent back here in time for it."

I started to laugh, the thought of getting to go home encompassing everything and lifting my spirits like nothing else could. I fetched Leo, who grumbled at having to leave the delights of such a large tree, and slid him into my satchel.

"So, where is this Arcanium skip-way?" I asked.

Taz still had his hand outstretched, but I wasn't sure if he was planning to walk me through the house like that or just getting used to doing it.

"My sisters couldn't be trusted to sneak through it," he said. "So this conservatory is my own personal portal. All I have to do is wish to be somewhere in Arcanium, and I am. But it only works for me so…"

He waved his hand at me, palm still out as an invitation.

I had to grin at that. "Nice and easy then."

As I took his hand, curling my fingers around his, the world shifted. Air rushed against my face and I got a glimpse of swirling grey mist before clamping my eyes shut. I had a split second of swaying disorientation, and silence.

Then:

"WHERE THE HELL HAVE YOU BEEN?"

CHAPTER EIGHTEEN
HOME UNTIL SOCIAL DUTY CALLS

I opened my eyes to find myself in Queenie's office, Taz's hand still clamped around mine.

The moment Petra's voice stopped ringing in my ears, I shook Taz off and eyed the group assembled. Queenie hadn't deigned to get out of her chair, intense displeasure scrawled across her deep purple lips.

Emil rarely ever sat down and was hovering by the door. Today was apparently a dark red boiler-suit day, but he had his tweed flat-cap covering his head so things were serious.

Standing in front of Queenie's desk, their faces set in varying displays of astonishment, were Ace, Milo and Petra.

"Sorry to barge in," Taz said, not sounding sorry at all. "We had a little snag so I had to skip us to my mother's."

Queenie's lips thinned even more than usual. "Explain. Now."

"We found the information we were sent in for," I said. Like Taz, I was taking great strength from being home again. *This I can handle.* "Am I okay to report in front of everyone here? Milo was there for all of it, so it's no revelation."

Queenie eyed Milo and gave me a nod.

"Right, well, the Old King arrived at Gallows Oak to oversee the Puzzle Tower event. I sort of accidentally got entered for it-" I hesitated as Petra made a high-pitched noise. "So we went through, and we won, but-"

"You won?" Emil's voice was quiet.

Taz grinned. "Yeah we did. Demi was brilliant."

I flushed. "It was a joint effort. But we also managed to follow- *someone,* and we found the 24 club meeting."

"How did you know it was the Forgotten 24 club?" Petra asked, her tone sharp.

Taz folded his arms. "Because the Old King himself stood up and said, welcome to the elite Forgotten 24 club. Sorry, go on, Dem."

"They had a load of trinkets on the table, so I lifted one. Director Cornelius basically lost his pocket watch and it was there, so I took it, although I couldn't be sure it was definitely his at the time if I'm honest. But he offered me the chance to choose the fate of one of the people at the party that night, so I told him he had to let Milo come here if he wanted, and um, Milo really wants to come here, I think?"

I looked to Milo and he nodded vigorously.

"Yes, please! I can work very hard, and I don't mind what I do. I'm very good at listening and I can-"

"Yes, yes." Queenie snapped. "I have had a very irate Cornelius telling me he would be 'dealing with you' if you ever stepped foot in his club again, so, Emil, we can probably strike that realm off Demi's FDP list for future assignments."

She said future assignments! She wouldn't have bothered if they were kicking me out. I didn't dare query it to be sure though as she continued.

"He was furious, although by all accounts they're having somewhat of a membership problem due to some broadcast on *The Faerie Net* so I doubt it'll be high on his list of priorities now. He did mention, however, that I've inherited one of his assistants and that I have you to blame for it."

Milo hung his head and I clenched my fists.

"I'd say you have me to thank."

The words leapt out of my mouth, earning me surprised looks

from everyone assembled. Except Taz, who for some reason looked horrified. Perhaps he still wasn't used to this side of me yet, which would be strange considering it was just about my only side these days, but I was too exhausted and elated to care right now.

Queenie pursed her lips. "That remains to be seen. We will honour your acquisition. I believe Gnat has requested an assistant as the librarian duties are somewhat overwhelming for him at present, so that will do for now."

"Thank you!" Milo gasped, his eyes shining.

I guessed Queenie might change her mind if he started blubbing, but luckily Taz jumped in.

"So he will have the same protections and allowances the rest of us assistants and mentees have?" he asked. "He will be free to come and go within the normal Arcanium restrictions, no caveats?"

Queenie nodded. "Yes, no caveats. No tricks. We do honour hard work here, Taz, whatever some may believe."

Taz had the decency to look shame-faced, but only for a moment before Queenie got bored of us.

"Right, out." She waved her hand at the door. "You've returned, you're unscathed and the assignment is complete. Go do whatever it is you do."

Taz grabbed Milo by the shoulder and jostled him out before he could start burbling more gratitude.

"Wait a minute!" Queenie bellowed.

Taz sagged as she held up a silver piece of paper that hadn't been in her hand a moment ago.

"Taz and Demi, you have an appointment to keep," she insisted. "The Queen has already noticed your absence and *demanded* your return."

Taz scowled. "Yeah, for a birthday party. It's hardly urgent."

Queenie's lips twitched.

"Yes, I've received my invitation. Most inconvenient lack of notice, but still. The Queen summons, we attend. Home, now."

"Arcanium is home," Taz muttered, but he didn't stick around to argue.

Out in the hall, Emil strode off to his office without a word.

"Are you okay?" Ace asked me, one hand settling on my shoulder.

It took me a second to realise he hadn't flinched. I was now apparently so used to Taz being able to grab my hand and manhandle me without getting zapped by my gift that I was letting my guard down.

Perhaps my gift is only in my hands after all.

I nodded at Ace and eased myself out of his grip as I faced Petra instead.

"I didn't mean for it all to go wrong," I said before she could speak. "I told you about the Puzzle Tower but I didn't realise it would be today. Yesterday? A lot has happened, I don't even know what day it is now what with all the skipping between realms. First they stole my orb to use as a token."

"Then we had to go through these poisonous water creatures." Taz stepped in. "A Reflectator, individual trial chambers and sort through a bunch of keys and codes. Demi beat this boy called Friese though, and he already hated us."

"Then they chased us," I continued. "We fled, and sent Milo for help, but we couldn't hold them so Taz skipped us to his mum's. We were only there what, an hour? Then Ace told us Milo had arrived here, so we skipped back and here we are. But we got the assignment done."

"That is a lot." Petra conceded with a small smile. "To win is an immense achievement, but we'll have to celebrate later. You and Taz have an appointment to keep."

She grinned as Taz groaned. I bit my lip and turned to find Ace standing beside Milo.

"Don't worry about us," he insisted. "Milo and I will get acquainted and I'll show him the ropes around here. No doubt you'll be back in a day or two and then we can all chill out for a change. Do you want me to take Leo?"

"That sounds amazing, thanks, Ace."

I handed Leo over, who grinned at Ace in recognition and clambered up to his shoulder. He would be safest here, especially as everyone kept warning me about Taz's sisters.

Before Taz could take my hand to skip back to the court, someone stepped out of the lift at the end of the hall. I recognised the blonde hair and the purposeful stride of the girl coming toward us, but I wasn't used to seeing her in anything other than a medieval-style gown.

"Hi, Alannah." I smiled as she stopped in front of us. "I didn't know you were back."

She smiled at me, but I noticed she gave Petra a cool glance and ignored everyone else.

"Hi, Demi. I hear you've been causing mayhem again."

I'd only met her a couple of times during my last assignment, but it was in her realm that I had found Leo, and she'd kept him safe when I needed to stop people from finding out about him.

I shrugged, flushing. "Kind of. How's your prince, and your charge?"

"My charge is fine as far as I know. My assignment was to ensure she became duchess, then queen, and now she is, so my role there is done."

"Ah, okay. Guessing the prince is still a pain?"

Alannah smiled, her lips curving with alarming wickedness. "No, he met a somewhat sticky end but it's no great loss. I'll see you around anyway, I have a meeting with Emil."

She nodded to me and strode on without a word to anyone else. Petra rolled her eyes after Alannah and gave me a look.

"Career family Fae right there. Okay, straight back to the Queen please, and Demi, we'll catch up when you're back."

I nodded. "Thanks, Petra. I'll do my best not to cause total carnage for the next day or so."

Petra only laughed at that and set off toward the lift.

"Before you go," Milo said. "I wasn't sure who to tell, or who to trust, but I overheard something and I need to tell someone."

His hands started twisting around each other, his bulky shoulders hunched and his lips pressed thin with anxiety. We all inched closer to hear.

"I was hiding in the entertainment complex behind the wall of games machines, and I'm sure it was Director Cornelius talking to the King- the *Old* King's advisor. They mentioned, um, threats on the lives of all the Queen's children, because without them, um, I mean you, her line is even more fragile."

Taz rubbed his chin with a heavy sigh. "I guess my mother has already thought of that. Wouldn't be the first time someone's tried to off the kids to clear the line. Lucky for me I'm not full Fae, so I probably don't count."

I hadn't known it wasn't the first time, and remembered the Old King telling his guards to find out which of the Queen's children was at Gallows Oak, but wisely said nothing. Instead, I focused on clearing all secrets between the group. If Milo was going to stay, to be friends with us, we needed the truth.

"Milo, we have to ask about the cocoa."

He froze. His eyes widened to swimming pools of horror and I almost told him not to worry about it, to pretend it never happened.

"I'm so sorry," he whispered. "You knew?"

I nodded. "Taz figured it out pretty quick. You lucked out with an insomniac."

Milo hunched over and covered his face with his hands. Ace stared in alarm, one arm hovering as if he was unsure whether he needed to offer hugs or be wary of him.

"I'm so sorry," Milo said. "Friese made me. He caught me making the cocoa and gave me something to slip into it. I tried to tip it onto the tray instead, but he caught me and compelled me to put it in, but I know that's no excuse. Then he said I couldn't tell because who would believe me, and I think he put some kind of restriction on me, because I wanted to tell you but the words wouldn't come out, and I couldn't make my hands throw the cocoa away-"

"Whoa, steady on." I eyed Taz, who shrugged. "Milo, breathe, please."

The breathing was marginally worse than the babbling, huge heaving sobs that went inwards rather than outwards. Ace found a clean tissue and tucked it between Milo's fingers before patting him on the back. I sought for the right thing to say and gave it my best shot.

"Milo, listen. You can't be blamed for what Friese made you do. It's not a matter of strength. If someone compels you, there's nothing you can do. We understand that, and if he restricted you from telling us, you couldn't help that either. We're not angry, are we?"

I gave Taz a savage nudge when he hesitated.

"Er, yeah, of course not."

"See?" I tried to sound soothing. "We'll say no more about it, but I just wanted to hear it from you, okay? We're not angry, and we're not holding it against you. If what you've said is true, then it wasn't your fault."

Milo hooted into the tissue and wiped his eyes on the back

of his hand.

"I'm Fae, I can't lie," he said. "But I can't thank you enough, you've all been so kind to me. I don't deserve it."

An idea came to me, a way to cut a load of going around in conversational circles reassuring him.

"Earn it then. Work hard in the library, be nice to people. Ace is alright, generally, so he's a good role model."

I gave Ace a cheeky grin to lighten the mood, freezing when he gave me a one-armed hug.

Still no sparks, phew.

"From you, that's practically a medal," he joked.

I managed to hold my smile but wondered if using my energy gift so strongly back at Gallows Oak had somehow extinguished it completely.

Taz raised an eyebrow as Ace let me go. "Well, as cosy as this all is, Demi and I have a death sentence to attend now."

"Ever the drama prince." I rolled my eyes.

Go and enjoy your party," Ace said. "Oh, and Happy Birthday, mate!"

Taz shrugged, but from the tiny smile on his face I could tell he was pleased. Milo mumbled his own good wishes, still blinking as if he expected us to turn around and tell him it was all a big hoax at his expense. I could empathise with that feeling well, and knew that Ace was the best person to reassure Milo, like he'd done for me when I first arrived.

Taz held out his hand palm up and I took it, my cheeks flaming now that we were in front of our friends.

The air rushed past my face and I kept my eyes open to see the brief swirl of grey that obscured my vision before we landed back in the now candlelit darkness of Taz's conservatory.

"Whoa, time changed fast," I remarked.

Taz nodded, stifling a yawn. "Realm-skipping does that.

Messes with your head so best just accept it. At least this means it's acceptable for us to skip the royal Fae dinner expectations now, as we've likely missed them."

I rubbed the back of my neck and wondered if there was somewhere I could crash without any Fae complications or trickery. Right now, the conservatory would do nicely.

Taz eyed me over before letting go of my hand.

"Come on, you look done in. I'll show you to a room you can use and have food brought up for you. If we can get through tomorrow unscathed, we'll be back home before we know it."

I nodded and followed him toward the tapestry. That was a plan I could wholeheartedly agree with.

CHAPTER NINETEEN
DRESS DILEMMA AND A NEAR MISS WITH A DOOR

I stared at the dress hanging on the wardrobe and squinted, twisting my head from side to side.

When the Queen had mentioned a birthday party for Taz, I hadn't thought anything about it, not in terms of myself. I wasn't even sure I'd been officially invited considering nobody had mentioned it since we returned from Arcanium. I certainly hadn't received an invitation like Queenie had.

I'd spent the day with Taz showing me the grounds of the court, jumping stones across the river and watching the wild Fae horses in the meadow beyond. Either Taz had awful balance for a Fae prince, or he was trying his hardest to make me laugh. He even gave me a chance to practice with my energy gift, as he was immune so it was relatively safe. I still had fears that I was slowly roasting his insides without us knowing, but I guessed the Queen would have thought of that.

I really hope she would have thought of that.

But now I stood in front of the wardrobe in my temporary bedroom at court, eying up the monstrosity hanging against it. The whole thing exploded pink. Baby pink, hot pink, dazzle-your-eyes-fluorescent pink; it was a disaster. There were ruffles. Puffs of lace protruded out.

The Queen had no doubt told someone to order me a dress, but surely she would have given some kind of instruction.

Unless she's having a laugh at my expense. This is Faerie, and these are Fae, whether Taz's family or not. Trickery and laughs at the expense of others is part of the job description.

"You won't get anywhere staring at it, dear."

I flinched and turned my head at the sound of a muffled feminine voice, but I couldn't see anyone in the doorway.

"Over here, dear."

I looked around the room but couldn't see a single soul.

"Um, where are you?" I asked. "And *who* are you?"

"Your wardrobe, dear, and it might help if you moved the dress a little."

I blinked. *This has to be another trick.*

I unhooked the dress from the wardrobe and threw it over the bed. When Taz had shown me to the room last night, there had been a perfectly normal wardrobe. It was still normal-looking, made of dark oak and had one door in the middle. But now it had a face in it. Not an actual face, but wood knots for eyes and a mouth that seemed to be frowning.

"That's better," it said.

Oh crap, the wood is talking.

I'd also slept in the room last night and put on new clothes when I woke, a black knitted cardigan and black jeans provided by Marthe from Faerie knows where, so the wardrobe had no doubt seen everything.

I bit my lip. Even though a talking wardrobe was unusual in terms of my limited experience, I was technically in its domain so I didn't dare be rude.

"Hi."

The mouth-knot widened into a smile.

"There we are, dear. Now, the dress may look a bit… *puffy,* but if you go in from the bottom and shimmy upwards, you should get there."

"Don't you have anything less puffy? Um, please?"

The wardrobe blinked its two eye-knots.

"No, dear. This was arranged for you by the royal family, so I'm afraid I can't be disobliging to their wishes. Pop it on and I'm sure it will look lovely."

I had two options, well, three if you counted not going to the party at all. I could go down in my current clothing, or I could put on the dress.

It's one night, and I can't leave Taz alone to fend off all the elite Fae the Queen will have invited.

I inched out of my clothes, acutely aware there was now a wardrobe watching me. That alone was weird, but the constant encouragement it gave me as I approached the horrid dress freaked me out even more.

"It'll look much better on, poppet," the wardrobe soothed.

I picked up the bottom hem of the dress and slid into the massive collection of folds. I struggled up, almost having a panic attack when I got stuck. The body was fitted and I thought I was going to suffocate, but I found the arm holes and broke through before turning to face the mirror.

"I look like a huge pink jelly! They're all going to laugh at me." I groaned.

"Nonsense, dear." Even the wardrobe didn't sound too sure. "Now sit in front of the vanity table and let the brushes do their job."

I shuffled across the room, still too in shock at the horrific dress to argue, and hovered by the chair.

"Um, is the chair- is it going to talk if I sit on it?"

The Wardrobe tutted. "Of course not, dear. It's a chair."

Of course not, how silly of me.

I sat obediently as the brush began to run through my hair of its own accord, accompanied by a comb. The sensation started to soothe my ruffled nerves until I noticed a rustle of red at the hem near my foot. I lifted the multitude of skirts to reveal a rose-red satin underskirt that shimmered with slicks of colour like my hair did.

I wonder who actually ended up getting me this dress.

I hadn't met Taz's sisters yet, but they'd been suspiciously absent. I'd not asked either, so I had no idea if they were all at some kind of fancy Fae school or being kept out of sight.

"Who ordered this monstrosity for me, specifically?" I asked the wardrobe.

"Lady Belladonna, at the Queen's request."

"She's Taz's sister I take it?"

The wardrobe's mouth twisted, the knot shrinking.

"Yes."

So they're the ones playing a horrid trick on me. Well, if they want me to wear this dress and be a laughing stock, I'll hold my head up and pretend I don't care.

That thought kept me going for several seconds, buoyed up by stubborn will until my bedroom door swung open.

BANG.

I jumped as the door slammed shut again, followed by a loud clicking.

"There you go, half-breed!" A high voice rang out. "Don't like the dress, don't come to the party."

An echo of laughter bounced through the cracks in the door, several voices joining in.

The hairbrush hovered in the air as I got up and rushed over to rattle the door handle. It wouldn't budge. I kept shaking it anyway, despite knowing the door was locked.

"Ex-*cuse* me, have you ever heard of manners, girl?"

I looked down to the find the keyhole mouthing the words.

A talking wardrobe, why not a talking door?

I pressed my hands to my face. "Please open. I have to be at the party, I can't let Taz down."

The keyhole twisted, the movement accompanied by a disgruntled sniffing noise.

"Lord Oakthorn is currently lower in the family hierarchy than Lady Belladonna, and *you* are not featured at all. I have been locked, therefore I will remain locked."

I stared at the disagreeable quirk of the keyhole mouth and imagined the door folding its non-existent arms in refusal.

"What, even if it never gets opened and I die in here?"

"I-" The lock paused. "I have been locked, therefore I remain locked."

The wardrobe tutted. "Keesley, let the poor girl out, you know how the Lady can be."

I wasn't waiting around for a talking keyhole to change its mind. I eyed the open windows instead and rustled over to lean out. A ledge ran underneath the frame right to the corner of the building. I might be able to balance on it if I was careful.

I swung a leg out.

"Oh no, don't you even think about it," the Wardrobe gasped. "It's not safe! Keesley, open up this minute."

I paused to glance over my shoulder, but the keyhole was still pulling a disagreeable expression. I clambered out onto the ledge, clinging to the window sill. My childish bravado vanished as I looked down.

The ground was stupidly far away. I could just about make out people arriving in fine carriages and beautifully elegant dresses and suits, some of them carrying presents. No doubt others would also give Taz ability gifts for his birthday, if they liked him. I continued looking down as elegant classical music floated through the air. One slip and I'd be dead.

This isn't like the Carrie's Castle books, I reminded myself as the ground seemed to grow further away with each passing second. *If I fall, no part of the house is going to catch me.*

It took most of my strength to haul myself back into the room, the sting of tears prickling my eyes. I froze, halfway in as a loud ripping sound tore the air. I looked down to find a snatch of pink ruffle caught on the edge of the sill. A very specific part of the sill, which was now twisted and warped in the shape of fingers pinching. I inched further into the room, each movement unravelling the dress.

Maybe the house is going to help me after all.

I swung into the room with all my might, gratified by the constant sound of stitches disintegrating. I walked a few paces then started spinning in a circle, the pink beginning to whirl off me like garish petals to reveal a red slip underneath. Even the skirts were red, and I could tell that Taz's sister had modified a dress, rather than had the pink one made specially, no doubt a lazy kind of spiteful. They didn't consider me as worthy of having a whole new monstrosity made, and for once I was glad of their arrogance.

Thank Faerie for cruddy stitching.

I pulled the last of the pink off with my hands and smiled down at the red fabric. The dress was strapless, a satin bodice with a simple slip-skirt covered in elegant folds of velvet that reached the floor. Apart from a couple of snags along the seams where the unravelling had gone too far, the dress was perfect. I looked up in time to catch the Wardrobe mouthing to itself with its eyes closed.

"Thank you." I gave it a look, but it just winked back at me.

"Don't look at me, dear, I'm not the clumsy one who ruined Lady Belladonna's dress."

The smiling knot betrayed the stern words and I took courage from that. The floating brush renewed its vigour on my hair, and I ignored the subtle fluff of make-up brushes feathering around my face. I turned all my attention to the lock, determination rising now that I didn't look a complete idiot.

"Is there anything I can do to get you to open the door, Keesley?" I asked.

The keyhole twisted. "No."

"Nothing at all?"

"No."

"Nothing you might like, or want? I can't do much, don't have much, but you never know."

Silence. Then, "I like riddles."

"Asking, or answering?"

"Asking."

"So, if I answer a riddle, you'll let me out?"

The keyhole swished from side to side.

"From inside I have walls but no windows or doors, a roof but no chimney and immovable floors. From outside, easy entrance is found with a key, as my lock is the only access to me."

I blinked, my mind racing over the words.

"But you'll never figure it out," he added primly. "And you only get one guess."

Walls without windows or doors. Can't get out through gaps in the top or the floor. I paced back and forth. *A lift? A coffin? But access is only through the lock with a key.*

I shuddered at the mere thought of coffins and locks, memories swelling up from not long ago where Elvira, the maniacal Fae who'd been with the Old King at Gallows Oak, had locked me in a massive box. I forced them away but even quicker I thought of the trial chambers, that pressing darkness crunching in around me.

I lifted a hand to my chest and focused on breathing through my renewed anxiety.

Think, idiot. People don't tend to go in and out of a coffin easily, and lifts often have hatches in the top. But the room beyond the trial chambers...

I frowned. That room had no doors and windows, no sign of any way out through the floor or the roof. But we did get in and out.

"Or maybe we need to somehow get them to lift the lid." Taz's words from then filtered through my head. *Lid, like the lid of a-*

"Is it a box?" I asked, aware if I was wrong I might have to consider the window again. "It is, isn't it?"

I can't realistically try the window, even if the house has helped me this far. But maybe I can orb Petra and ask her to get a message to...

The keyhole quivered for several seconds before emitting a disgruntled click. I pressed the door handle once more and my heart leapt as the door swung open.

"Thank you, Keesley! Thank you, and you wardrobe and brushes and windows and anyone else I'm sorry if I've missed you."

I dashed out of the room and down the hall, still expecting the house to work against me. I waited for corridors to turn into dead-ends and rugs into quicksand, but it presented me almost immediately with a set of stairs.

Waiting at the bottom was a golden curtain. Strains of music from behind it beckoned me forward, a delicate lull of strings and flutes swelling on the other side. I took a deep breath and dipped around the edge of the fabric.

The pale marble floor of the Queen's throne room was decorated with swirls that moved in a circular pattern, not wide sections like a snake but tiny lines that glimmered gold and silver amid the pale surface. High above, the vaulted ceilings were left open to the elements, no doubt due to the Queen's ability to control any weather element she chose in her own court. Stars twinkled above in the inky sky, excessively and unnaturally large. I eyed the decorations, and the ribbons tied around collections of flowers, the colour scheme apparently dark purple and pale gold.

On the far side of the room opposite the doors, the Queen sat on a marble throne surveying the scene.

I wonder if everyone else sees the same thing as me, or if the house is still showing everyone what they imagine.

I scanned the crowd, aware of several unnervingly glamorous groups of people staring at me. I wondered if they could tell I wasn't Fae like them, but then I saw Taz a little way away. He was wearing a purple suit so dark it was almost black, but embroidered with pale gold patterning. Underneath the jacket his shirt was also gold, but muted so that the warm tones of his honey brown hair were still noticeable.

He matches the room.

I breathed sharply to dislodge the sudden flutter in my chest, an ill-timed reaction. Even though we were friends and nothing else, I had to admit the whole Fae elegance seriously suited him.

I lifted up my skirts and hurried across the room with the startling realisation that I wasn't wearing any shoes. Or socks. Or tights. I had no idea if the brush had a chance to finish whatever it was doing to my hair either, so Faerie only knew how wild I looked right now.

I came to a stop in front of him, noticing that the embroidery on his suit formed loads of little acorns and oak leaves. I caught his eye instead of ogling, aware that he was looking me up and down in return.

Staring at me.

A blush crept over my cheeks.

"I know," I gabbled. "My hair's probably a mess and I'm not

wearing any shoes, but I had good cause."

He swallowed. "Uh, yeah. You look fine. Um, why?"

"Fine" isn't what any girl wants to hear, even from a friend. "Why what?"

"Oh, why don't you have shoes on?"

I folded my arms. "Your sisters locked my bedroom door with me still behind it, I'm assuming with a key, although in this place who knows? I ripped part of the dress trying to climb out the window, or technically trying to climb back in again. Then I had to answer a riddle to get the door to open and I kind of rushed out when it did without thinking."

That wiped the strange look off Taz's face quick enough. He straightened up and eyed the ballroom, falling deceptively still.

"They what?"

"Locked the door. They shouted something taunting through it and ran off laughing. Well, I'm assuming it was your sisters. Keesley mentioned a Lady Belladonna."

"Keesley?"

"My keyhole. I mean, not mine, but the one on the door of the room I'm using."

There's a conversation I never imagined having.

Taz's fists clenched. "I should have made them swear to leave you alone. I thought because my mother had approved you being here, they'd know better."

Realising I probably shouldn't have told him about any of it, I groaned.

"Don't go doing anything drastic. It's fine, I'm out. Let's sit down, watch people dance around for a bit."

Taz shot me a look, but when I moved toward the row of gold-painted chairs set against one wall, he followed me and flopped down on one.

"I'm going to strangle them," he hissed to himself. "One by

one. I'll make their stupid Fae eyes pop out of their stupid Fae heads. I told them all you were off-limits."

I eyed the room. "And you thought they'd listen? Well, they certainly have an astonishing effect on your vocabulary."

He made a dismissive growling noise in his throat and I decided not to needle him any more for a while.

The ballroom sparkled in a whirl of gem-adorned finery as the dancers moved across the marble floor. I spied a table groaning with food, but also noticed that nobody was eating any of it.

Is it just for show? I stared around at the room full of too-perfect people. *Most likely.*

A cluster of girls stood nearby doing the time-honoured practice of gathering close together and giggling behind their hands as they looked mine and Taz's way. I couldn't be sure if they were laughing at me or at his scowling and the hunched 'child sulking at a party' routine.

Perhaps they fancy him, or more likely his title.

Friese and Penelope stood on the opposite side of the room, dressed in resplendent finery, his dark red suit with silver-lined waistcoat matching her elegant satin ballgown. They were talking to a girl who had her back to us, but I didn't need her to turn around to recognise the conker brown hair. Diana looked over her shoulder at us, and all three of them laughed.

"Is it strange her brother isn't here?" I mused. "Usually she and Kainen are joined at the hip."

Taz shrugged, his expression still moody. "Dunno. Why, are you disappointed?"

"No, just holding a conversation with myself apparently."

Again the group looked over at us and laughed. I would have done the grown-up thing and ignored them, but another boy cut through the crowd to join their huddle. My skin rippled with chills and I sat up straighter, anger tickling my connection awake. I slid my hands under my thighs, feeling the warm tremor inside my gut that suggested it wouldn't take much for my new gift to start crackling.

"What is it?" Taz had noticed my sudden wariness.

"That boy with Diana and the others."

"That's Jack Harmony, he's my seventh cousin I think."

That distracted me momentarily. "You think?"

"Fae royalty is somewhat extended. Do you know him?"

I nodded. "I should say so. He's the one who gave me my 'gift'."

CHAPTER TWENTY
NO REST FOR THE FORGOTTEN

Taz's face twisted with fury in an instant, his eyes flashing green as he started to stand up.

I grabbed his arm.

"Don't do anything drastic," I warned. "Not in a room full of gossip-hungry Fae."

He gave me a sulky look, but slouched back in his seat. A girl about our age approached from across the room, her ice blonde hair neatly pinned and her pale pink dress accompanied by matching slippers, ribbons and jewels. Unlike the way my dress had looked originally, her gown was pure elegant silk instead of a pink disaster, without a puff or ruffle in sight.

I could also tell she only had one object in mind, her gaze fixed with resolute determination on Taz. I should have expected it, that people would want to dance with him, but somehow I couldn't help the tremble of anxiety in my gut at the thought.

When the girl got within earshot, Taz flicked a glare up at her and sent her scurrying away toward the drinks instead. I tried not to smile. Tried really hard.

"She was probably going to ask you to dance." I told him.

He grunted. "I don't dance."

I left him to his brooding, aware that Diana and Jack were still looking over and laughing openly at us. I flinched when Taz's head appeared next to mine.

"One day, I'll curse him for you," he whispered.

I shivered as his breath brushed my ear. "You can do that?"

"There are a few perks to being of royal blood, and ability to curse is one of them. Not easily done, and there are consequences, but I will. We'll wait for our moment though. No sense- what was it? No sense making a scene in a room full of gossip-hungry Fae."

I stuck my tongue out at him, but the thought of something horrid befalling Jack did cheer me up a fair bit.

"What would you do then, make his nose fall off?"

Taz grinned. "Make something fall off maybe."

I snorted, in the most unladylike way, as Diana appeared in front of us. I couldn't deny her dress was stunning, a simple satin sheath dress in black, with matching suede heels. She also looked like she'd been decked out in the family jewels, with a V of diamonds glinting at her throat and a small tiara nestled in her hair.

"Shall we set aside any silly misunderstandings for the evening and be adults, Taz?" she asked with smile, ignoring me. "I thought you might want to ask me to dance."

I froze as Taz stood up, not sure if he was going to lose his mind entirely and agree, or lose his mind entirely and do something awful to her instead. Then again, if he couldn't dance perhaps him saying yes would be an awful enough indignity in Fae circles. He eyed Diana up and down, predatory intent shining in his eyes.

"No." He turned to me instead, his face breaking into a grin as he bowed low. "Do *you* want to ask me to dance?"

He looked so happy at being dramatic that I started laughing.

"Well, I doubt anyone else is going to ask you now," I told him. "Since you've been glowering at everyone, even that nice looking girl in the big pink bow."

Diana looked on, her sheer horror at being snubbed rendering her silent for once. Nearby, several pairs of eager eyes were watching with gleeful anticipation. They didn't care who got snubbed as long as somebody did.

Taz cast a look around the entire room, slow and purposeful, before holding his hand out to me and making his stance clear.

The tiniest flicker of mischief inside me told me to refuse, or at least hesitate to raise the drama levels. After a couple of seconds, I took his hand and tried not to catch the looks on anyone else's faces as he led me toward the dance floor.

"I don't usually dance," he warned. "But you might not get to another royal ball for a while, and seeing Diana's face when I said no felt so good."

"You're evil sometimes," I told him.

Behind my blasé nonchalance was a huge heart of vulnerability beating right underneath the surface. I placed my hand in Taz's and put my other on his shoulder, staring at the pale lines of my fingers against his dark purple jacket. Being this close to him when we weren't fleeing imminent danger had so many awkward nerves hopping through me that I couldn't bring myself to look at him, and I didn't quite know why.

I thought I recognised the song as one they played on a lot of Faerie orb-channels, but then violins started and Taz pressed his hand onto the small of my back. I glanced up to find his face set with grim determination.

"Just follow my lead, okay?" he whispered.

I heard the loud snort of the man from the nearest couple as they launched into the dance.

I do recognise this song. With a broad smile, I took a few well-practiced steps and fell into line with the rest of the dancers. *Finally, some part Xavio's mental training regime is paying off.*

Taz missed a couple of steps but caught up with me, his eyes wide with shock as he had to spin me. I grinned wider, nerves dissipating, pleased that for once in the mad world that was Faerie, I knew how to do something right.

"Xavio insisted on teaching us how to dance," I told him as we stepped close. "He seemed to think it was important. I guess being able to dance and show off will always be a big deal to Fae though."

Taz seemed to struggle with that for a moment as he spun me in a wide circle, claiming my hand and my waist a second later. Each touch sent fizzles of awkwardness through me, but I tried to relax into the dance and act like this was completely normal, just two friends dancing together.

"That display with Diana was just for the politics anyway, I take it?" I asked.

In the hesitation that followed, the demented part of my brain wanted him to say no.

He shrugged, waltzing us through the weaving crowd.

"That was the least I could do after what she did to you. Also, I'm hoping you're the least likely to stab me or gift me against my will in here."

I faked a wistful sigh. Okay, mostly faked. Taz and I were friends, and I'd accepted he wouldn't ever be interested in me any other way. But when a good-looking boy goes to the trouble of snubbing your enemy in favour of you, there's bound to be a little bit of residual emotion tied in with the gratitude.

"Fake flattery rarely ever works on me," I told him. "Er, why has everyone else left the dance floor?"

I missed a couple of steps as the crowd disappeared from around us, leaving Taz and I the only ones dancing. His hand tightened on my back as though he knew I was a split-second away from running.

"The Queen's doing no doubt." His mouth quirked to the side, resigned. "A ploy to show me off as her pet half-breed project. Just keep dancing, the song will end in a second."

I wasn't entirely sure I wanted to be part of this show, but I couldn't abandon him now.

We continued moving, not talking and not quite meeting each other's eyes as we span and returned to dancing face to face. I focused on his shoulder, aware of his fingers firm on my waist as he twirled us in another sharp circle. Our eyes met and the noise around us fell away. Almost.

A note of discord filled in the air, tearing my attention away from Taz. The music fumbled, jarring as the musicians stopped playing. Then silence fell.

I lifted my hand and threw out a protection warding on instinct as a roar filled the throne room, Taz doing the same. I could sense the moment his warding met mine, the unspoken agreement between us letting them weave together for extra protection.

Taz grabbed my hand and spun around so we stood back to back. There was no time for any uneasiness at the hand-holding as a man charged toward the throne with a blade aloft.

The Queen didn't so much as twitch, but her attacker rebounded in mid-air as if pulled by an invisible cord. He skidded away across the floor and sailed out of sight through the throne room doors.

The Queen shot the quickest glance in our direction then rose to her feet. Slow, purposeful, regal. With a flick of her head, she raised the knives, forks and spoons from the food table. The plates rolled onto their delicate edges. The crowd watched in hesitant silence, on edge and waiting for the thin thread holding chaos at bay to snap.

"You think she's going to use them as weapons," Taz muttered. "But bet you any money she's clearing them out of the way. They're family heirlooms from the fourteenth century."

I could see Diana and Jack inching toward us now. Diana had her hand up, possibly holding her own protection warding above her.

What happens when two enemy protection wardings cross each other without permission from the wielders?

I didn't have time to find out as the Queen's voice filled the hall, booming over the muttering of the crowd.

"Anyone who dares cross me or mine will make themselves an enemy today. The party is over. Leave, or consider yourself against us."

I eyed the crowd but Diana and Jack were getting ever closer. I took a deep breath to calm the anger rippling through me, tingling my energy gift awake. I owed Diana payback for how she'd treated me, Jack too.

A loud bang rolled around the room as someone sent a wave of flame across the crowd. I winced as it hit our warding, but the blow only turned to a warm breeze against my face. My connection strained against the attack but held firm.

Someone else sent a bolt of lightning toward the Queen and a collection of girls now standing near her. I guessed these were Taz's sisters, but they were Fae, they probably had gifts rolling out of them like sweat.

Taz squeezed my fingers, catching my attention.

"How do you feel about attacking if I defend?" he asked, his tone grim.

"What are you thinking?"

"I can hold our warding but let your gift out, so you can attack but nothing can come in. Do you think you can control it enough to keep people away from us?"

I nodded. "I think so, as long as nobody annoys me. Then again, you're impervious so we should be fine. Who am I keeping people away from?"

"Me and you, screw everyone else."

"Taz!"

"Okay fine," he huffed. "If you get a chance to protect the Queen, or my sisters I guess, then go for it, but not at the expense of yourself, okay? No heroics. Unless I'm in trouble. Save me, I like me."

I couldn't help a snort bursting out at that, but straightened up as gifts started to zap and sizzle around the room.

When Diana stopped a few metres away from us, I faced her, taking in the cruel, Fae smile. Jack hovered beside her with a wary eye fixed on the fighting crowd.

"I've been looking forward to this, *Sparky,*" Diana crowed.

I dug deep and strengthened my connection, the tingling blooming up my arm and flowering across my shoulders. I'd slept and eaten. I was safe with Taz holding our warding and I owed both Diana and Jack a display of the 'kind' gift they'd given me.

"Ready?" I asked.

Taz squeezed my fingers. "Ready, let them have it."

I visualised my gift shooting out, the energy leaving my fingers and zinging Diana's head, just a little jolt, enough to lift her hair on end and make her jump. She shrieked and reached up to pat it down with her spare hand. Something whizzed right behind her and I realised she had temporarily let her protection slip.

Before I could taunt or warn her away from trying anything, she glared at Jack.

"What did you do?" she shouted above the din.

He returned the icy look. "You told me to give her a shocking gift, so I did."

"What did you actually say?"

I glanced over my shoulder at Taz, who shrugged. I could see sweat shining on his forehead now and realised the protection must be taking him a lot of effort to wield given that other gifts were bouncing against us at alarming speed.

"I did what you said!" Jack argued, folding his arms while Diana's hand apparently held the protection around them single-handed. "I gave her the ability to shock people."

"You *idiot!* I said give her a gift that shocks people, as in any time she touches them, not an ability when she chooses."

"Well, you didn't say that. You should have been clearer. I didn't sign on for this, Diana."

I couldn't help grinning, despite the mayhem firing all around us. Someone skidded across the room from a blow to the chest and bounced like a pinball off various people's protection wardings.

"We should get to somewhere safe," I told Taz.

He sagged. "Your best idea yet. Whoa, what is he doing here?"

I turned my head to see where he was looking and my jaw dropped.

Xavio strolled through the crowd, regardless of the mayhem happening around him. My old mentor had a visible rainbow bubble keeping him safe and, given the happy smile on his face and the occasional rounding of his lips, he was probably humming Tchaikovsky's *1812 overture* complete with cannon sound effects, his favourite.

"Um, Dem?" Taz's back pressed against mine. "He's headed straight for us. Do you trust him? If he pushes against our protection, I'm not sure I can hold it."

"Yeah, as much as I can trust anyone. He's got no reason to harm us."

Xavio drew up beside us and, with a simple flick of his finger, made Diana's protection warding force her and Jack toward the exit.

"Happy birthday, Oakthorn," he said, his voice strident above the battle raging on. "Nice to see you're keeping busy, Demi."

I pulled a face at him. "Not quite the time now I don't think."

He nodded. "Quite right, you should head back to Arcanium, where it's safe."

Taz seemed stunned into silence, I couldn't quite tell why, but despite his bravado earlier, I knew he wouldn't want to leave until his family was safe.

"We'll stick it out, thanks," I insisted. "But maybe from a safe distance."

I panicked as a woman darted at us, her face pulled into a snarl and a jet of dark bubbling liquid streaming from her mouth. I threw my hand outwards, as if I alone could stop her. The jolt whipped from my fingers, flicking through her liquid and sending it splattering in an explosion of inky droplets across the room. They caught a couple of people without wardings raised who started to scream, wiping at wherever the substance had landed.

"Oh, I didn't mean to do that!" I gasped.

The woman eyed me, but Xavio clapped his hands and thrust them forward, sending her zooming across the room as easily as someone might flick off a fly.

"I have a gift for you, young Oakthorn," he announced.

Taz's fingers were all but cutting through my bones now. I tried to shake him off but he refused to let go.

"I- now?"

I heard the disbelief in his voice, but he didn't know my mentor's random behaviour like I did.

"Easier to go along with it," I told him. "Can you open the protection to let someone in?"

He nodded and I twisted around so that we were both facing Xavio.

"Room in and out for you only," I warned, aware this was the person who'd taught me almost everything I knew. "And only if you mean us no harm."

Xavio chuckled. "Very wise. I'm glad I taught you something at least."

He stepped across the invisible boundary, or at least I assumed he had as he arrived in front of us without being repelled. He kissed the top of my head without any warning, so quick I barely had time to flinch.

"I gift you with my blessing," he said.

A subtle prickle of magic crept past my skin, but a quick look down and I couldn't see or sense anything new lurking inside me.

"Um, thanks?" I blinked. "Blessing for what?"

He winked, and I knew full well that was all the response I was going to get as he turned to Taz next. Taz clenched his eyes shut, a sure sign of trust.

Taz trusts him because I trust him. I kept a flicker of my connection lingering, just in case.

Xavio clasped his hands behind his back and leaned forward to brush the lightest, quickest peck on Taz's head. Taz cringed like someone had thrown a toilet bowl over him and I tried not to smile.

"To you I gift the ability to transmute the state of matter, all except animal, Fae, fairy, human or hybrid living material. Have fun with it."

"Whoa, really?" Taz opened his eyes and gawped.

Without another word, Xavio turned and walked away. I could have sworn he was whistling *The Nutcracker*, his hands still clasped behind his back. As he disappeared through the doors at the other end, Taz glanced around the room. Several were still holding protections or trying to fight, but the Queen and Taz's sisters looked okay still.

Mostly okay. One of Taz's sisters was being bundled onto a stretcher. Taz's gaze fixed on her, his jaw bunching.

"My mother will clear the room quick enough now one of them has been hurt," he said. "We're getting out of here. Whatever you do, don't let go of me. Don't get separated."

I nodded. "Okay, what you going to do?"

"Practice."

He lifted a hand in front of him. I waited, then frowned, unsure.

"Are you-"

The dark purple carpet runner that hemmed the dance floor turned into a moat. Several people tumbled into the aubergine water, which gouged a hole in the floor until a current swept them across the ballroom and out of the door.

Someone ran at us but I saw the Queen throw up a hand, and the man fell down choking. She was beside us before I could so much as blink.

"Out, now," she roared.

Taz looked like he was about to hesitate, to argue, but I tugged on his hand and he nodded. We dodged the fighting groups, Taz's eyes pinched as he held the protection around us. I threw out the occasional jolt to clear the way, but every cell of my body was beginning to feel the exhaustion of using my gift. I could only imagine how weary Taz would be.

"I can take over the warding," I offered.

He shook his head and increased the pace. Once we were heading up the staircase, the noise of the fight still echoing behind us, he let go of my hand and lifted both of his to keep the protection going. I thought I recognised the corridor, but couldn't be sure until a familiar voice filled my ears.

"There she is, slinking back like an alley cat," Keesley grumbled.

Taz glanced at me.

I shrugged. "Don't ask me."

"No boys in the room!"

I swept past, ignoring the indignant squawking, but even Keesley fell silent as Taz shut the door behind us.

"We'd best sit up a while," he said, rubbing his hands over his face. "I don't want to leave you alone, just in case anyone comes looking for trouble."

I nodded and pulled two chairs to the window for us to collapse onto while Taz fetched a couple of cups of water from the decanter on my dressing table. I could still hear the distant clash of fighting raging on downstairs, but a loud crack of thunder rumbled overhead. The battle sounds seemed to cower in response, growing fainter until I couldn't hear them anymore.

We sat down and I pulled my phone out of the side pocket of my satchel. The movement was a remnant of old behaviour, even though I knew human communications didn't reach into Faerie.

I looked up to find Taz frowning at me.

"Hot date?" he asked, turning his gaze to the shadowy world outside the window.

A streak of lightning tore the sky, turning it grey and navy for a second before hailstones began to pelt down in a heavy drumming.

"No, just seeing if there are any messages. But then human messages can't get through in Faerie, so it's habit more than anything. Ace was texting me a lot actually over the mentee break." I spun the phone around in my hands, my gut tense as I forced myself to keep talking. "Um, Taz? Can I ask you something?"

It was as good a topic as any to bring up while the rest of the Fae elite tried to destroy each other downstairs. Even if it was an excruciating one.

"Sure." He nodded. "It's going to be glacial while my mother is in this mood by the way. Are you cold?"

I shrugged despite sitting next to him with bare, shivering shoulders. Taz wriggled out his jacket and wrapped it around me.

"There. What's the question?"

I shrunk into the jacket as though it could shield me from the embarrassment of what I intended to ask next. The faintest whiff of his apple shampoo reached me from the collar as I forced myself to ask.

"How do you tell if a boy likes you? Like, likes you likes you?"

Taz stayed silent a moment. "He'd try to spend time with you because you don't make him want to scream and run away." His lips lifted then. "You're thinking about Ace texting you a lot?"

"I guess. He's always checking in, sending me smiley faces and putting kisses at the end of his messages. He even called me pretty a couple of times last term, and why else would he say something like that?"

Taz grinned. "To be nice? I guess that could be a sign, but Ace is into boys, so I'm thinking not."

"Oh." I wasn't sure how to take that. "Would he be okay with you telling me, or should I not say anything?"

"Everyone knows, he's never been shy about it. I'm surprised you didn't actually."

I sighed. Despite the awkwardness of someone maybe fancying me, especially someone I didn't feel that way about in return, it was still a teeny bit of a sting to find out they most definitely didn't. Still, much easier to take a bit of a sting than to worry about upsetting him by saying no.

"Disappointed?" Taz asked, his tone soft.

"No." I shook my head. That I could be sure of. "Relieved, and feeling really up myself now."

He laughed. "I think when a boy likes you, he'll find a way to tell you."

I glanced over to find him looking back at me, his eyes dark in the absence of light from the ferocious storm clouds roiling above. I could only just make out how wide and expectant they were.

"How?" I had to ask, even though my voice was barely audible and my insides were going weirdly squishy.

"Little things."

"Like what?"

Taz leaned an inch closer and opened his mouth, but it wasn't his voice that tore through my ears.

"Out of my way!"

The furious holler echoed out in the hall. Taz scowled and sank back in his chair.

"Brace yourself for the Queen of Mean routine," he muttered.

The door handle rattled.

"Appointments only!" Keesley seemed determined to irritate everyone, not just me, which I guess was something.

A feral snarl filled the air, followed by what sounded like a cartoon kettle screeching. The door bounced open, revealing the Queen in a black pantsuit with a cape and a shining black breastplate, a Fae regent dressed for war. I managed to brave staring at her long enough to make out strands of barbed wire adorning her hair.

"Why are you not in your room?" she demanded.

As I was already in my room, I guessed she meant Taz and wisely kept silent.

"First place kidnappers would look," he retorted.

The Queen's face shivered with many emotions before she took a long 'you-can't-pulverise-your-only-son-to-bits' breath.

"You shouldn't be in here unchaperoned either way," she said.

Taz folded his arms. "Why not? I can't hang out with my friends now?"

"Boys and girls are rarely just friends. Both of you are going back to Arcanium first thing in the morning."

"Good!" he snapped back. "Where we belong."

I flinched at the bite in his voice but the Queen was clearly used to it.

"Quite." She stalked toward the doorway and turned back. "You behave yourself and go back to your room. The last thing we need is to bring grandchildren into this."

"Oh, orbs alive!" I gasped.

I covered my face with my hands in horror, but the Queen was gone.

"Ignore her," Taz said, his cheeks bright pink and his teeth clenched. "She just has to have the last strike no matter what. Fae are impossible."

I shook my head in disbelief.

"It's not just Fae, believe me. Old people really do only think about one thing, don't they. What happened to let kids be kids?"

Taz wiped a hand over his face. "Apparently war makes grown-ups of us all."

"Very poetic. We'll get you that on a t-shirt."

Taz smirked at that, the deep groove lifting from his brow.

"Cool, but you don't have to get me a birthday present or anything."

I grinned to hide the mortification still burning my cheeks, mindful to keep a nice healthy gap between us now.

"Too right I don't, considering you never even told me it was your birthday."

He slumped with a sigh. "So, Xavio was your old mentor?"

So, we're just ignoring the moment back there? Okay. I settled back in my chair.

"Yeah. He's a bit odd, but he's kind. Very pro-Queen and pro-human."

"I've heard him mentioned, but never actually met him before you. I reckon he gave me this gift to protect you."

I shook my head. "No, we're not that close or anything. I was kind of teacher's pet because I studied hard and had no friends, but we don't know each other. It's not like he ever gave me a fairy gift, just a penknife when I left for Arcanium. Maybe he's trying to get in your mum's good books for something."

Taz raised his eyebrow but didn't comment.

"So, transmutation gift?" I prompted.

He nodded and leaned forward to grab my cup. With his other hand outstretched over it and his eyes narrowed, I watched him concentrate. A few seconds later, he tipped the cup upside down. I waited, but nothing leaked out.

"Transmutation - turning solids to liquids and vice versa." He tipped the cup right way up again and focused. "See, liquid to solid and back to liquid again."

I peered into the cup, impressed. Not so impressed when Taz bounced the cup so a slosh of liquid jumped up and splattered on my nose. He roared with laughter, and I had to smile at seeing his mood improve.

"So, what about my power?" I asked. "Could we make like liquid zap-power, like I did with that woman's inky stuff during the fight?"

Taz sighed and rubbed the back of his neck. "I don't know, Sparky. We should try sometime. But not tonight."

I shook my head and stared out over the stormy grounds, wind lashing the trees. The Queen was clearly furious, and any gift-testing mishaps now would probably result in me getting my head chopped off. Besides, it was kind of nice sitting with Taz, listening to the storm rage outside.

"No, not tonight."

CHAPTER TWENTY ONE
HOMEWARD BOUND

"That's so cool!"

I stared in awe as Taz turned my coffee to a solid and back to liquid again.

"It's not so bad, as gifts go." He grinned, clearly very pleased with himself. "It'll take me a while to work up to changing big things, like last night with the carpet runner nearly did me in, but it'll get stronger."

I'd woken early after the night of the battle, only to find out that Taz had told Marthe to keep an eye on me and alert him when I was up. The moment I was washed and dressed, he was waiting outside my room to walk me down to breakfast, but I appreciated his protectiveness. We'd not encountered the Queen yet, and he reassured me that his sisters were already elsewhere, not wishing to be home for longer than necessary. Outside, the sky hung like a bruised mass of weighty cloud, a reminder that things were far from resolved.

We sat in the huge cosy kitchen on wooden chairs, eating hot rolls and pastry. To round it off I took an apple from the huge fruit platter, not trusting any of the more exotic fruits I didn't recognise, and sat back with a sigh.

"Do we have a plan yet?" I asked.

Taz nodded. "My mother insisted I wasn't to leave as she wants to escort us back, probably to make herself look like a good parent. So we're stuck here until then."

I smiled at the thought of classes and the library, of Ace no doubt bombarding Milo with all the delights Arcanium had to offer, the Braunees and the canteen. My room.

Taz stood up with a groan.

"Come on. She'll find us wherever we are, so we might as well make the most of your time here. What do you fancy, beach? Mountains? Forest?"

"You can choose any location?" I jumped to my feet, the apple forgotten. "What's your favourite?"

I would have been happy hanging out in his conservatory, but I wasn't about to knock a day trip into Faerie if he was offering.

"They're all good. Let's go to the beach. If we get far enough away, we might see sunshine again. Close your eyes and spin around three times."

I eyed him. "Really?"

"No." He grinned. "Not really."

I whacked him on the shoulder but hesitated as he held out a hand. He hadn't mentioned our brief 'moment' the night before, so I could only assume I'd imagined it.

No point bringing it up and making things weird.

I took his hand, ignoring the awkward swooping of my insides as he curled his fingers around mine. I closed my eyes against the grey ether that came with realm-skipping, but almost immediately the gentle splash of waves made me open them again.

"Wow."

I dropped Taz's hand and rotated a circle.

A vast expanse of golden sand stretched in all directions but one, lit under a bold white sun. I ignored the urge to take off my shoes and socks and run my toes through the grains, turning my attention instead to the crashing sea, too cornflower blue and sparkling to be real.

"Is this still your mum's part of Faerie, like the actual court?"

I asked.

Temptation got the better of me as I pulled my trainers off, my socks balled up in one hand. Taz flicked a glance at me, shading his eyes with his free hand. In the mixture of shadow and the glare from the sun beaming down, the green in them looked toned down so his eyes matched the water.

"Of course." He looked out at the waves. "When have you ever seen a beach like this except in dreams, films or imagination? If the sun is shining and the sea is calm, it means some part of the Queen is in a good mood. It's probably the part of her that's been spoiling for a fight, wanting the Old King to finally make his move so she can end this."

I tried not to feel disappointed. Faerie was real, just as the human world and Arcanium were, but somehow when Taz spoke about it, he reduced it to a cheap illusion trick.

"Fairies are all about glamour, but sometimes it can pay off," he muttered, softening the sombre mood. "This is one of my favourite places in Faerie though, so I wanted you to see it."

"It's beautiful."

As we set off side by side along the shoreline, I scuffed my bare feet through the wet sand.

"Dem?" Taz paused to clear his throat. "About last night..."

Uh-oh.

I turned to find him right in front of me. I tore through the scant recesses of my social experience for something light-hearted to say, but of course I had nothing.

A breath of wind gusted past us and a curl of my hair pinged against my cheek. Taz smiled and lifted a hand to brush it back. With my insides threatening to go squish, I tried to remember how breathing worked as he glanced sideways.

"Oh, sorry." He stepped back and pointed to a figure further along the beach. "Even before we've started it's time to go back.

It's actually been kind of okay being stuck here with you around."

No!

I wanted to scream it, to force him to kill the suspense either way, even if he just wanted to stay friends. But the Queen stood waiting for us, her delicate shoulders clad in a grey cloak like something out of a gothic film and dark make-up decorating her face. In that moment, aside from the honey brown hair, she looked more like Queenie than Taz's mother. I pulled my shoes back on, wincing at the gritty sensation, and we picked up the pace.

"It's been kind of okay being here," I agreed, trying to hide how unsettled I was. "Well, except for your sisters locking me in my room."

"Yes, that should have been avoided. I'll get them back one day for that."

"Or when your party turned into a battle."

"That should have been avoided too, although it got me a new gift. I still doubt he'd have bothered giving it to me if I weren't protecting you. You managed your gift so well though."

"We make a good team."

As I turned to walk toward the Queen, Taz's hand shot out and landed on my wrist.

"She's told me I have to come straight back here," he said. "We're just dropping you off and I'm picking some things up from my room. There's training she wants me to do here apparently and she doesn't trust me to come straight back."

My heart sank. I pushed my free hand into my pocket so Taz wouldn't see my fingers starting to tap. It was a ridiculous reaction, especially when I had other friends at Arcanium besides him, but he was my *best* friend.

Who am I going to sit with in class, or talk to? Who else will practice with me?

I forced my face into a frown, hoping that would hide the multitude of emotions thundering through me.

"Oh, okay. I guess that could be helpful, maybe she'll give you another gift or something, if you behave."

Taz snorted and let go of my wrist, leaving buzzing warmth where his fingers had been.

"When do I not behave? Come on."

I followed him across the sand to join the Queen.

"Before we return, a few instructions." She gave Taz a serious look before turning to face me. "No more assignments for you for the moment, Demi. You shouldn't have had to do any anyway at your age, and no going anywhere other than Arcanium or here, if you have to."

"Are you saying I can't go back to my family for a while?" I asked, somewhat hopeful.

"I gave your family the highest level of protection when we came to collect you, but you can't return I'm afraid, at least not for now. It might draw attention, especially after your rather bold denouncement of the traditional ways on *The Faerie Net*."

I nodded with my cheeks turning red.

"Okay. Can I still ring my mum though? She'll worry otherwise."

"Yes, that should be fine on a human device, but no straying too far from the arcade either."

I hadn't spent much time outside Arcanium since starting there anyway, so this was no great loss, although Taz, Ace and I sometimes sat on the stony beach on days off with fish and chips or doughnuts.

"Okay, that's all I want from my family anyway pretty much."

The Queen's lips twitched. "Families can be difficult."

Taz snorted, but refrained from commenting. I noticed that he didn't meet his mother's gaze too readily either.

"Place your hands on my shoulders, please," the Queen instructed.

I stood on her left and did as I was told, using the lightest touch possible and hoping my hand wouldn't leave any marks on her fancy cloak.

"Close your eyes," she insisted. I closed mine. "Properly closed, Taz."

I bit down the urge to smile, knowing Taz would be scowling up a storm already. I could almost hear the thoughts springing in his head, no doubt that he'd done this a thousand times before without her. I realised then that I'd never heard her call him Taz before either, only Oakthorn.

A soft whisper of air brushed past my cheeks, ruffling my hair.

"There we are." The Queen shrugged my hand off her shoulder. "Oh, you're too kind."

I opened my eyes and squinted against the glare. The sun coming in through the ceiling of glass dazzled me, but my vision cleared quick enough to recognise my surroundings. A long walkway leapt over a perilous drop and led to a circular platform. The despatch floor in Arcanium looked exactly the same as it had when we left for Gallows Oak, except for the reverent hush of several trolls all down on one knee.

I found Trevor in the crowd and he risked a wink in my direction before lowering his head once more.

"There is no need for propriety," the Queen insisted. "I am merely dropping two Arcanium members back. Oakthorn, I'll have a quick word with Queenie. Meet me in her office once you have your things."

Taz started scowling and opened his mouth, no doubt to

argue something, so I ambled across to Trevor to give them some privacy.

"Escorted by the Queen no less." Trevor chortled, keeping his voice low. "I've been on standby ever since you left, just in case I had to come get you. My Moira was most impressed when we saw you on *The Faerie Net* as well."

I groaned. "I'm never going to live that down, am I?"

"Probably not." Trevor paused, scratching his head. "My little one still wants to meet you someday too, but I said you're very busy."

"Of course, meeting her would be fine, nice I mean, really nice."

I bit my lip. I had no idea what I should say, but Trevor smiled as if he knew.

"She's a terror, but luckily Glynnis takes everyone."

I floundered. "Glynnis?"

Trevor fiddled with the bar on his rickshaw.

"She runs the Arcanium day-care. Most trolls live in, part of the on-call nature of the job, but some Arcanium FDPs and mentors, support staff and the like also live here. All Arcanium kids not employed go to Glynnis."

"I had no idea."

Trevor shrugged, his easy smile never fading. "Why would you? You're a bit young yourself to have a little one I'd have thought. Oh, Taz is waiting for you."

I turned as Trevor pointed past me. Taz stood with his arms folded and a disagreeable frown on his face, but his gaze was stuck somewhere in the distance, his thoughts elsewhere. The Queen was already gone, off terrorising Queenie until Taz was ready to leave again. The idea of the two women in the same room both trying to be polite amid their attitudes made me smile.

"Well, let me know when your- what's her name?" I asked

Trevor.

I was sure this was at least proper social behaviour to ask for names of people's kids.

"Moira, after her mum, but we just call her Moss."

"Well, when you have time let me know and I'll come up and meet her. I'd like to."

I surprised myself with how truthful that was. Trevor had been so uncomplicated and frank with his support, and I wanted to meet his kid. I lifted my hand in farewell and walked toward Taz.

"Did you know Arcanium has a nursery?" I asked.

Taz frowned, but his mind was still distracted. "What? Oh, yeah. I help out there sometimes with reading hour."

Wow. How much about my friends is there that I still don't know?

I got into the lift and shut the grill as Taz punched the button for the library. I'd hoped to sneak off to my room before Petra collared me, but no doubt he had his reasons for choosing the library first. I also had no idea how to say goodbye to him or how long he was meant to be going back to his mother's court for. The sinking sensation in my gut had nothing do with the lift shooting downwards, but the realisation that Taz wouldn't be around for a while. With my hand hidden in the sleeve of my cardigan, I tapped my thumb back and forth over my fingers.

Whatever happens, he's my friend. Ace and I will still be able to orb him and catch up.

The thought didn't make me feel any better. Taz had been my rock since I arrived at Arcanium, the person who'd shared all the adventures. He helped me in classes with Faerie stuff I didn't know, and stayed up late studying with me.

I clenched my fist and tried to calm myself down. He was going home for a bit, like we did over the mentee break.

It won't be forever. It can't be.

We found Ace and Milo in the library sitting side by side at one of the tables. They were hunched over a large hardback book with their heads almost touching, Ace's black hair nestled against Milo's shaggy brown locks. They looked up as we approached, their expressions sheepish. Milo's cheeks were a definite shade of pink, but Ace leapt out of his chair like it was made of eels.

"Welcome back." He gathered Taz and I into a hug. "Glad to be home?"

Even though I still wasn't great with the whole being randomly hugged thing, the knowledge that it was definitely a purely friendly hug made me smile.

"Hell yes." Taz sighed. "But not for long sadly. I figured you'd be here."

Ace nodded and sank back into his seat.

"Good call," he agreed. "How was your party? And what do you mean, not for long?"

Taz flicked me a look, his mouth turning up at one corner. "The party turned into a Fae battle, as all the best ones do. But I got a transmutation gift out of it."

Milo and Ace stared.

"It's a long story, kind of," I added. "But we know now that we need to be careful and stay on guard. First the Forgotten try to take over Arcanium. Then the Old King arrives at Gallows Oak publicly to thunderous applause, and several court Fae attack us at Taz's party. There's going to be a war."

Ace rubbed his forehead. "That doesn't sound good."

"But at least it's not going to be today, that we know of," Taz said. "I'll be back in a minute, I need to drop by my room and get my stuff."

"Get your stuff?" Ace asked.

"Yeah, the Queen is calling me home for a while. Apparently, she has training for me. I'll pop back down in a minute to say a proper goodbye."

He strode across the library toward the lift, and I watched him until he was behind the golden grill and out of sight. The weirdest urge to go after him tugged at me, like an anchor pulling against my ribs, but I stayed where I was.

He won't go without saying goodbye to me. I was almost certain of that.

"Um, I should get to work," Milo said.

He strode off toward the librarian's desk like Knucker tentacles were at his heels, the hoodie wrapped around his waist flapping behind him like a mini cape. Ace gave me a hesitant look and flopped back in his chair.

"So, did we miss anything while we were away?" I asked.

At least he doesn't know about my assumption that he liked me. I'm pretty sure Taz won't blab about that.

Ace shrugged, his gaze drifting down to the book in front of him although his eyes didn't so much as twitch over the page.

"Well, Petra and Alannah had a huge spat, I'm not even sure what about but it involved you, like almost coming to using their gifts on each other. Oh, and Emil wants to see you when you're ready, but you can sleep and eat and things first if you need to, it didn't seem urgent. I think it's just a check-in."

"You didn't ask Petra what the fight was about?" I asked. "Seems a bit severe a reaction for a simple argument."

Ace shook his head. "No, she was in a foul mood, I didn't dare."

"Oh well. I'm sure she'll tell me if I need to know. How's Milo settling in?"

Ace tipped his head back, a subtle quirk catching the corner of his mouth.

"Good, he's actually really smart. I found him a room near mine, and we sat up really late talking about things. He hadn't seen any of *Demolition Ducks* so I made him watch the whole first season."

He looked over to where Milo was methodically sorting through a pile of books, his head down. I eyed them both with renewed intensity, remembering what Taz told me. Milo glanced up then, meeting Ace's eye and giving him a shy smile.

I was so busy focusing on them that I almost missed Ace's head shooting up, his gaze fixed over my shoulder.

"Hi, Petra," he said.

I turned in my seat to find my mentor hovering behind my chair. Ace made himself scarce and I smirked as he headed straight toward the librarian's desk.

I faced Petra, unsure if I was in for a telling off or a celebration now the immediate dangers were done.

"Follow me." She beckoned without any hint of a smile and set off across the library.

Telling off it is then I guess.

CHAPTER TWENTY TWO
GOODBYE, FOR NOW

I followed Petra across the library. She led us to a small room off the main chamber that looked more like a school music room with a keyboard in the far corner on a stand, but Petra only leaned down to turn on a large fan. It whirred loudly into life, almost swallowing all hope of further sound into it.

"We should be okay to talk here," she said. "Can't be too careful who's listening these days, even inside our own domain."

She leaned against the wall and I gratefully dropped onto a wooden stool. Petra folded her arms and gave me an expectant look.

"Tell me everything in detail then. There are rumours of a rift in Faerie, and I was speaking to Emil when Alannah came in without knocking and announced without any secrecy whatsoever that you'd been involved in a battle. Then she saw me and clammed right up."

I frowned. "How did she know?"

"How indeed. Tell me everything."

I bit my lip. It wasn't that I didn't trust Petra, but I'd learned to keep things to myself from a young age. I took a deep breath.

She's my mentor, this is what she's here to do.

"I'll skip the bits about Gallows Oak that you already know," I began. "In short, the Old King was there, or the 'usurper' as the Queen calls him. He was holding court at the Forgotten 24 club when we found it, then I heard the Director, Cornelius, talking about how he has a contact who has the ear of the King and that the Queen's time is over."

I hesitated, but Petra's frown didn't give me any indication of what to expect once I was done.

"It all kicked off so Taz got us to the Queen's court. He can realm-skip there, kind of like a royal security thing, but he didn't have enough energy to get us back here after."

"Taz has certain privileges," Petra said. "The charm he wears around his neck allows him to realm-skip into Arcanium at will, but I see you're the one wearing it."

I looked down to find Taz's pendant still hanging for all to see around my neck. The flush fired straight to my cheeks like paintballs.

Oh hell, what will people think? I was still wearing it at the party and everything.

I remembered the sour glances from Diana as she ignored me, the hushed whispers and giggles from the crowd that looked at us. I would have to give it back before he left but the damage, if there was any, had been done. I shook the thought from my head and focused on the details I'd not yet gotten to.

"Well that aside, while we were at Taz's party, we were dancing-"

"You and Taz? Or in general?"

Why is that in any way relevant?

I stumbled on, trying to pretend to myself that my blushing wasn't getting worse.

"Um, me and Taz, but anyway. It all happened a bit fast. Someone tried to attack the Queen and then it was mayhem. Diana Hemlock was there, and she's been out for me since I started here, and some boy called Jack. He was the one who gave me this energy gift I have, but only out of spite because Diana made him. It backfired because they were arguing he'd done it wrong."

Petra blinked and I tried to rein in my babbling.

"That's all I know, but it looks like the Forgotten and the Old King are getting ready to make a public move."

"They're testing the boundaries," Petra sighed. "I probably shouldn't divulge this, but they've taken control over a couple of distant parts of Faerie, as in the Queen can't access them right now because the Old King has the power there. If that keeps happening, the Queen's hold will weaken. She has many who are loyal to her in Faerie, but not necessarily the Lords and Ladies who still hold dominion over some parts of the land."

I remembered the room full of court Fae from last night, and the Queen saying the whole court was like a political shark tank.

"Did you overhear anything?" Petra took a step forward. "It could be important, even if it seems little to you."

I grasped my head with both hands. "Sorry, I think that's it. I didn't think to listen to conversations or anything, but perhaps I should have. Sometimes I don't think I'm actually very suitable for this FDP thing."

I meant it as a flippant joke, but the tremor of fearful belief leapt up all the same.

I looked up to find Petra kneeling right in front of me. The closeness almost sent me bashing backwards through the wall. A vision of having to explain the shattering plaster to the facilities team swam into my mind, *'my mentor loomed in front of me so I broke your wall, sorry'*.

"Stop stressing." Her usually strident voice was soft. "Demi, do you know why I chose you as my mentee?"

I blinked at her. "Chose? I thought you got assigned to me. Why would you choose me? I'm hopeless. I'm guessing I don't need to tell you about my debut on *The Faerie Net* either."

Petra raised her eyes upwards but her smile remained.

"Faerie knows why I chose you," she chuckled. "And yes I

did see. I was horrified and proud in one swoop. In all seriousness though, Emil was going to take you on himself, but I saw how you handled your first assignment, then all the trouble you got into for the sake of this place."

Petra's dark eyes danced and she rocked back to sit cross-legged, lessening the closeness and my tension.

"You make friends," she said. "You have this weird skill for diplomacy and reason that doesn't come along as often as it should. Emil said he was going to take you and I said no, I was. He asked me why and I told him the same thing, people end up liking you even when you don't know what the hell you're doing."

I tried to process that. "You chose to mentor me because I'm hopeless, but you think people like me anyway?"

"You're not hopeless. You may not have background knowledge, or be naturally good at everything, just like I'll never become a singer, but you're not hopeless as a person. Look, this whole emotional thing doesn't come easy to me."

I slumped on my stool, almost sliding straight off it. Petra grinned but didn't comment.

"It doesn't to me either," I admitted.

"Exactly, except people like you all the same. You're kind and fairly selfless, so I know I can trust you to do the right thing. That means my job will be more about showing you how to do it safely and protect against the untold dangers."

"I'm not sure about that."

Petra laughed. "I just passed Beryl Eastwick, you know the sister that never smiles?" I nodded, although I'd seen Beryl smile once or twice and thought that was a bit unfair. "She was raging about being sent on an errand for a bag of Jelly Babies, told me my mentee was getting ideas above her station."

"Oh." I bit both my lips together to keep the smile in.

"I asked her if she knew why they were so important," Petra continued. "She just got this really indignant glower and told me that you were apparently having them sent every week to your realm-skipper. That's when I knew I'd chosen the right mentee. Then that absolute diva Alannah comes marching up saying that she's met you briefly and she wants to take over mentoring you. She's not even a mentor. I said no, and she didn't take it well."

"Well, thanks." I rubbed the back of my neck.

Why on earth would Alannah want to mentor me after we only met a couple of times, all of which I was totally clueless?

Petra slid to her feet and stood up.

"It's like an instinct thing," she added. "I knew you were my mentee and that was that. But don't ever let anyone tell you that you're not worth anything. You're apologising for not remembering things when you've done a huge assignment, and brought us information from Gallows Oak we wouldn't have had otherwise."

My insides warmed at the thought of her reassurances and Petra returned my smile, her shoulders relaxing.

"Anyway, enough of the deep and meaningfuls. Thank you for trusting me with this info. There won't be any assignments for you for a while, but I hear you're not able to go home for the moment either?"

I nodded and followed her out of the room back into the main chamber of the library. Petra saw my face as she led the way toward the lift.

"Don't like home?" she asked.

Normally I would have muttered something non-committal, but Petra was my mentor and she'd chosen me. As we waited for the lift, I told her the truth.

"I have two sisters that enjoy tormenting me. My mum tries to be fair, but I've always been different and they make sure I'm punished for it. Arcanium is my home now."

"Well, okay that sucks," she admitted. "Not Arcanium being home but the sisters thing. At least you don't have to go back for a while then. Still, no doubt you could do with learning to defend yourself. How about I teach you a move that uses the opponent's weight against them? Then you can basically flip any of them without much effort."

I had to smile. "You've seen me run. They'd catch me and lock me in a cupboard or something."

Petra's responding grin wasn't exactly encouraging, but I started to wonder if either of my sisters would survive in a straight fight against her, let alone stand a chance of winning.

"I'll teach you to pick locks," she assured me with a determined glint in her eye. "It'll be fine."

Warmth swept through me at the sheer determination in her voice.

For whatever reason, she chose me as her mentee. She must believe in me at least a little bit.

I remembered Keesley then, but knew picking locks could be a fantastic skill for a girl who was scared of being trapped in tight spaces. As we waited for the lift, I remembered it was polite to ask the other person questions occasionally, even though I found it invasive and daunting.

"Do you have any sisters?"

Petra shook her head. "Nope, five brothers."

"Wow. Is that how you learned to fight?"

"In a way. Being the only girl and the youngest, they refused to let me play any games with them, or do anything remotely dangerous. So, I rebelled. Now not one of them can take me."

"Okay, that's kind of awesome."

Petra laughed. "Before long I'll have you up to a similar level, don't worry."

The previous warm feeling tiptoed out as self-doubt stormed in. I couldn't imagine ever being as talented as Petra, having seen her ability to turn items into whatever she needed and the sheer skill she had in combat training. Either way, it would mean a lot of hard work.

At least that'll keep me busy while Taz is away.

The lift arrived and Petra pulled the grill aside only to have Taz almost mow her down on his way out.

"Steady on," she grumbled.

She stepped into the lift and shut the grill behind her, but I called out before she could hit any of the buttons.

"Petra? Thanks for choosing me and for being kind. Not many people are these days."

She rolled her eyes but I saw the subtle twitch at the corner of her mouth.

"Don't be dim. Meet me in the training room in an hour. We need to start preparing you for your future."

The lift shuttled off taking half of my agonised groan with it. I'd stupidly assumed I would have some time to relax in my room, or here in the library with Ace and Milo, before I had to exert myself. I turned away from the grill only to find Taz holding out a dusty old book to me.

"I thought this might be useful to give you before I leave," he said. "It's the Almanac of Lineages, so it shows all the historical families in Faerie. Figured I could at least tell you which families tend to be on which side. Not always obviously, but still worth knowing. That way you won't go making any ill-advised friendships without me."

I took the book with a smile. "Thanks. From what I've heard over the past few days, there are dark times ahead so I'll take all the knowledge I can get."

Taz rubbed his face and started walking toward the main

desk. I kept pace with him, anxious that the time to say goodbye was finally here.

"The wider world of Faerie is definitely having trouble," he agreed. "I'm also intrigued to find out how it is that Milo can realm-skip at will, so I asked Emil on my way back down here. I didn't mention what Milo can do, but apparently he turned up in the Ogle, when nobody but Queenie, Emil or my mother can realm-skip in and out. That's some serious power."

I frowned. "We know he wasn't really responsible for the cocoa, and I don't think we can ever hold that against him. But if you're saying he's got big gifts, then perhaps we need to be careful, especially as Ace has taken a liking to him. Also, if you could not tell anyone about what I told you last night, about what I thought? That'd be great."

I looked around, checking through the gaps in the bookshelves to make sure there weren't any eavesdropping ears. If there was ever an opening for Taz to bring up last night again, that was it.

"No worries." He laughed. "It's not like I'm going to be here for a while to say a word. Trust nobody but me from now on though, and try not to get into any trouble before I get back."

I bit my lip, hesitant to show how tumbled my insides were. Taz had been my constant since I'd arrived at Arcanium, and doing any of this without him around was going to be so weird.

"How long do you think you'll be gone?"

He shrugged. "Could be a couple of days, could be a year. If I behave myself, she'll get bored and let me come back sooner. Meanwhile, we should try to figure out what's going on. I can find things out at the court, and you can keep an ear to the ground here."

"Okay, so you'll keep in touch and stuff." I tried to keep my voice level. "I'll find out what I can without getting kicked out or anything, but you can orb me first then."

I tried not to think of that like a blatant flashing 'call me' sign, but somehow the image wouldn't get out of my head.

"I don't have an orb," Taz reminded me. "The only way for me to communicate out would be through the Queen's network, and she can monitor those. I swear it's like she has a link to all the house communication lines right in her head, she knew everything when we were growing up. But I'll try and get messages to you as often as I can."

I won't even be able to speak to him.

I gulped against the lump in my throat, horrified that my eyes were starting to prickle.

"Oh." I reached around my neck for his pendant, more for something to do than out of morality. "I should give this back as well while I remember."

I flinched, my hands still hovering at the back of my neck as Taz threw an arm around my shoulders. I didn't need to look at his face to know he was grinning at me.

"Don't worry," he said. "Keep it for now in case it brings you luck. And I'll be on my best behaviour so I can get back as quick as possible. The times ahead aren't going to be easy, so I'll probably be back before you know it. Just don't forget me while I'm gone."

I stood frozen with my arms still half-lifted to my neck as Taz pressed a lightning quick kiss to the top of my head.

My mind went completely blank. Not, 'can't think of anything to say' blank, but utterly frozen while my insides rioted. He laughed, as if he knew, and let me go.

"Be good until I get back, Sparky."

Without another word, he strode off toward where Ace and Milo were transfixed on the same book, but they didn't seem to be moving their eyes at all. From this distance, I could just see the smirks on their faces.

He kissed me. I regained the ability to move my body. *And I'm standing here staring at him like an idiot.*

Petra had mentioned training. I should find her.

Training. Right.

I opened the grill and stepped into the lift, pressing the button for the residents' floor and sighing as the lift shot upwards.

I had to believe that Taz wouldn't be gone forever, and training with Petra would be the perfect distraction. Dark times were coming, but I was back home and my second assignment had been a success, kind of.

I stepped out of the lift onto the study floor and walked toward the training hall.

"Hey, Demi," Hutch Hutchinson called out from one of the classrooms. "Saw you on *The Faerie Net,* nice job sticking two fingers up to the establishment!"

My cheeks burned as he led a round of applause, but I noticed a fair few of his classmates joining in. Even Avril, the tutor, gave me a warm smile before calling for everyone to pipe down.

Despite their approval, I knew the Forgotten wouldn't be so delighted with my appearance on *The Faerie Net.* They were still out there, along with Elvira and the Old King, planning their next move. Taz's party was only the beginning, and at Gallows Oak the Old King had mentioned going after the Queen's children next.

Let them try. I strode into the training hall to meet Petra, determination beginning to crackle inside me. *Whatever comes next, I'll be ready.*

ACKNOWLEDGEMENTS

I thought I was lucky to have one book, but here I am doing it again! As always, the biggest thanks go to my amazing editor and loveliest friend Anna Britton, who is still doggedly stopping me from making all sorts of linguistic and plot errors and cheering me on whenever I assume I've suddenly forgotten how to write (and quite often how to human as well… <3)

Also special thanks go to Debbie Roxburgh for ploughing through the ideas for the stories to come and cheering on my book babies – also for making sure I don't do anything dim to the characters that I end up regretting later on!

To my writing family as always, your support means everything to me - Samantha Williams, Sally Doherty, Marisa Noelle, Emma Finlayson-Palmer, Katina Wright, writing Twitter, everyone who joins #ukteenchat, Stuart and the WriteMentor crew, Rebecca F Kenney for the AMAZING covers, the bookshops that took a chance on stocking my first book when I had absolutely no idea what I was doing, and many more!

So thank you all for keeping me going, and here we go again!

ABOUT THE AUTHOR

While always convinced that there has to be something out there beyond the everyday, Emma focuses on weaving magic realms with words (the real world can wait a while). The idea of other worlds fascinates her and she's determined to find her own entrance to an alternate realm one day.

Raised in London, she now lives on the UK south coast with her husband and a very lazy black Labrador who occasionally condescends to take her out for a walk.

Aside from creative writing studies, an addiction to cake and spending far too much time procrastinating on social media, Emma is still waiting for the arrival of her unicorn. Or a tank, she's not fussy.

For the latest new and updates, check the website or come say hi on social media:

www.emmaebradley.com
@EmmaEBradley

www.ingramcontent.com/pod-product-compliance
Lightning Source LLC
Chambersburg PA
CBHW061617190726
48288CB00007B/2355